"Stay right where you are…"

Stretched out on the floor in front of Grayson, Chloe just felt sexy. The feeling only intensified as he took a seat and started to draw.

It seemed like only seconds had passed when he tossed down his pencil and picked up his brush. The way he painted was twice as sensuous as the way he drew. The brush was like an extension of his hand, and the canvas her body. Wherever his hot gaze landed, she felt the stroke of his brush. Her feet. Her legs. Her breasts. Her warm center.

He made her feel beautiful. Breathtaking. And wicked.

She now understood what it meant to be "captured on canvas." Right now she was Grayson's. For all eternity she wanted to be…

"Grayson's."

She didn't realize she had spoken until his hand halted in mid-brushstroke. His gaze found hers, and he dropped the brush and slowly rose from the stool and looked down at her with hungry eyes. She remained perfectly still.

A willing sacrifice on the altar of Grayson…

PRAISE FOR THE DEEP IN THE HEART OF TEXAS SERIES

THE LAST COWBOY IN TEXAS

"4 stars! The larger-than-life world of Katie Lane's Deep in the Heart of Texas series offers colorful, rowdy characters and passionate love stories that are easy to enjoy and hard to forget."
—*RT Book Reviews*

A MATCH MADE IN TEXAS

"Fun-filled and heartwarming...a wildly sexy romance with a beautiful love story [that] old and new fans definitely do not want to miss."
—BookReviewsandMorebyKathy.com

FLIRTING WITH TEXAS

"4½ stars! [A] complete success, blending humor, innovative characters, and a wonderfully quirky town with an unlikely and touching love story."
—*RT Book Reviews*

TROUBLE IN TEXAS

"Sizzles with raunchy fun...[Elizabeth and Brant's] dynamic provides the drama to complete this fast-paced novel's neatly assembled package of sex, humor, and mystery."   *—Publishers Weekly*

CATCH ME A COWBOY

"Lane gives readers a rip-roaring good time while making what could feel like a farce insightful and real, just like the characters themselves."   *—Booklist*

MAKE MINE A BAD BOY

"I absolutely loved Colt! I mean, who doesn't like a bad boy? Katie Lane is truly a breath of fresh air. Her stories are unique and wonderfully written...Lane, you have me hooked."

—LushBookReviewss.blogspot.com

GOING COWBOY CRAZY

"[This book] really reminded me of an early Rachel Gibson...or early Susan Elizabeth Phillips. Faith became a sassy, intriguing heroine...The chemistry between these two ratchets up to white-hot in no time."

—TheSeasonforRomance.com

HUNK FOR THE HOLIDAYS

Also by Katie Lane

The Overnight Billionaires

A Billionaire Between the Sheets
A Billionaire After Dark

Deep in the Heart of Texas series

Going Cowboy Crazy
Make Mine a Bad Boy
Small Town Christmas (anthology)
Catch Me a Cowboy
Trouble in Texas
Flirting with Texas
A Match Made in Texas
The Last Cowboy in Texas

Holiday novels

Hunk for the Holidays
Ring in the Holidays
Unwrapped

Waking up with
A BILLIONAIRE

KATIE LANE

FOREVER

NEW YORK   BOSTON

Copyright © 2016 by Cathleen Smith
Excerpt from *A Billionaire Between the Sheets* copyright © 2015 by Cathleen Smith

Cover design by Elizabeth Turner
Cover photography by George Kerrigan
Background image © Shutterstock
Cover copyright © 2016 by Hachette Book Group, Inc.

Forever
Hachette Book Group
1290 Avenue of the Americas
New York, NY 10104
forever-romance.com
twitter.com/foreverromance

First Edition: July 2016

Forever is an imprint of Grand Central Publishing.
The Forever name and logo are trademarks of Hachette Book Group, Inc.

The publisher is not responsible for websites (or their content) that are not owned by the publisher.

The Hachette Speakers Bureau provides a wide range of authors for speaking events. To find out more, go to www.hachettespeakersbureau.com or call (866) 376-6591.

ISBN: 978-1-4555-3320-6 (mass market); 978-1-4555-3319-0 (ebook)

Printed in the United States of America

OPM

10 9 8 7 6 5 4 3 2 1

To my Ridge, the most precious grandson
in the whole wide world

Acknowledgments

Writing is a solitary job, but it takes a village to get a book published. And I'm very fortunate to have such a great village:

My agent, Laura Bradford, who keeps my feet firmly planted on the ground so my head can remain in the clouds.

My editor, Alex Logan, who fits together all the puzzle pieces and keeps me on the right track.

All the copy editors, proofreaders, cover artists, publicists, and sales reps at Grand Central, who work so hard and efficiently at their jobs.

The Land of Enchantment Authors, who are not only my writing support system but also my dear friends.

The ladies of the Dog-Eared Divas book club, who never let me forget the reason I started writing in the first place—the desire to give my readers the same feeling of contentment I get when I finish a good book.

My family, which loves me despite the craziness of deadline week, and keeps me smiling and feeling so blessed.

And last but not least, my readers. Your love of my characters and stories is what keeps me seated at my laptop and tapping away. Thank you for all your support. Mwah!

*C*HAPTER ONE

*T*he lobby looked like a Concord grape that had been stomped beneath a boot heel. Variations of the color purple were splattered everywhere. The polished marble floors. The plush velvet couches. The contemporary light fixtures. The highly polished surface of the reception desk. Even the dress of the svelte blonde who sat behind it. And if there was a color that Chloe McAlister hated most, it was purple.

Purple was the color of her childhood bedroom. The color of Napa Valley at dusk. And the color of bruises. Deep, painful bruises that faded from view, but never from one's heart. Standing in the midst of all that purple, Chloe felt slightly sick to her stomach. For a second she thought about turning tail and walking right back out the tall glass doors with their stenciled-on lips. Unfortunately, if she wanted to overcome the past, she needed to deal with the present. At the present moment, she needed money.

Fidgeting with her bangs, which she'd just butchered that morning, she walked to the receptionist's desk, where the blonde was talking on the phone. The receptionist watched her approach, her gaze sliding over Chloe, who no doubt stuck out like a withered raisin on the vine in her basic black secondhand dress and scuffed high-heeled boots. The blonde looked away. The snub didn't bother Chloe. She had spent the last six years of her life trying to blend into the woodwork, trying to be someone no one took note of. She stepped up to the high counter of the desk and cleared her throat.

The blonde ignored her and continued her conversation. "I think he's so much sexier now. I mean he was sexy before, but now he's like a hundred and ten on the hot-o-meter. And the way he looks at you with those eyes. It's like he's consuming everything about you all at once—and not just your looks, but your secret desires and naughtiest wishes too."

Chloe rolled her eyes. "Excuse me."

The blonde stopped talking and sent Chloe an annoyed look. "I'll have to call you back, Tiff." She placed the receiver in the cradle. "Can I help you?"

."I'm here to see Mr. Grayson Beaumont."

"Do you have an appointment?"

"No. But I'm friends with—"

The woman didn't let her finish. "It doesn't matter who you're friends with. You can't just walk in and ask to see one of the owners of the biggest lingerie company in the world. You have to have an appointment. We can't just take walk-ins. What do you think this is…Supercuts?" She swept her hand in a dismissive gesture. "Come back when you get a clue."

Chloe's hands tightened into fists. But before she could do something really stupid—like pop the rude receptionist in the mouth—a delivery guy pushed Chloe out of the way with a bouquet of white roses in a huge rubber ducky with a little blue sailor's hat. While the ducky was cute, the roses were all wrong. Chloe would've filled the sailor duck with Shasta daisies and ocean breeze orchids. Or at least something more whimsical and fun.

"Another flower delivery for Deacon and Olivia Beaumont," the guy said. "And I've got three more in the truck." He set the ducky on the counter, but when it blocked his view of the receptionist, he moved it to the floor at his feet. "With all the deliveries I've made in the last two days, you would think that the Beaumonts just gave birth to the next crown prince of England." He smiled at the blonde and winked. "So have you thought about it, beautiful? Are you ever going to agree to have drinks with me?"

The blonde tipped her head coyly. "I told you that I have a boyfriend." She sounded about as sincere as when she'd asked Chloe if she could help her.

The delivery guy rested his arms on the high counter and flexed his biceps. "So what? I'm talking about drinks, not marriage. What is one drink going to hurt between friends?"

"Well, maybe just one drink." The blonde pulled a business card from the holder and wrote down her number while the flower delivery guy tried to peek down the neckline of her dress. With both preoccupied, Chloe saw an opportunity and took it.

Bending down, she scooped up the floral arrangement and headed for the elevators. The old security guy who sat on a stool didn't even raise an eyebrow. In fact he got up and pushed the elevator button for her.

"You know that Mr. and Mrs. Beaumont aren't here, right?" he said. "They're both home with that brand-new baby, so you'll have to leave it with their assistant, Ms. Wang—or I guess I should say Ms. Melvin. She got married to one of the company lawyers not too long ago. Me and the missus got invited to the wedding, and let me tell you, that was quite the shindig. But not as big of a shindig as when Mr. Nash Beaumont married that pretty little writer."

Chloe had been invited to the wedding. In fact she was supposed to be a bridesmaid for Eden, alongside their other friend Madison. But that was the bad part about blending into the woodwork. It was hard to keep your friends. Especially when Eden had just sold her first book and gotten married to a panty billionaire, and when Madison was one of French Kiss's supermodels.

"That's sure one big rubber ducky." The security guard continued to talk. He reminded Chloe of her grandfather— white hair, a ready smile, and lots to say. "You know what they named him?"

"Uh…no." She glanced over her shoulder and was relieved to see the delivery guy still flirting with the receptionist.

"Michael Paris," the security guard continued. "Michael, after the man who started the French Kiss lingerie company, and Paris because that's where the idea for the company came from. And because Paris and Helen are famous lovers—and all the Beaumont men are named after famous lovers." He counted off on his fingers. "There's Michael Casanova, who started the company, and his brother, Don Juan. And then there's Don Juan's three sons—Deacon Valentino, Nash Lothario, and Grayson Romeo—who inherited the company and run it now."

This wasn't news to Chloe. Everyone knew about the Beaumonts' middle names. It was hard not to when each brother had his own lingerie line named after him. Women all over the world wore bras and panties from the Valentino, Lothario, and Romeo Collections—Chloe included. But only because she got them free from Madison. Okay, and maybe because they were pretty.

The elevator doors opened, and she thanked the guard

before she hurried in. Once inside, she peeked through the roses and tried to figure out what button to push. The shout of the delivery guy—"Hey, who took my ducky!"—had her taking a chance on the top floor. But before the doors could completely close, a distinguished older gentleman in an expensive gray suit slipped in.

He tapped a floor button before he glanced at his watch and shook his head. "Late again. My mother would be rolling in her grave." He straightened his already perfectly knotted tie and finally noticed Chloe. Or not her so much as the bouquet she hid behind. "I'm going to assume that there is someone inside that rose garden." With no other choice, Chloe shifted the ducky and peeked out. The man's eyes widened. "Holly Golightly."

"Excuse me?"

"My apologies," the man said. "But your resemblance to Audrey Hepburn took me by surprise. Holly Golightly was the character she played in the movie *Breakfast at Tiffany's*." He cocked his head and pressed his index finger to his bottom lip. "The resemblance is uncanny—same symmetrical facial features, short, dark bangs, and expressive eyes." He lowered his hand. "Please tell me you model."

She shook her head. Although that wasn't exactly true. She had modeled once, and for French Kiss, but not on purpose. And she'd signed the release only because she needed the money and her entire face had been covered by a big floppy beach hat.

"That's too bad," the man said as he pulled a card from his pocket. "If you ever change your mind, be sure to call me. Samuel Sawyer." Since her hands were full, he tucked the card in the roses just as the elevator doors opened. He stepped out and gave her a knowing look over his shoulder. "Maybe when you call, you can tell me why you stole the ducky."

The top floor wasn't nearly as purple as the lobby. The hallway carpet was a neutral beige, and the office doors a natural wood. Next to each door was a gold nameplate, and it didn't take long to find the one she was looking for. She stared at the name and was surprised at how nervous she suddenly felt.

Grayson Romeo Beaumont held no threat for her. In fact, of all the men she had met in her life, Grayson was the least threatening. He was shy and soft-spoken, with a calming effect on women that had had Chloe nicknaming him the Woman Whisperer. Not that his whispering had worked on her. After her one and only boyfriend had been physically abusive, she didn't trust her own instincts where men were concerned. Just the thought of Zac had her knocking on the door a little harder than necessary.

The door flew open. The man who stood there wasn't the man she'd expected to see. This man wasn't a clean-shaven billionaire in a designer suit that had cost more than Chloe's yearly rent. This man had a scruffy beard and thick brown hair that fell to his shoulders. He wore a white button-up linen shirt that was covered with smudges of paint, and faded jeans with rips in the knees and tattered hems that partially covered his long, bare feet.

She lifted her gaze from his tanned toes to his purple eyes. Not the ugly purple of squashed grapes, but the deep bluish purple of the bachelor's button flowers that grew in her grandfather's garden. There were only three men she knew with eyes this color. One was at home with his new son, and the other was on his honeymoon. Which left one. Except this man didn't act like the youngest Beaumont. Especially when he barked at her.

"Flower deliveries are dropped off at the front desk." He slammed the door.

Chloe stood there for a moment in confusion before a smile lit her face. It seemed that the Woman Whisperer had finally decided to show his true colors, and not surprisingly, she was much more comfortable with this volatile Beaumont than with the shy, calm one she'd met six months ago. Without bothering to knock again, she turned the knob and walked in.

The executive suite didn't look like an office. It looked more like a painter's studio. A messy painter's studio. A splattered white tarp covered the floor, a mishmash of furniture and props was piled in a corner, and canvases were stacked against one wall. The other wall held a black backdrop. In front was a purple divan like the ones in the lobby. A divan she'd seen in Grayson Romeo's paintings. But in all his other paintings, a gorgeous naked woman had been draped over the divan. Today the long sofa held something else entirely.

Chloe squinted at the small red apple for only a second before her gaze turned to the man behind the easel. The few times she'd seen him sketch, his movements had been fluid and graceful, like his pencil was a figure skater gliding across ice. She had assumed that he would paint the same way, but she'd been wrong. His movements were brisk and brutal as he jabbed his brush into the acrylic paint palette he held before slashing it at the canvas as if he wanted to slice it in two.

"I guess painting apples is not as much fun as painting women."

His head jerked up, and she set the ducky bouquet down on a table cluttered with paints and brushes and waggled her fingers. "Hey. Remember me?"

The paintbrush fell from his fingers and hit the floor, splattering black paint all over the hem of his jeans and his bare foot.

She smiled. "I guess you do."

It took only a second for him to recover and for his eyes to narrow. "What do you want?"

Chloe let her smile drop. "I get it. You're not exactly thrilled to see me. And after the way I acted on our road trip to Eden's parents' house, I can't really blame you. I admit that I was a wee bit bitchy."

"A wee bit?"

She held up her hands. "Okay, so I was a lot bitchy—especially when you were doing me a favor."

"I didn't do it for you. I did it for Madison."

Chloe understood that. Madison could get men to do just about anything. And not just because of her voluptuous body, but also because of her kind heart and sweet nature. She was the antithesis of Chloe's skinny body and belligerent attitude. Which probably explained why they were such good friends. Madison was the one who had introduced Grayson to Chloe. The one who had brought him to Zac's apartment after Zac had beat the crap out of Chloe. The one who had talked him into driving Chloe to a safe place until Zac was arrested. And maybe that was why Chloe had been so mean to Grayson. She hadn't liked that he'd seen her at her weakest. She didn't like being weak. But she especially didn't like people witnessing it.

"Well, anyway," she said, "I'm sorry."

She knew it wasn't the best apology, but she expected some kind of acknowledgment. Instead he set down the palette before he grabbed a rag and leaned down to wipe the paint off his foot. She might've sworn off men, but that didn't stop her from appreciating the view. Grayson had always had a nice body—long, lean, and well proportioned. She just hadn't remembered his ass being so hot.

He straightened. "Is that why you came? To apologize with a ducky bouquet of roses?"

She cleared her throat, along with the image of his butt in the worn jeans from her mind. "No, the roses were being delivered to your brother. I just used them to get up here. The real reason I came is to let you know that I've changed my mind." She forced a bright smile. "I've decided to let you paint me."

He didn't reply. Instead he just stared at her, and she realized that the snobby receptionist must've been talking to her friend about Grayson. His intense eyes felt like they were looking right through her and reading all her dark secrets and desires. And the last thing Chloe wanted was someone discovering her dark secrets. She looked away and started organizing the paint tubes on the table by color. Who knew that there were so many shades of yellow?

"So what changed your mind?" he asked. "I believe your words were, 'The last thing I'd want to do is be exploited by a paint-by-numbers billionaire.'"

She cringed. Obviously she'd been bitchier than she remembered. Instead of apologizing again, she tried a compliment. "Well, that was before I saw some of your work. You don't exploit women as much as immortalize them."

He snorted. "Sell that to someone else. You aren't the type of woman who cares about being immortalized or famous."

She finished organizing the paint tubes and centered the rubber ducky bouquet on the table before turning to him. "You're right. I don't want to be immortalized. In fact, I don't want you to paint my face."

His eyes studied her with their disconcerting intensity. "The last time you didn't want your face shown, it had to do with bruises. What's your reasoning this time?"

"I'm shy."

His gaze sizzled down her body. "And yet you're willing to strip naked for me."

The possessive way he said *for me* had heat sweeping through her body, flushing her cheeks and settling in wet warmth beneath her Romeo panties. Annoyed by her reaction, she snapped, "Look, do you want to paint me or not?" She glanced at the divan. "It would have to be more exciting than painting a wormy apple."

One of the things that annoyed her about Grayson was that she could never get a good read on his emotions. But for once she read the pain that crossed his handsome features extremely well. It flickered through the lavender fields of his eyes for just a moment before it was gone. He set down the paintbrush he'd been cleaning and moved out from behind the easel.

"Sorry you made the trip for nothing," he said. "But I'll have to pass. I don't paint women anymore." Then, without another word, he walked out.

Long after the door slammed, Chloe stood there feeling stunned. Not only because she wasn't going to get the money she needed but also because of his parting words. He no longer painted naked women? It didn't make sense. Anyone who saw one of his paintings knew that the man had been born to celebrate the beauty of a woman's body. And now he was going to give that up to paint fruit?

Curious about what had changed his creative thinking, she stepped around the easel to study his painting. She expected to see a perfect, shiny red apple. Instead there was nothing on the canvas but a big black X.

It appeared that women weren't the only things Grayson couldn't paint.

$\mathcal{C}$HAPTER TWO

$\mathcal{G}$rayson had lost it. He knew this and had known it for the last six months. But he just hadn't known how much he had lost it until Chloe McAlister had walked into his studio wanting to pose for him. Until that moment he'd thought there was a chance that he could pull himself back from the deep, dark abyss that threatened to consume him. After all, he was the levelheaded Beaumont, the one who could stay calm in any given situation. But he didn't feel calm now. He felt as if he'd toppled right over the edge of insanity and was flailing around trying to grab on to anything that would save him from hitting rock bottom.

He headed for the elevators. He had just bought a brand-new Bugatti sports car, and he planned to drive until the desperate panic that clawed at his guts subsided. But on the way down to the parking garage, the elevator stopped at the lobby. And when one of French Kiss's top models stepped in, he changed his plans.

"Gar-a-son?" Natalia said in her thick Russian accent.

"Is that you? I had heard that Paris made you a little more…how do you say in English…hungry? Just look at you. You look like my uncle Bo-o-oris." She stroked a hand over his beard. "But much younger and much sexier, of course."

Grayson ignored the doors opening at the parking garage and pulled her into his arms and kissed her. She didn't protest. The times he had painted her, she'd made it perfectly clear that any advance would be more than welcome.

"Oooh, you are hungry," she whispered against his lips as she curled her arms around his neck and her leg around his waist. Grayson guided her back against the wall of the elevator.

He wanted to feel desire, or passion, anything that would stop the panic. But all he felt was disappointment. Not in Natalia. She was a beautiful woman and kissed like she modeled, with enthusiasm and heat. No, his disappointment was in himself for using her. He didn't use women. At least he never had before.

He'd started to pull away and apologize when the elevator doors opened and he found himself looking into the big brown eyes that had started his downward spiral. Eyes that rolled up in disgust. At one time he had found the habit endearing. Not anymore. A road trip had cured him of any endearing thoughts toward the woman. Paint her naked? Not in this lifetime. He'd rather be locked in a closet with a rabid wolverine then spend hours in a studio with Chloe.

With his eyes still locked on hers, he deepened the kiss, causing Natalia to moan and Chloe to release an exasperated grunt as she stepped into the elevator.

Natalia finally noticed that they were no longer alone and stepped away. "Gar-a-son"—she swatted his chest—"you make me forget myself." She turned her full model-smile on

Chloe as she pushed the tenth-floor button. "What is it with American men and elevators?"

Chloe sent him the same look she always seemed to give him—hatred mixed with contempt—and pushed the button for the lobby. "I think it has to do with having a woman cornered with no means of escape."

Natalia laughed. "Perhaps you are right." She glanced at Grayson. "Although I have no desire to escape." Only seconds later the elevator stopped, and she gave him a quick kiss on both cheeks before she got out. "I have to meet with Samuel in the design studio, but I should be done by five. Call me."

Grayson should've gotten out with Natalia—not just to explain that he wouldn't be meeting her later but also to get away from Chloe. Instead he watched the doors close and realized that now he had no means of escape.

"New girlfriend?" she asked.

She stepped closer, and just that quickly his creative brain became consumed with her perfect features. What oil paint colors would he need to mix to re-create the creamy porcelain of her skin? The flushed peach of her cheeks? The blooming rose of her lips? And if he used a thousand different shades ranging from burnt sienna to gold ochre, he would never completely capture the depth and entrancing beauty of her eyes. It was too bad that her beauty was only skin deep.

The thought had his logical brain regaining control, and his gaze moved to her choppy, uneven bangs. "New bad haircut?"

She fidgeted with her bangs. "I know. I really butchered it. I guess I should check *beautician* off my career list." She shot him a glance. "So what happened in Paris to screw up your painting mojo?"

It was his worst fear put into words, and he felt like she'd kicked him with her pointy-toed boots right in the balls. As soon as he caught his breath, he tried to deny it. Just as he'd been denying it to himself for the last six months.

"You think I can't paint? Well, I can paint anything I want to paint. I just don't happen to want to paint you."

Chloe's eyebrows lifted beneath the fringe of uneven bangs. "So you'd rather paint apples? Although that X looked nothing like an apple to me."

His eyes widened. "You looked at my painting?"

She shrugged. "I was curious."

While he struggled to get his anger under control, the elevator arrived at the lobby. Chloe lifted a hand as she stepped off. "Good luck with that apple."

The sarcasm in the words sent his temper right off the charts, and he stepped out with her. But before he could tell her that a lot of talented artists painted fruit, the security guard took her arm.

"I'm sorry, miss, but I'm going to need to know what you did with the floral arrangement."

Hearing the guard, some muscled guy in a white polo with a flower on the breast pocket came hurrying over. "Is she the one who took my ducky?" He pointed a finger at her. "Give me back my ducky!"

Grayson wasn't sure why he did it—maybe because he had never liked bullies—but he stepped in front of Chloe. "What's going on?"

The flower guy gave him the once-over. "I don't need some street bum butting into my business."

The security guard spoke up. "That's not a street bum. That's Mr. Beaumont." He turned to Grayson. "I'm sorry for the disruption, Mr. Beaumont, but this man says he had his flower bouquet stolen." He looked at Chloe. "And I did see this young woman with a big ducky of roses."

"But I didn't steal it." Chloe looked at Grayson. "Tell them."

For the first time since she had strolled into his studio, Grayson felt in control, and he wasn't about to give up that feeling. He squinted. "I'm sorry, but do I know you?"

She rolled her eyes. "Very funny. Now tell them that I brought the floral arrangement to your office."

Thoroughly enjoying himself, he smiled. "What exactly would I do with a ducky filled with roses?"

Just that quickly the belligerent young woman Grayson remembered so well made an appearance. And for some strange reason, he was happy to see her. "How about shove it up your ass!"

"Don't you dare talk to Mr. Beaumont like that." A blonde hurried up. Grayson didn't recognize her face, but he did recognize the standard purple dress and heels that all the receptionists wore. The woman pointed a tangerine-colored nail, which clashed with her dress, at Chloe. "This is the same woman that was trying to sneak into French Kiss earlier. She thought she could see a Beaumont without an appointment." The woman looked at him and batted her eyelashes. "As if you would want to talk to someone with a bad haircut and faux-leather boots. Which is exactly why I told her to take a hike and come back when she had a clue."

As much as he was enjoying toying with Chloe, this woman's arrogance didn't sit well. Especially when he had grown up poor and knew what it was like to have bad haircuts and cheap clothing pointed out by the wealthier kids. He was about to put her in her place when the doors opened and two police officers walked in. Upon seeing them, Chloe raced toward the opposite doors.

The policemen gave chase, and Grayson figured that his fun was over. It was one thing to let Chloe get hassled by a security guard and another to let her get arrested and thrown in jail. Unfortunately, by the time Grayson got out to the street, the police officers had Chloe on the ground and were handcuffing her. Or trying to handcuff her. As he might have expected, she was putting up one hell of a fight.

"Get your hands off me! I did nothing wrong."

"If you did nothing wrong, ma'am, then why did you run away from us?" The officer who had her on the ground finally got ahold of her wrist and pulled it behind her back.

"Let her go," Grayson ordered as he walked up.

The other police officer stepped in front of him. "Back off. This is none of your business."

"It's exactly my business. I'm Grayson Beaumont, and I own French Kiss."

The officer looked him over and laughed. "Sure you are. And I'm Donald Trump. Now go about your business before I haul you in for interfering with an arrest…or for loitering."

Grayson glanced down at his tattered, paint-splattered jeans and couldn't blame the officer. He did look like a vagrant. "Look, I can prove it." He made to pull out his wallet, but then remembered that he'd left it in his studio. Unfortunately, the officer didn't take kindly to Grayson reaching for something behind his back, and grabbed Grayson and shoved him against a parked car. Grayson's reaction was more reflex than anything. When you grew up with two older brothers who loved to box, you had to have good reflexes. He didn't intend for his elbow to clip the officer's jaw and send him stumbling back. Before Grayson could ask if the guy was all right, the other officer joined the fray, and Grayson found himself lying facedown on the sidewalk next to Chloe.

He grunted as the cop's knee dug into his back and cuffs were slapped on his wrists. "You want to tell them who I am?"

Chloe squinted. "Do I know you?"

Grayson didn't know why he laughed. He should've been pissed that she had turned the tables on him. And he was pissed, but he could also see the humor in the situation. He continued to laugh as the police officer got him to his feet. The other one helped Chloe up. Of the two, he acted a little more friendly.

"So what's your name?" he asked her.

For the first time since Grayson had known her, Chloe actually looked scared. She swallowed hard and cleared her throat a few times before she glanced at Grayson. "Chloe McAlister."

"And do you have any identification on you, Ms. McAlister?"

She shook her head. "I don't drive."

That surprised Grayson. Growing up in a small town in Louisiana, he had started driving his dad's beat-up cars when he was twelve. Not that Deacon had known Nash let him drive. Nash and Grayson kept quite a few things from their volatile older brother.

The officer nodded, then had her spell her name and give him her birth date before he did the same with Grayson. While he radioed in the information, the other officer tried to control the crowd that was forming.

"This is all your fault, Grayson," Chloe grumbled.

He adjusted his cuffed hands and leaned against the cruiser. "How do you figure? I wasn't the one who stole the ducky."

"No, you were just the one who wanted to be an ass and not tell the security guard that I didn't steal it. What happened to you? I thought you were the nice Beaumont brother—the one who always does the right thing."

He had always done the right thing. Whether it was

getting good grades in school or eating all his peas, he did what was expected of him and never complained. When you were being raised by two headstrong older brothers, compliance was the easiest route. So he had kept his mouth shut and gone along. If something had bothered him and he needed an outlet, he would go to his room and sketch or paint. Through his art he learned to express all the emotions that he couldn't express in a household filled with men. His paintings were his release...or at least they had been. Now he couldn't even paint an apple.

It seemed that Chloe was right. He had lost his painting mojo. Which left him with no outlet for the tumultuous emotions that swirled around inside him. Although being arrested had released some of his anger. In fact he felt pretty good at the moment, much better than he'd felt in months.

"Maybe I'm tired of being the perfect Beaumont," he said.

"I didn't say you were perfect. I said you were nice. Now you're just as grumpy and mean as I am. And let me tell you, it's not very becoming."

He grinned. "I don't think anyone can be as grumpy and mean as you are—"

"Mr. Beaumont!"

Grayson turned to see Deacon's executive assistant, Kelly, weaving her way through the crowd. She wore the standard purple and gray that all employees wore, but Kelly always accessorized with her favorite cartoon cat, Hello Kitty. Today a headband printed with the little white cats held back her long black hair.

"What's going on?" she asked. "Jason and I were coming back from my doctor's appointment when we noticed the crowd."

A crowd that was getting bigger. People were jostling

each other for a front-row position. Something that Grayson wasn't real thrilled about. Deacon didn't like bad press, and one of his brothers getting arrested wouldn't look good on the cover of a tabloid. Which was why Grayson was so relieved when Kelly's husband, Jason, appeared. As one of French Kiss's most competent lawyers, he immediately assessed the situation and took charge.

"I'm Mr. Beaumont's attorney," he said to one of the police officers. "I'd like to know what he's being charged with."

That seemed to get the officer's attention. His eyes widened, and he pointed a finger at Grayson, speaking in an overly loud voice. "He really is a Beaumont? But what woman would want to wear panties he designed?"

"Just about half of the female population," Kelly piped up. "The Romeo Collection is our most popular line."

After only a moment's pause, he quickly took Grayson's handcuffs off. Unfortunately, it was too late. The crowd had been alerted to his identity. Phones appeared and started clicking. If he had been Deacon, he would've given an eloquent speech and made it clear that it had all been a misunderstanding. If he'd been Nash, he'd have flashed a charming smile and said something amusing. But Grayson had never been good at eloquent speeches or charm. So he just stood there as the cell phones snapped. Although he was taking the attention much better than Chloe. She had turned away and was cowering next to the police cruiser.

Once Grayson's hands were released, he spoke to the officer. "Take her handcuffs off. She didn't steal the bouquet. She delivered it to my office."

"She gave you flowers?" Jason asked. "And here I thought the scruffy look you've been sporting since you got back from France would turn women off." He flashed a grin. "Obviously I was wrong."

"They weren't for me." Grayson watched the officer take the handcuffs off Chloe and felt a little annoyed at the red marks the cuffs had left on her wrists. "They're for Deacon and Olivia."

"Speaking of your brother," Kelly said, "he just called and wants to know why you're not answering your phone. I think he's a little worried that you won't be able to handle things while he and Olivia are on parental leave and Nash is on his honeymoon."

Grayson didn't blame his brother for being worried. He was more than a little worried himself. While Deacon and Nash were completely involved in the business, Grayson had always been more wrapped up in his art. He didn't have a clue how to be a boss. Let alone run a company. Unfortunately, he didn't have a choice. Deacon needed to be home with his new son. And Nash needed to be with his new wife. Which meant that Grayson needed to pull his head out of his ass and quit hanging out in his studio. Even if he could paint, he didn't have time to. Nor did he have time to drive his new sports car or deal with Chloe McAlister.

Although once she had her handcuffs off, she didn't waste any time making her getaway. Without one word of goodbye, she hurried down the street with a hand shielding her face.

"Hey"—the other police officer came around the cruiser—"why did you let her go?"

His partner shot Grayson an annoyed look. "It turns out that this guy is a Beaumont and the girl did deliver his flowers. Which is something he should've mentioned to begin with."

The other policeman didn't seem to be as put out by the misinformation. In fact he immediately became apologetic. Of course, Grayson hadn't elbowed him in the eye. "So sorry about the misunderstanding, sir." He waved a hand at the building behind them. "I love your lingerie—I mean I love your lingerie on women. I bought some for my girlfriend, and she looked hot."

Instead of replying, Grayson continued to watch Chloe as she made her way up the steep street. What had made her change her mind about posing for him? She didn't like him. She had never liked him. It had been hell getting her to sign a release for the picture French Kiss had used for the catalog. She'd finally given in when he'd offered her a boatload of money. And maybe that was why she was back. She needed money. Although that didn't seem likely. If she needed money, all she had to do was ask her friends Eden and Madison. They would gladly give her whatever she wanted. Of course, Nash had once offered her money, and Chloe had turned him down flat. So maybe she was too stubborn to ask for help.

"Is she your girlfriend?"

The question had him looking at the officer. Not only did he look interested but so did Kelly and Jason. No one at French Kiss, besides Grayson and Nash, knew she was the model who had graced the cover of the summer swimsuit catalog. Chloe had insisted her name not be released.

"No," he said. "She's not my girlfriend. She's not even a friend."

The officer nodded. "I'd keep it that way if I was you. When I looked her up on my in-car computer, I didn't find a thing—-no tickets, driver's license, vehicle registration, rental agreement, or credit cards. Nothing. And with the way she shied away from the cameras, I'd say that Chloe McAlister isn't her real name."

CHAPTER THREE

Chloe didn't waste any time putting some distance between herself and the snapping cell phone cameras. She could only hope that no one had gotten a good picture of her. Not that it would make a difference now. In a few weeks, she'd be long gone. And the years of looking over her shoulder would be only a bad memory. No one would think to look for her in England.

Chloe didn't believe in fate, but it had certainly seemed like the stars were aligned when an Englishwoman stopped by the Fisherman's Wharf stand where Chloe sold flowers to tourists and struck up a conversation about lavender. They'd talked for a good hour, and for some reason, Chloe had done something she never did: She'd talked about the past. Not the bad parts, but the time she'd spent in her grandparents' flower gardens and how they had taught her all about annuals, biennials, and perennials. What flowers needed full sun and what flowers needed little. Using tea or coffee grounds in the soil to acidify, and eggshells for valuable nutrients. At the end of the conversation, the woman had given Chloe a card and offered her a job at a gardening nursery she owned outside London. All Chloe had to do was get there.

Unfortunately, tickets to England weren't cheap. Not to mention the money she would need to live on until she got her first paycheck. Damn Grayson for losing his painting mojo and turning into such an ass. Now she would need to figure out another way to get the money.

Her thoughts were so wrapped up in her money issues that she almost walked into a teenage girl sitting on the sidewalk. The girl was strumming a guitar with a fast-food cup of change in front of her. She didn't look to be over sixteen and had the same desperate, hungry look that Chloe had once had.

Regardless of her financial troubles, Chloe pulled a ten-dollar bill out of her purse and placed it in the cup. The girl stopped playing, and her eyes filled with gratitude. Which had Chloe jotting down the name of the flower stand on Fisherman's Wharf and handing it to the girl.

"I'll be leaving in a couple weeks, and the owner will need someone to help her. She doesn't ask questions, and she pays in cash."

The teenager took the paper, then hesitantly asked, "You were a runaway?"

Chloe added another couple of dollars to the cup. "I still am."

After leaving the girl, Chloe headed to her apartment. It was a small studio, and for the rent she paid, it was quite a steal. Especially in San Francisco, where rent was as high as the Golden Gate Bridge. At one time she had lived there with Madison and Eden. But Madison had moved to a high-rise apartment downtown that went with her new top-model profile, and Eden had moved in with Nash. Now it was just Chloe who lived there.

When she arrived, Mr. Garcia was standing in front with his little dog, Scamper. She tried to keep her distance from the other tenants. But Mr. Garcia was hard to ignore. He was a suspicious old guy who viewed himself as the building watch. He took one look at her and started his interrogation.

"What are you doing off work? I thought you sold flowers on the wharf during the day."

"I do, but I took the day off."

His eyes narrowed. "You're not going to start selling drugs, are you?"

"No, sir," she said as the terrier raced over to greet her. Chloe didn't like dogs. They were too easy to get attached to. But it was hard to ignore Scamper's big brown eyes. So she bent down and gave his ears a quick scratch. The dog immediately rolled to his back and exposed his belly for more scratches as Mr. Garcia continued.

"It wouldn't surprise me if you were into something shady. Especially with that tattoo and hole in your nose."

Chloe touched the side of her nose that had once held a diamond stud. Zac had called it an engagement diamond when he'd paid for it and her piercing, but really it had been more like the ring placed in a bull's nose to control it. She had stopped wearing the stud after he'd been arrested for running a prostitution ring.

The thought made her realize that Mr. Garcia was right. She had been involved in something shady, all because she had once been as desperate and hungry as the little guitar-playing girl. But never again. Never again.

She gave Scamper one last scratch before she rose. "I promise I'm not selling drugs or doing anything illegal."

"Then explain why that detective was looking for you."

It took a real effort to keep her fear from showing. Although her voice quavered when she spoke. "What detective?"

"The one who showed up here this morning."

"What did he want?"

"He wanted to know if a Selena Cameron lived in the building."

Selena Cameron. It had been so long since she'd heard the name that it sounded foreign, like it belonged to someone else. And technically it did. It belonged to an adorable baby in a fuzzy blanket. A sweet toddler in a frilly dress. A happy little girl in her father's arms. It didn't belong to a disillusioned young woman who wanted to forget the painful past.

"So what did you tell him?" she asked.

"I told him that I'd never heard of a Selena Cameron, and then he whipped out a picture." Mr. Garcia squinted as he studied her. "The hair was longer and lighter, but the face was the same."

Since the jig was up, there was nothing for her to do but accept it. She glanced at the front door of the building. "So is he waiting inside?"

Mr. Garcia looked surprised by the question. "Hell no. I'm not gonna let some stranger waltz into our building." He paused. "Just like I'm not gonna give a stranger any information on the tenants who live here—I don't care if he is a cop. We neighbors have to stick together."

She released her breath in a rush. "Thank you, Mr. Garcia."

He only nodded before he pulled Scamper down the street.

Once he was gone, Chloe hurried up the steps of the building. Relieved though she was that Mr. Garcia hadn't thrown her under the bus, she still didn't have any time to lose. The man looking for her wasn't a cop, but she didn't have any doubt that he was a private detective.

Once inside her apartment, she locked the door and then looked around to see what she would need to pack. Pots of flowers covered every available surface. There were orchids, African violets, begonias, hibiscuses, amaryllis, and a white peace lily that stubbornly refused to bloom. Probably because there was little peace in Chloe's life. When she left, she would need to figure out what to do with the flowers. Maybe she would give them to Mr. Garcia as a thank-you for not giving her away to the private detective. Of course, the detective would be back. Which was why she couldn't stay there.

Chloe headed to the closet and pulled down her duffel bag. She didn't have a lot of clothes to pack but, thanks to Madison, she had two dresser drawers filled with lingerie. She chose only her favorite sets of panties and bras, skipping over the light pinks and lavenders for the darker reds and blacks. After tossing in a few toiletries from the bathroom, she grabbed the framed picture on the nightstand.

Eden had given it to her for her twenty-first birthday. It was of her, Eden, and Madison at the Bay City Marathon. They were standing by the finish line with their arms wrapped around each other. For once Chloe looked happy. Maybe because she'd goaded Madison until she finished a half marathon. Or maybe because Eden had just informed them that she was engaged to Nash. Or maybe because she had finally started to hope. Hope that she could forget the past and move on. She'd been wrong. There was no forgetting who she was. Or where she came from.

Placing the picture on top of her folded clothes, she zipped the duffel bag and then headed to the kitchen and the cookie jar where she kept the tips she'd made waitressing at

The Lemon Drop bar. She knew exactly how much money was in the jar. She counted it nightly. She also knew that it wouldn't be enough for a plane ticket to England, let alone enough for rent and food until she got her first check.

A pounding on the door interrupted her thoughts. She froze for only a second before she raced into the living area and stuffed the money in her duffel, then grabbed it and her purse and headed for the fire escape. She had the window open and one leg slung over the sill when the lock clicked and the door swung wide. The curvaceous blonde in the red designer dress was a welcome sight.

"I knew you were running from me." Madison placed a red-nailed hand on her hip and pointed the key she'd just used at Chloe. "And I'm telling you, Chloe McAlister, that I've had about enough of your shenanigans. If you don't want to be my friend anymore, just say so."

Chloe dropped her duffel and pulled her leg back in the window before sinking down to the couch in relief. "I don't want to be your friend anymore."

Madison didn't even blink at the callous reply. "Don't be silly. Of course you want to be my friend. Who wouldn't want to be friends with a famous French Kiss model?" She pulled a bag out of her huge leather purse and tossed it to Chloe. "A model who can get her friends the newest line of lingerie before it even hits the stores."

Chloe rolled her eyes. "Would you please stop with the lingerie, Maddie? My drawers are stuffed full already."

"A girl can never have enough lingerie...or diamonds...or furs." She sat in the chair and waited with an expectant look until Chloe finally opened the bag. She rolled her eyes again when she pulled out the nightshirt.

Madison clapped her hands with glee. "Isn't it cute? It's the newest casual sleepwear from the Romeo Collection."

"I think anyone could figure that out." Chloe glared at the word written across the front. *Romeo's*. The possessive noun made chills run down her spine...and not in a good way. After Zac, she certainly didn't need to be another man's possession. Not that Grayson wanted to possess her. In fact he didn't even want to paint her. She folded the nightshirt and placed it on the coffee table, already deciding that it would be something she left behind.

Madison must've read her distaste. "I should've known that you wouldn't like it. Nash's collection is more your style, while I'm a Romeo girl through and through."

""I hope you don't have a thing for Grayson," she said. "Since he got back from Paris, he doesn't seem very stable to me." Chloe realized her mistake when Madison's gaze narrowed on her.

"When did you see Grayson?" After only a second, her eyes widened. "You came to Eden's wedding after all, didn't you? I knew you couldn't resist." She held a bejeweled hand to her chest. "Wasn't it so romantic? I mean Eden's beautiful gown and the way Nash kissed her at the end and swept her up in his arms, carrying her down the aisle just like a prince and his princess. I swear I thought I was going to swoon. And speaking of swooning, I don't think Grayson looks unstable. I think he looks hot."

"You can't tell me you like the beard?"

Madison shook her head. "It's not the beard. It's something about the look in his eyes. He left looking sweet and innocent—sort of like his lingerie collection—but he came back looking dangerous and..."

"Desperate." The word just popped out, but it was accurate. Grayson did look desperate.

"I was going to say *sexy*. But as sexy as he is, Grayson and I are just friends. Unlike Natalia. I just left a lingerie fitting, and all Natalia could talk about was Grayson. I guess he kissed her in the elevator and now she's in love with him—of course, she was in love with Nash six months ago. I think it's that hot Russian blood."

Just thinking about the elevator kiss annoyed Chloe, and she wasn't sure why. "Well, maybe she can take care of Grayson's wild desperation."

Madison laughed. "I doubt it. Natalia doesn't seem like his type. And since he was gone for six months to Paris, you have to wonder if he didn't find someone there that changed him."

The theory made sense. A woman *would* explain why Grayson's personality had changed so drastically and why he had lost his painting mojo. Love could really screw a person up. Chloe was a perfect example. After falling in love with Zac, she had turned into the worst form of herself imaginable.

"Do you have any chocolate?" Madison got up from the couch, but froze when she noticed the duffel bag by the opened window. Her eyes zeroed in on Chloe. "Are you taking a trip? Because if you're taking a trip when you refused to go with me to Cancún for the modeling shoot, I'm going to be so-o-o mad at you."

A lie would make things so much easier. Unfortunately, she couldn't think of one good lie. So she told the truth. "I'm leaving, Maddie."

Madison looked more than shocked. She looked as if Chloe had just drowned an entire sack of kittens. "What? But why?"

Chloe reverted to the tough, belligerent kid who had survived on the streets. "Because I'm sick of this town."

"But I thought you loved San Francisco."

Chloe did love San Francisco. She loved the bridges with

their towering heights and glittering lights. She loved the smell of the sea on the cool breezes coming off the bay. She loved the bell-ringing trolleys that glided over the hilly streets. And the resiliency of a city that had rebuilt itself after numerous fires and earthquakes. But she couldn't say that. "Maybe at one time, but I need something a little more exciting. And I'm not talking about Scrabble Night with you and Eden. I'm talking about real excitement."

Madison's eyes reflected her hurt. "You don't like Scrabble Night?"

Just that quickly Chloe lost her tough facade. "Okay, so Scrabble Night was fun, even if you always try to cheat with pig Latin words. But you've got to realize that I'm only twenty-one. I need to be around people my own age and...party." She threw her arms wide to emphasize her point and ended up knocking over her peace lily. Potting soil spilled all over the floor. Never one who liked messes, she quickly got up and hurried to the closet for the hand vac. When she turned, Madison had her duffel bag open and was holding the picture of them at the Bay City Marathon.

"I'm not buying the entire excitement thing," Madison said. "You are the oldest soul I've ever met, Chloe. I don't know how many parties I've invited you to, or how many modeling photo shoots in exotic locations. And you always would rather stay home with your flowers." She put the picture back in the duffel and zipped it closed. "But I get it. You aren't ready to tell anyone your secrets. Just like I wasn't ready to tell anyone mine until I met you and Eden."

Madison's secrets were nowhere close to Chloe's. Madison had grown up in a large family with a mother who switched out fathers like underwear. Chloe had only one father. At least that's what she'd thought until she turned fifteen.

"But once I confided in you and Eden," Madison contin-ued, "it was like this huge weight had been lifted off my shoulders. I suddenly realized that I was selling myself short by being an escort. I'm worth more than just a fur coat and fancy baubles." Her eyes turned dreamy. "Although I do love fur coats and fancy baubles." She shook her head. "Anyway, I just want you to know that, whenever you want to confide in someone, I'm here for you."

It was hard to keep tears from filling her eyes. But Chloe knew that if she let one fall, Madison wouldn't let her go. So she clicked on the hand vac and knelt down to clean up the potting soil. Once she was done, she picked up the peace lily and placed it back in the plastic pot, then filled the pot from the bag of soil she kept in the corner.

"Here." She handed it to Madison. "Maybe you can get the stupid thing to bloom."

Madison accepted it with sad eyes. "Is there anything you need before you leave?"

It was hard to get the words out. Chloe wasn't good at asking for help. "Actually, I need a place to stay until I leave and a loan. Just until I get my first check—"

Before she could finish, Madison had her in a bear hug. "Of course you can stay with me. And I would love to give you some money."

"Not give. I'll pay every cent back."

Madison released her and laughed. "You are as prideful as they come, Chloe McAlister. Which is just another reason why I love you. Now would you please find me some choco-late? I'm feeling the need for a sugar high."

They ended up polishing off an entire bag of Chips Ahoy! cookies, but it didn't give them much of a high. Madison was sad because Chloe was leaving, and Chloe was sad because she had to leave. Once Madison was gone, Chloe changed into her jean skirt and black T-shirt for work, then carried the remaining plants downstairs and left them next to Mr. Garcia's door. She didn't leave a note. Goodbyes were much easier without them. When she went back to her apartment for her duffel bag, the Romeo nightshirt caught her eye, the glittery name on the front standing out like a sign on the Vegas strip. Without another thought she picked it up and stuffed it in her duffel. Not only because it was her last gift from Madison, but also because it would serve as a reminder.

Never become a man's possession.

CHAPTER FOUR

After being mistaken for a bum and almost arrested, Grayson went straight home and shaved off his beard. Not all of it—he left a little stubble—but enough to make him feel as naked as his nudist neighbors, the Huckabees. He thought about trimming his hair, but then vetoed the idea. He was as bad at cutting hair as Chloe.

Or whatever her name was.

Grayson had thought that Chloe didn't want her face photographed or painted because of some silly girlie insecurity about her looks. But after what happened today, he had to wonder if the police officer was right and Chloe wasn't who she said she was. It seemed likely, given that she didn't have any identification or records. And if it was true, whom was she hiding from? The law? Her family? Another abusive jerk like Zac?

The questions stayed with him as he showered and dressed in a gray designer suit, then drove back to the office. He was almost relieved when his phone rang and gave him something else to think about. But his relief was short-lived when he answered his hands-free cell phone and Deacon's voice came through the car speakers.

"So I'm going to assume that I don't need to come bail you out of jail."

Grayson cringed. "I guess Kelly told you?"

"It happened right in front of our corporate office. Did you expect our employees to ignore the fact that one of their bosses was lying on the ground in handcuffs? When I asked you to take over, Gray, this wasn't what I had in mind."

As tired as Grayson was of being the perfect Beaumont brother, he hated disappointing Deacon. After their mother died, Deacon had given up a lot to make sure Grayson and Nash hadn't gone without. Not only had he worked to provide them with clothes and food, but he'd also given up his savings so Grayson could go to art school. Grayson owed him. And causing problems for French Kiss was a shitty way to pay him back for everything he'd done.

"I'm sorry, Deke," he said. "It was all a misunderstanding."

"So you're okay?"

"Yes, I'm fine, and everything is straightened out—"

Deacon erupted. "Straightened out? How can things be straightened out when one of the owners of French Kiss is plastered all over the Internet with the captions *Billionaire Bashes Cop* and *Rowdy Romeo Gets His Panties in a Twist*?"

Grayson tightened his grip on the steering wheel and blew out his breath. "Shit."

"Yes, I couldn't agree more. You've gotten yourself into a pile of shit—and subsequently, the company."

"But I didn't mean to hit the guy. I was trying to help…this woman and things got out of hand."

"We both know that the truth doesn't matter. The public only knows what it reads. And the damned online rag-mags have you pegged as a derelict jerk who beat up a police officer."

Grayson might be able to dispute beating up a police officer, but he couldn't dispute looking like a derelict or acting like a jerk. He had promised Deacon he would take care of things while Deacon was on baby leave, and all he'd been doing so far was moping around feeling sorry for himself because he couldn't paint.

"Okay, so what do we need to do to fix it?" he asked. He wasn't surprised when Deacon quickly answered. His big brother had an answer for everything.

"We can't get the pictures back, but we can show the public the real Grayson Romeo Beaumont."

The real Grayson Romeo Beaumont? Good luck with that. Grayson didn't have a clue who that guy was. At one time he'd been a creative painter. Now he was just an embarrassment to his family. Although Deacon didn't seem to think so.

"Let's show them the sensitive guy who defends women. *Entertainment Tonight* has been wanting to do a segment about the upcoming fashion show. Get Kelly to call them and see if they can squeeze it in tomorrow. I'm sure they'll jump at the chance to ask about the pictures."

"And what should I say?"

"Keep it simple and truthful. Just say it was all a misunderstanding and you were trying to help the woman. Who is she, anyway? The pictures weren't very clear."

Grayson didn't know why he'd kept Chloe's identity from his brother. Maybe because Deacon would ask more questions than Grayson was willing to answer. He didn't want to talk about Chloe. In fact he didn't even want to think about her. He was through with the woman. Let her keep her secrets.

"She's nobody," he said, before changing the subject. "So how's fatherhood?"

"A piece of cake. Everyone acted like a new baby was such hard work, but frankly, I don't see it. All the little guy does is sleep." Since the baby had been home for only a day, Grayson didn't know if Deacon had a true grasp of what being a new parent entailed. But he didn't point that out.

"Well, give Olivia and Mikey a kiss for me, and I'll try to stop by tomorrow night."

"Good. I'll expect an update on the interview. Oh, and before you do it, make sure you shave and get a haircut. After coming back from Paris, you look like shit."

Grayson laughed. "This coming from a man who used to have a beard down to his chest and whose favorite clothes were camouflage."

"True, but that was when I didn't have a multibillion dollar company to run." He paused. "Maybe I should come into work for just a little bit this afternoon."

"Absolutely not. You need to be with Olivia and the baby. Besides, I've got this covered."

It might've been an overstatement. Grayson didn't have anything covered. Especially not his personal life. But for his brothers, he would do his best. He got his first chance to prove himself when, on the way from the parking garage to the executive floor, the elevator stopped at the lobby. The same receptionist from the day before sat at the desk, her back to the front doors as she chatted on the phone. Her obvious lack of respect for her job prompted him to step off the elevator and walk to the desk.

"I know I have a boyfriend, Tiff, but I'm telling you that this flower guy is so hot." Grayson cleared his throat, and she glanced over her shoulder. When she saw him, her eyes widened. "I've got to go." She hung up and smiled brightly. "Mr. Beaumont. Don't you look handsome."

"Thank you..."—he glanced at her nametag—"Miss Daniels."

"You can call me Stacy." She fluttered eyelashes that were so long they looked cartoonish. "Is there something I can do for you, sir? I heard about what happened with the police. I knew that woman was trouble the first moment I set eyes on her."

It was the truth. Chloe was trouble. But that didn't excuse this woman's behavior.

"As a matter of fact, there is something you can do for me," he said. "You can start treating the visitors to French Kiss with the same respect you give me." When she looked completely baffled, he explained. "When someone walks in and asks to see either me or one of my brothers, you will treat them with courtesy, kindness, and respect. I don't care if it's a bum off the street or the president of the United States."

The lightbulb went on, and she made an attempt to defend her actions. "But she didn't have an appointment."

"That can be explained nicely without making a judgment about people's clothing or looks. Make sure it doesn't happen again or you're gone." Grayson turned to leave but then stopped and issued one more order. "And that phone is for business calls only."

When Grayson reached the elevators, he found the security guard grinning.

"That one has always been too sassy for her britches." He pushed the up button, then looked at Grayson. "I want to apologize for yesterday, Mr. Beaumont. I had no idea that the police would attempt to arrest you. Some folks don't know how to handle a badge. Especially when you were only trying to save that pretty little gal. To be honest, I never did believe she was trying to steal the ducky of roses."

"She wasn't," Grayson said.

The guard lifted his shaggy gray brows. "It would've made things a lot simpler if you had mentioned that earlier."

The elevator doors opened, and Grayson glanced at the guard before he stepped in. "Just for the record, there's nothing simple about that pretty little gal."

When Grayson reached the executive floor, he headed straight to Kelly's desk. If anyone could help him get through the next couple of weeks, it was Kelly. She could be a little bit of a loose cannon at times, but she was also loyal and efficient. She knew everything there was to know about French Kiss...gossip included.

"So there's the cop-abusing Beaumont," she said as soon as she saw Grayson. "My, but you clean up nice. You looked horrendous in your Facebook pictures."

He stepped up to her desk, which was cluttered with Hello Kitty figurines and sports paraphernalia. Both she and Jason were huge sports fans and spent most of their free time at games. "Make sure you thank Jason again for intervening, and I was thinking that I'd take over Deacon's office while he was gone. I'm not very good at this boss thing and was hoping you could help me."

Kelly grinned. "I wouldn't say that. You handled Stacy Daniels pretty well."

Holy crap. Gossip did travel fast in an office. Grayson ignored the comment and moved on. "So I'm going to need you to see if I can get an interview—"

"Done." Kelly handed him a memo. "*Entertainment Tonight* is sending a camera crew tomorrow morning, and the piece will be aired tomorrow night."

Grayson shook his head. "Deacon couldn't let me handle things, could he?"

Kelly laughed. "Are you kidding? In case you haven't figured this out, your brother's a huge control freak. The entire office is betting that he won't make it a week without coming back."

Grayson didn't think his brother would make it a week. In fact he wouldn't be surprised if Deacon walked down the hallway any second. But while Grayson had the ball, he might as well run with it. "So I thought we should have a few of the models at the interview. Call Madison and Natalia and see if they can be here."

"Fine, but I'm pretty sure *ET* is going to be more interested in your arrest than in your fashion show." She got up. "I'll get you some coffee. I think you're going to need it. Not only do you have to get ready for the interview but there's also a million phone calls and e-mails you need to return."

"Great." He walked into Deacon's office.

While Grayson had chosen a small office with good light for his studio, Deacon had chosen Uncle Michael's huge corner office with panoramic views of the Golden Gate Bridge and the bay. The decor of the office had once been of dark woods, bold paintings, and deep purple fabrics. Now it was furnished in a more contemporary style of glass and chrome with a light gray couch and lavender throw pillows. But the paintings were still the ones that had hung in Uncle Michael's office. They were all of Paris. The Eiffel Tower. The Seine. And the quaint little lingerie shop that had been his mother's inspiration for French Kiss.

Before Althea Beaumont had married Grayson's father, she had traveled to Paris. It was there she'd met Uncle Michael. His uncle had fallen head over heels in love with the beautiful Althea and brought her back to Louisiana to

introduce her to his family. It was a mistake. His mother
had taken one look at Donny John Beaumont and lost her
heart. And her dream of making lingerie. Instead she had
raised three sons before she lost her life to cancer. Or she
had raised two sons. Grayson had been only eight when his
mother died.

When Grayson had lost his ability to draw, he had gone
to Paris, hoping to find inspiration as his mother had. But all
he'd found was disappointment and a deep, nagging ache for
the mother he couldn't remember.

Ignoring the pain, he turned and walked to Deacon's
desk. He spent what was left of the afternoon answering
phone calls and e-mails, rescheduling meetings until after
Deacon and Nash came back, and coming up with answers
for any questions that *ET* might ask about the incident with
the police. Until now he had always avoided the business
side of French Kiss, preferring to deal with the creative side.
But now that his creative side had deserted him, he discovered he enjoyed the monotonous tasks and wasn't even
aware of how late it was until Kelly poked her head in.

"I stayed late to try and get things organized for you, but
now I've got to go home and have sex with my husband before the ovulating window of opportunity closes. That's why
I had the doctor's appointment this morning: Jason and I are
trying to get pregnant. And it's a lot harder than I thought it
would be. You have to take your temperature and keep track
on a calendar and pee on a stick." When Grayson cringed,
she laughed. "I guess that was too much information for a
single guy."

"Just a little. But I wish you luck. And tell Jason that I
want to meet with him in the morning to go over contracts."

"Will do. See you in the morning." She closed the door.

After Kelly left, Grayson pulled up the pictures of the

new designs. Besides taking on Deacon and Nash's job, he still needed to get the holiday catalog out. Which meant he might be spending the night in Deacon's office. Especially after seeing the pictures Miles had taken. Miles was an excellent photographer, but he'd missed the mark on the Romeo Collection. The pictures looked too sweet. Too romantic. They needed edge. While he was studying the pictures, Madison breezed into the office, looking like the sexy lingerie model she was in a clingy red dress and sky-high heels.

He rose and walked over to greet her. Of all the models, he liked Madison the best. She was a straight shooter with a heart of gold. He still couldn't figure out why she was such good friends with Chloe. "You're working late, Maddie."

She kissed his cheek. "So are you. I'm surprised that you aren't in your studio painting. But I guess there's a lot to do with Deacon and Nash both gone." She pulled back. "So you decided to shave the beard."

"It was time. Is there a problem? I hope you're not here to cancel on the *ET* interview tomorrow. Your and Natalia's presence will take some of the heat off me."

"No, I'll be there. I just stopped by because I have a dilemma that I thought you could help me with."

He leaned against the desk and crossed his arms. "Shoot."

"I want you to call Nash and make sure he doesn't let Eden talk him into cutting their honeymoon short."

"But why would they cut their honeymoon short?"

Madison gave a guilty shrug. "Because I made the mistake of calling Eden and telling her that Chloe is skipping town."

CHAPTER FIVE

*M*ondays were a slow night at The Lemon Drop, and since the tips were dismal, Chloe probably should've called in sick. She was a nervous wreck all night waiting for some private detective to walk in the door looking for her.

"Got a late date?"

She turned to the man who sat at the table in the corner. Jeff was a regular at the bar and had been since his wife left him. He wasn't the type of guy who was looking for solace in a bottle. He just wanted someone to talk to about his wife's desertion, and for some reason he'd chosen Chloe. Which made her very uncomfortable, especially since she'd found out he was an FBI agent. All she needed was someone from the federal government getting suspicious about her identity. Still, she couldn't bring herself to ignore the poor guy.

"Excuse me?" she said.

Jeff took a sip of his beer. "You keep looking at the door. I just thought you were expecting someone."

Obviously she needed to do a better job of hiding her anxiety. "No," she said. "No date, hot or otherwise." She finished wiping off the table next to his before she picked up her tray and walked over. "And what about you? Don't you think that it's time to start dating again?"

He shook his head. "I don't think I'm ready. I let one of my friends at the Bureau fix me up with his sister, and it was a disaster. I talked about Shelly all through dinner."

"Well, that explains why it was a disaster. Women don't want to hear about past loves."

"I gathered that after she went to the bathroom and never came back."

His dejected look had Chloe trying to make him feel better. "Well, it's her loss. If she had given you a chance, she would've realized what a great guy you are. Although I do think that it's time to forget Shelly and move on, Jeff."

After only a moment, he nodded. "You're right. I need to move on. Shelly certainly has. She hasn't even texted me since she left."

Chloe wiped the table around his beer. "Which only proves that she's not a good person and you're better off without her. I'm sure there are tons of nice women who would love to date a handsome FBI agent."

He lowered his eyes and fiddled with the damp napkin under his beer bottle. "So what about you? Would you like to go out some time?" He looked up and grinned. "I've already told you everything that happened between me and Shelly, so I'll have to talk about something else."

Jeff was exactly the kind of guy she should date. He was nice and clean-cut and didn't look like he had an abusive bone in his body. Unfortunately, she was leaving. And even if she weren't, her life was too screwed up to add an FBI agent to the mix.

"I'm sorry, Jeff. I can't."

"It doesn't have to be serious," he rushed on. "We could just go get coffee. Or a drive to Napa Valley."

Just the mention of the Wine Country made panic well up inside, but before she could decline the offer, a voice spoke from behind her.

"I think the lady said no."

The smooth Southern drawl had Chloe whirling to find Grayson standing there. He looked very different from the bum she had talked with earlier in the day. He'd shaved his beard to a light dusting of scruff, and his long hair was combed back from his forehead and smoothed behind his ears. He wore a suit, but without a tie, his light lavender dress shirt unbuttoned at the throat. Unlike this afternoon, he looked every bit the billionaire.

"When do you get off?" he asked. Or more like demanded. And the demanding tone had her bristling.

"That's none of your business." She hugged the tray to her chest and headed to the three businessmen a couple of tables away. But as she took their empty glasses and asked if they wanted another round, she could feel Grayson's penetrating eyes on her. And sure enough, when she headed to the bar to drop off the glasses and place her order, he was sitting on a barstool watching her.

She tried to ignore him, but it proved to be impossible. The intensity of those eyes made her make one blunder after another. She screwed up orders. Brought back the wrong change. And slipped in a puddle of beer that someone had spilled on the floor and landed hard on her butt, breaking three empty margarita glasses when she dropped her tray.

Both Grayson and Jeff got up to help her but, unfortunately, Grayson got to her first. "Are you okay?" He held out a hand.

"Just dandy." She ignored the hand and glared at him. "What do you want?"

"Rum and coke."

She rolled her eyes. "I'm not talking about a drink. Why are you here screwing up my night?"

"We need to talk." He glanced at Jeff, who hovered over them. "In private."

She couldn't help it. She was curious. "Fine." She got to her feet, careful to avoid the broken glass. "I get off at midnight."

He nodded. "I'll be waiting outside." He pulled out his wallet and tossed a twenty on the bar.

"You didn't have a drink, so you don't owe anything."

A smirky smile lifted the corners of his mouth. "Just call it a tip for entertainment." As he turned to leave, Jeff snapped his fingers.

"That's it! I've been sitting there racking my brain trying to place you, and it finally hit me. You're one of those panty billionaires. The one who paints pictures of naked women."

Grayson looked at him, his eyes devoid of any emotion. "You're wrong. I don't paint." He turned and walked out.

Why that statement should bother Chloe, she didn't know. It shouldn't make any difference to her if Grayson could paint. And yet she couldn't stop thinking about it. Not as she continued to serve drinks and fend off Jeff's attempts to get her to go out with him, and not while she helped close up the bar. She finally stopped thinking about it when the owner informed her that she owed him twenty dollars of her tips for the broken margarita glasses. Which had her a wee bit snappy when she stepped outside and found Grayson leaning against the hood of a gray Bugatti sports car.

"What?" she said as she strolled over. "Are all you Beaumonts color challenged? Gray and purple. Purple and gray."

"My SUV is black." He opened the door of the car and waited for her to get in.

"I'm not going anywhere until you tell me what's going on."

"Get in, Chloe." He paused. "Although I'll make a bet that isn't the name that goes with your Social Security number, is it?"

It wasn't that hard to mask her fear. She'd spent most of her life masking her fear. With a mere shrug, she got into the car. The inside was like a cockpit upholstered in purple leather. There were cutting-edge dials and gadgets galore. But she paid little attention to them as she shoved her duffel bag in the small space behind the seats. She expected Grayson to start interrogating her as soon as he slipped into the driver's seat. Instead he buckled his seat belt and pushed a button on the dash. The engine growled, then quickly settled into a low purr.

"Where are you taking me?"

He pulled away from the curb. "Put on your seat belt."

It was good advice. Grayson drove faster than her cousin Gavin when he'd first gotten his license. His hands and feet worked in perfect harmony on the gearshift and pedals as they flew through the streets. On one steep hill, the car seemed to take flight, but the landing was so smooth that she might've imagined it.

"You drive like a maniac." Chloe reached for her seat belt and buckled it. "What happened to the cautious guy who drove me to Grover Beach and never once went over the speed limit?"

He downshifted around a corner. "Maybe he got bored with going slow."

"Well, it's better to be boring than dead," she said, even though she couldn't deny that there was something exhilarating about speeding through the city in the sleek sports car while most people slept safely in their beds. As the speedometer inched higher, so did the beat of her heart, and when they finally hit the Bay Bridge and he opened the car up full throttle, she couldn't help her quick intake of breath. She glanced over to see if Grayson had noticed and found those piercing eyes on her.

"Admit it," he said, "you like going fast."

She rolled down the window and let the cool air whip over her flushed face. "Maybe," she said above the wind and the pounding of her heart. "But I liked Zac too and look where that got me."

There was a long pause before he spoke. "Is that why you're leaving? Are you afraid of Zac getting out of jail?"

Her gaze collided with his. "Who told you I'm leaving?" Only a second later, she answered the question herself. "Madison."

He passed a huge semitruck, the red lights on the side of the trailer reflecting in his eyes. "You should know that Maddie has never been able to keep a secret. Not only has she told me, but she also told Eden. Now Eden wants to come home from her honeymoon to talk you out of it. And I'm not going to let you ruin my brother's honeymoon because you're running scared."

"I'm not running scared," she lied. "I'm just done with San Francisco. That's all."

"Right. Which is why you hid from all those people taking pictures." He glanced over at her. "So who are you?"

It wasn't an easy question to answer, so she didn't. And much to her relief Grayson didn't push it.

His shoulder lifted in a slight shrug. "It doesn't matter to me. In fact, I don't even care if you leave. You've been a pain in my ass ever since I've met you. But I refuse to let you throw a wrench in Eden's honeymoon like you did her wedding."

She turned to him. "How did I throw a wrench in her wedding?"

"You refused to be her bridesmaid and didn't even have the common courtesy to show up."

It was hard not to be flooded with guilt, but she refused to give in to it. "Eden is better off without me as a friend."

"I don't doubt that for a second. Unfortunately, for some reason, Eden doesn't feel the same way. She's convinced that you need her help, and she's not going to let you leave town without a fight."

It sounded like Eden. She was a goal-setting overachiever who refused to give up on people. Even a grumpy pain in the butt like Chloe. Unfortunately, Chloe didn't have a choice. She had to leave.

"No one can talk me out of it," she said.

Grayson released a tired sigh. "I was afraid you were going to say that." He took the next exit and turned around. When he was back on the freeway heading to San Francisco, Chloe tried to alleviate his fears.

"Look, I'll call Eden tonight and talk her out of coming home. Believe it or not, I didn't want to ruin her wedding, and I certainly don't want to ruin her honeymoon. I like Eden. And that's why I tried to cut things off between us. In case you haven't noticed, I'm bad luck."

Grayson snorted. "Oh, I've noticed."

It was one thing for her to say it and another for him to agree. "Now wait a minute. You're not trying to blame your inability to paint on me, are you? Because I had nothing to do with that. Whatever happened to your creative mojo must've happened in Paris because it was only after you came back that you started acting so weird." She glanced over at him. "So was it a girl? Come on. You can tell me. Unlike Maddie, I know how to keep a secret. Did you fall in love with a sweet little mademoiselle and she didn't return your love?"

He continued to stare at the road, although, even in the shadows, she could see his jaw tighten. "There's no sweet little mademoiselle."

"Don't tell me it's a monsieur," she teased.

He shot her a mean look. "Don't push it, Chloe—or whatever your name is."

"It's Chloe," she said. "At least, it is now. And if it's not a woman that screwed up your mojo, then what do you think caused it?" When he didn't answer, she crossed her arms and slumped down in the seat. "Fine, but if you want to paint again, you need to figure out what the problem is and face it."

He glanced at her. "Sort of like you face your problems?"

She looked away. "Point taken."

After that they didn't talk. Grayson drove like a bat out of hell, and Chloe just sat there and stared out the windshield. When they got back to San Francisco, she asked him to drop her off at Madison's. But instead of heading for Madison's high-rise, he took her in the opposite direction.

"Hey, where are you going?" she asked. "I thought you knew where Madison lives."

"I know where she lives," he said. "But I need to stop by my house for a second and check on Jonathan."

"What or who is Jonathan? Is that another Beaumont or a dog?"

"It's a bird."

She looked at him. "I didn't picture you as a bird kind of guy. Rottweiler, yes. Bird, no."

Five minutes later he turned into the driveway of a pretty

three-story row house. He pressed the remote clipped to his visor, and the garage door opened before he pulled in right next to the black Range Rover he'd used to drive her to Eden's parents' house. Eden's parents had offered her their home as a safe house until Zac was arrested, and the reminder made Chloe feel even more guilty about skipping Eden's wedding.

"Look," she said. "I promise I'll talk Eden out of coming back." She swallowed her pride. "And I want to thank you for driving me to Grover Beach after Zac . . ." She let the sentence drift off. "Anyway, I appreciated it."

Grayson turned to her. She'd thought that all Beaumonts were flawless, but being this close, she realized her mistake. Grayson wasn't perfect. His nose had a bump on the bridge, the curves of his top lip were slightly uneven, and his chin had an indention in the center. Although most women probably wouldn't call that a flaw. There was something sexy about it. Something that made her want to slide her tongue along the whiskery cleft. Her gaze traveled to his uneven top lip. It really wasn't a flaw either. She lifted her eyes to the bump on his nose.

But before she could assess the imperfection, she got lost in his eyes. Captivating eyes that seemed to pull all the stress and worry from her and replace it with a feeling of . . . desire. Desire to lose herself in the lavender fields of his eyes and never return to her harsh reality. Without even realizing what she was doing, she tipped her head and moved closer. Her mouth was a breath away from those imperfect lips when the garage light clicked off. Once hidden in darkness, Grayson's eyes no longer held her spellbound, and she pulled away.

Damn. He is the Woman Whisperer.

Feeling completely foolish, she scrambled for something that might distract him from the fact that she had been about to kiss him. "Umm...I guess I'll just wait here while you check on your bird."

After what felt like an eternity, he opened the car door and got out. But instead of heading inside, he walked around the hood of the car and opened her door. "Come on, I want you to meet Jonathan."

She should've stayed in the car. The desire strumming through her veins wasn't good. Unfortunately, she was curious. Not about the bird, but about Grayson's house.

It wasn't what she'd expected. For some reason she'd thought his house would be filled with art and color and as messy as his French Kiss studio. Instead the living area on the third floor was very white, very contemporary, and very neat, with muted paintings of the ocean on the walls. As if reading her mind, he explained, "I haven't changed much of anything since my sister-in-law Olivia lived here." He walked to the balcony and opened the sliding glass doors. He peeked out, then closed the door and turned to her. "I guess Jonathan Livingston Seagull is roosting elsewhere for the night."

Chloe couldn't hide her surprise. "A seagull? I thought you were talking about a parakeet or a parrot. You can't have a seagull for a pet."

"Tell that to Jonathan. I can't seem to get rid of the bird." He walked into the kitchen. "So do you want something to drink? Something to eat?"

Since she had burned off the Chips Ahoy! cookies hours ago, she was starving. But she wasn't taking any chances on the weird thing that had happened in the car happening again.

"No, thank you," she said. "I really need to get going. Madison is expecting me."

"Suit yourself." He pulled a bottle of water out of the

fridge and unscrewed the cap. She watched as his lips opened slightly and kissed the opening of the bottle. Watched as his tanned, whiskered throat bobbed with each swallow. He lowered the bottle and studied her, and she hoped the lighting was dim enough that he couldn't see the flush on her cheeks. "So I can't talk you out of going." It was more a statement than a question, so she didn't answer. With an exasperated sigh, he set the bottle of water on the counter. "Then I guess I don't have any choice."

Chloe didn't comment. She'd figured out a long time ago that few people had choices. Most were just pawns in someone else's game.

He headed for the stairs, and she followed behind him. On the second level, he turned toward an open door. "I thought you might like to see the rest of the house before we go."

The bedroom was more like Grayson's studio. Clothes littered the floor. The king-size bed was unmade. Paint tubes covered the top of the dresser. And canvases rested in stacks against one wall.

"Let me guess," she said as she stepped in. "This is your room."

Grayson studied her with his intense eyes. "Actually, for the next week, it's your room." He walked out, and there was a click as the door closed behind him, followed by the sound of a dead bolt sliding into place.

CHAPTER SIX

*I*t was kidnapping. There were no two ways about it. Grayson was keeping a woman against her will. Something he'd never thought he would do. Of course, he'd never thought he'd stop painting either. And yet he couldn't even paint an apple. Obviously he had changed...and not for the better.

He made sure that the dead bolt he'd installed on the door before he'd gone to The Lemon Drop was secure, then went back upstairs and turned on the television to try to drown out the pounding and yelling coming from his room. It didn't help. And finally he picked up his cell phone and called his home number.

She picked up on the first ring. "Have you lost your mind!"

Since it certainly felt like it, he ignored the question and moved on. "It's only for a week. Once Nash and Eden are back, you can do whatever you want."

"You realize that, since you left me with a phone, I can call the police, right?"

"You could, but we both know that you won't. I think your fear of the police was proven this morning."

There was a long stretch of silence before she spoke. "I really hate this new Grayson." She hung up.

He stared at his phone. Yeah, he hated him too.

It was a restless night. He tried to watch some late-night television, but nothing held his attention. So he finally went to bed. He slept in Nash's old room, the one right next to his, and every sound that came through the wall had him wondering what she was doing. She had stopped pounding on the door and yelling. Now she seemed to be moving around, opening drawers and then slamming them closed. It was annoying to think of her going through his stuff, but he had little choice. His bedroom was the only one with an adjoining bathroom.

After what seemed like hours, there was silence. The silence freaked him out even more. But silence had always freaked him out. Having grown up with two rowdy brothers, a carousing father who came in at all hours, and a snoring grandfather, he was used to noise. After Nash had moved in with Eden, the house had suddenly been quiet... and empty. At first Grayson had thought the quiet would help him paint. But it had the reverse effect. The quiet seemed to suck all the creativity right out of him, and he was left with his logical brain. A brain that always ended up in the same place.

His mom.

He'd seen enough pictures of her to know what she looked like. In fact every feature was stenciled into his brain. Even now he could pull up her image in vivid detail—the deep indigo of her eyes, the uneven curves of her lips, and the delicate bones of her body. But while he could visualize her, and even sketch her, he couldn't pull up one memory.

Not one. Not of her eyes filling with love. Of her lips pressing to his cheek. Of her arms hugging him close.

Which made no sense. He had been young when she died, but not so young that he shouldn't be able to remember one thing about her. Especially when he had other memories. Like catching his first fish with his father when he was four. And crashing on his bike when he was five. And winning a drawing contest when he was six. He remembered every detail of those events, from the color of the scales on the fish to the color of his first grade teacher's dress when she handed him the blue ribbon. But not his mom. No matter how hard he tried, he couldn't find memories of his mother.

Grayson's thoughts were interrupted by the faint sound of snoring coming through the wall. He listened for a moment before a smile broke over his face. Then he rolled over and went to sleep.

He woke to early-morning light. It took a few blinks to remember he had a guest. Or more like a captive. Surprisingly, he liked the idea of Chloe's being his captive…maybe a little too much. Climbing out of bed, he headed for her room. He opened the door to discover what she had been doing last night. He stared at the paint splattered all over the wall above his headboard. He hated to admit it, but Chloe painted better than he did. Beneath the painting Chloe slept. She had taken off her sneakers and jeans and was sprawled on her stomach. The hem of her T-shirt rode up, and he could see her red panties and the half moons of her bare butt cheeks. One had a streak of purple paint.

Grayson's right hand twitched, but he ignored the involuntary movement and closed the door. He showered and got dressed in another gray suit. He had a multitude of things to do that day, including the interview. But before he went to work, he collected some food for Chloe. He wasn't much of an eater, so the pickings were slim. He chose the nonperishable items—a jar of peanut butter, a box of stale crackers, a couple of PowerBars, and three diet colas that had been left in the refrigerator months before by one of the models who had posed for him.

He put the food in a grocery sack, then retrieved her duffel bag from his car and took both back to his room. When he opened the door, Chloe had rolled to her side and was hugging the same pillow he slept on. He studied the sweet curve of her leg wrapped around the soft, down-filled pillow for only a second before he set the bags on the dresser. The zipper on the duffel bag was partway opened, and something glittery caught his attention. He had never been much of a snoop, but he couldn't help sliding the zipper the rest of the way open.

The glittery name on the front of the shirt had him glancing over at Chloe. He could understand her having the nightshirt from his collection: As a model Madison got first choice of lingerie and had no doubt shared with her friend. Even the panties Chloe wore were from French Kiss. But if Chloe was leaving town and had packed only one small bag, why would a nightshirt with his name be included?

The question stayed with him all the way to French Kiss's corporate office, but he couldn't come up with a single answer...except for one. Maybe Chloe didn't hate him as much as he thought. He had barely started to digest the notion when his cell phone rang. He pulled into his executive parking space and answered.

Chloe's voice came through the receiver loud and clear. "I like smooth peanut butter, not chunky. And I don't drink cola—especially diet. Are you saying I'm fat?"

Grayson couldn't help the smile that spread over his face. He should've known that being held hostage wouldn't stifle her spunk. "Not even close, but I was out of chocolate milk and Fritos." As soon as the words were out, he wanted them back. But it was too late. Her reply came only seconds later.

"You remembered?"

Yes, he remembered. There was very little of their road trip that he had forgotten. He remembered the skinny jeans she'd been wearing and the way they hugged her butt when she'd run into the gas station to buy her chocolate milk and Fritos. He remembered the way her soft-looking top had fluttered in the breeze when she came back out, showing a peep of her stomach and the top of her tattoo. He remembered her falling asleep, and the way the sunlight had reflected off the red in her dark-brown hair and the diamond stud in her nose. But most of all he remembered her sullen attitude and biting remarks. Which made him veto his theory about why she had his night-shirt in her bag. Chloe didn't like him. She barely tolerated him. Which made his reply short and snappy.

"I've got to go." He hung up.

When he got to Deacon's office, Kelly greeted him wearing a Hello Kitty belt and holding a full morning agenda. "You have a meeting at nine with Miles for the catalog," she said as she followed him into the office. "At ten you have a meeting with Samuel, and at eleven the film crew from *ET* will be here. I thought you'd want to do it in the design studio. Madison and Natalia will meet you there. And after that you have a meeting with Deirdre Beaumont about the charity event she's planning."

"Great. Thanks, Kelly." He glanced at his watch. He had exactly thirty minutes to take care of some personal business. "What time do you think it is in Greece?"

"I don't know. You want me to find out?"

"If you would. And if it's not in the middle of the night, get Nash on the phone for me."

"Will do."

It turned out that it was only evening in Greece, a perfect time to call a honeymooning couple. Or so he thought until it took forever for Nash to answer, and when he did, he sounded out of breath.

"If I've interrupted something, Nash, I can call back," Grayson said.

Nash laughed. "I'm not having sex, Gray. I'm running."

"On your honeymoon?"

"Eden thought we needed to get out of the room," he said. "Although if she keeps teasing me with those tight running pants, I'm going to continue our honeymoon right here."

"Nash!" Eden's voice came through the receiver. "Would you cut it out? I'm trying to find my rhythm."

"I can show you some rhythm, baby—ow-w-w. I wish your brothers had never taught you how to frog someone in the arm. That hurt like hell."

Grayson laughed. "Now you know how I felt when you and Deacon punched me in the arm."

"I never punched you as hard as Eden punches me. I swear I'm going to have to turn the woman in for abuse." His voice got a sweet tone. "Just kidding, honey, I would never turn you in for abuse, even though that riding crop did sting a little—"

"Nash!"

Nash laughed. It was a good laugh. One that didn't carry any of the pain it once had. As much as he missed having his brother living with him, Grayson was glad he had found happiness.

"So what's up, Gray?" Nash asked. "Are there problems at French Kiss?"

He probably should've mentioned his arrest, but that

could wait until Nash got back. "No problems. Actually I called to talk with Eden."

Without hesitation Nash handed over the phone. "Here, baby, Gray wants to talk to you."

A few seconds later, Eden got on, sounding completely out of breath. "Hello?"

"Sorry to bother you, Eden, but Madison mentioned that you were thinking about cutting your honeymoon short so you could come back and talk Chloe out of leaving, and I wanted to let you know that there's no need to worry. Chloe isn't going anywhere until you get back."

"She's not? How did you change her mind?"

Grayson could've lied, but he didn't want Eden getting her hopes up that Chloe was going to stay in San Francisco. "I kidnapped her."

There was a pause. "I'm sorry, Gray, but I must have a bad connection because it sounded like you said that you kidnapped her."

"That's exactly what I said. It was the only way I could figure out how to keep her here until you got back from your honeymoon."

The next pause was quickly followed by shouted words that made his ears ring. "I love you, Grayson Beaumont! And if I was there right now, I would give you a big kiss—"

Suddenly Nash was back on the phone. "What the hell, Gray? Are you trying to seduce my woman?"

Before he could answer, Eden must've grabbed the phone. "Don't pay him any attention, Grayson. I'll explain everything later. Just keep Chloe there until I get home and can talk her into staying."

"Are you sure that's smart? She hasn't exactly been the best of friends."

"Chloe's a good person. She just hides all her goodness

behind a tough exterior. But now that I have more time, I'm going to get her to drop the tough act and let people love her. Thank you so much, Gray. You just gave me the best honeymoon present ever."

"Excuse me." Nash's voice came through the speaker. "I'll show you the best honeymoon present ever." Eden squealed, and it sounded like the phone was dropped. Figuring that the call was over, Grayson hung up, satisfied that he had saved his brother's honeymoon.

Unfortunately, the rest of his morning didn't go as well. The photographer for the catalog was not happy when Grayson told him that he wanted edgier photographs for the Romeo Collection. In fact Miles was so pissed that Grayson would question his "creative eye" that he stormed out of the office. Which wasn't good when they had only a few weeks before the catalog needed to be out. And to top that off, the interview was a complete disaster. Not because Grayson flubbed any of the questions about his near arrest— he seemed to do okay answering those. No, the problem came when Natalia couldn't seem to keep her hands to herself.

While Madison sat next to him and answered any questions the interviewer tossed her way, Natalia wrapped herself around Grayson like a cat around a scratching post and seemed unable to answer one question without including him.

"Oh, I love everything French Kiss gives me to wear." She smiled seductively at Grayson. "But especially Gar-a-son's."

"Yes, I get a little nervous on the runway, but not if I'm with Gar-a-son."

"Am I dating Gar-a-son?" She smiled slyly. "I never kiss and tell."

By the time the interview was over, Grayson was so sick of his own name he wanted to change it. Instead he smiled politely until the *ET* crew had left the design studio, then he very calmly informed Natalia that they weren't dating, because he couldn't date a French Kiss employee. It wasn't exactly the truth. French Kiss didn't have an official interoffice dating policy—more than likely because Deacon couldn't have a rule he hadn't followed. After they inherited French Kiss, he'd promptly fallen in love with the CEO. Unfortunately, Natalia didn't take the news well. She burst into tears and raced from the design studio.

"I wouldn't worry about it," Madison said after Natalia was gone. "She's always been overly dramatic. Although I would worry about Miles. From what I hear, he's thinking about quitting."

"Great," Grayson muttered before he headed back to his office for his next appointment. He could only hope that his meeting with Deirdre would go better than his first two. Of course it was doubtful, since Deirdre Beaumont intimidated the hell out of him. She was his uncle Michael's widow, Olivia's mother, Deacon's mother-in-law, French Kiss's head designer's girlfriend, and an obstinate, opinioned socialite who was used to getting her own way. And she was not used to people showing up late for her meetings.

"Did you lose your watch, Grayson?" she asked as soon as he stepped into the office. She was sitting in Deacon's chair as if she belonged there, leaving him to take the chair in front of the desk.

"I'm sorry, Mrs. Beaumont. The interview with *ET* ran over."

Her eyebrow lifted. "Hmm, well, you're here now, so let's get started. And please call me Deirdre. After all, we're family."

"Sorry," he said. "My mother was a stickler for showing respect to one's—" He stopped when he realized what he had been about to say. Unfortunately, it was too late.

"Elders," she finished the sentence for him, looking as if she had just swallowed a lemon whole. "Yes, well, be that as it may, this *elder* would like to be called Deirdre."

He cleared his throat and loosened his tie. "So how can I help you with the benefit…Deirdre? Did you need money? Some of French Kiss's employees to help you pull it together? All of my resources are at your disposal."

She smiled slyly. "I was hoping you would say that. Because your resources are exactly what I need."

Just that quickly he started to panic. How had he forgotten the last benefit that Deirdre had put together? The Romeo costume with tights that she'd wanted him to wear had been damned humiliating. Which was why he'd had to switch costumes with Nash. But since Nash wasn't here, there would be no getting out of whatever she had in store for him this time.

He swallowed hard. "Exactly what kind of benefit is this?"

"Since your mother passed away from cancer, I thought it was fitting to champion that cause." She smoothed out her cream-colored pants and crossed her legs. "At the time I offered my services to the American Cancer Society, I thought I would have all the Beaumont brothers at my disposal to help with the charity event. But then Nash decided to get married, and Olivia got pregnant with my most precious grandson." Her gaze locked with his. "So that only leaves you."

The feeling that crept up his spine could be described only as fear. He cleared his throat. "I don't think that's true. Nash will be back in a week, and after talking to Deacon, it sounds like he's got the baby thing under control so he shouldn't have any problems helping out as well."

Deirdre's eyebrow lifted. "Really? Is that what he told you?"

Grayson nodded. "I guess all Mikey does is sleep."

"Hmm?" Her coral-painted lips tipped up in a knowing smile. "I think that Deacon is figuring out who is in control as we speak." The smile faded. "So where was I? Ah, yes, you were telling me that you would be more than happy to offer all the resources I need for the charity event. And since you are the talented one of the bunch, I've decided that an art show featuring your paintings will be the perfect way to help raise money for cancer research."

Grayson felt the bottom drop out of his stomach. Art was the last thing he wanted to think about. "I'm sorry, Mrs. . . . Deirdre, but I don't think that's going to work."

Her spine stiffened. "Of course it's going to work. I realize, with Nash and Deacon gone, you have a lot to do here. So I don't expect you to pull it together. I'll be in charge of finding the venue, caterer, and so forth. All you have to do is donate the paintings." She opened her purse and pulled out a pen and day planner. "What day would be good for me to come to your house and see your collection of paintings? How about tomorrow at two?"

"No!" The word came out a little too loudly. When she glanced up in confusion, he tried to cover his mistake. "I mean I don't keep my paintings at my house."

Her eyebrow hiked up. "Really? Then where do you keep them? Because I stopped off at your office and didn't see anything but some bad paintings of apples. Were you teaching one of the models to paint? Because the woman has no talent whatsoever."

Grayson felt his face heat. "I'm sorry, Deirdre. I'm afraid

that I don't have enough paintings for a show. I gave you most of my paintings to auction off at the Lover's Charity Ball."

"But that was six months ago. Certainly you've painted more by now."

"I'm afraid not. But what I can do is get another artist to donate paintings for the benefit."

Her eyes darkened, and he thought she was going to storm out like Miles and Natalia. He should've known better. Deirdre Beaumont didn't storm. After only a moment, she calmly made a note in her planner before she got up and walked out.

Which was much more terrifying.

It was like she had just marked him for a hit.

CHAPTER SEVEN

$\mathscr{C}$hloe should be steaming mad. Surprisingly, she wasn't. At least, she wasn't anymore. She had been thoroughly pissed after Grayson had locked her in his room. She'd screamed and ranted and thrown a major fit, which included slapping paint all over Grayson's pristine white walls. After she did that, her anger sort of fizzled out.

There was something very freeing and cathartic about painting, and she now understood why Grayson felt lost without it. Painting gave you a medium to express all your pent-up emotions. And that's exactly what Chloe had done; she'd released all her anger in streaks and splats of paint. Not just her anger at Grayson, but also her anger at life. The wall became a huge abstract self-portrait of her past pain. The slash of purple represented her bruises from Zac. The blossom of pink, the frilly dresses her father had bought his only daughter. The blue, her mother's face on her deathbed. And the huge splatter of red over the pink and blue, her mother's betrayal.

Once the painting was finished, she'd promptly fallen asleep and slept better than she had in a long time. When she woke, she realized that having been kidnapped by Grayson wasn't such a bad thing. Except for Grayson, no one knew where she was. Which meant that she was safe until her plane left.

After eating the stale crackers and peanut butter, she set about cleaning up the mess. Not that she was solely responsible for it. Grayson was one messy dude. He didn't hang up his clothes, organize his T-shirts and underwear in separate drawers, or pair up his shoes in the closet. In the bathroom he didn't put the cap on his toothpaste, separate hair products from over-the-counter medicine in the cabinet over the sink, or put his toilet paper on the holder. So she spent the next couple of hours doing those things for him.

She organized the silk shirts, gray suits, and purple ties in his closet, then categorized his paint-splattered T-shirts, worn jeans, running shorts, boxer briefs, and socks into different drawers of his dresser—tossing the socks that didn't have mates. She lined up his paint supplies by color and brush size before moving to his nightstand. In the top drawer, she found sketchpads and all different types of sketching pencils. She went through the sketchpads and found them empty. Grayson really had lost his ability to create. She put the sketchpads back and opened the second drawer of the nightstand.

There was only one sketchpad in this drawer, and it looked as if it had seen better days. The front cover was worn and aged, and the wire binding discolored and misshapen. The first drawings weren't very good, but still better than what Chloe could do. They were all of a dog sitting or sleeping. Gradually the drawings became better, with more action—the dog running, jumping, catching a ball. But it was the sketch after these that showed the artist's true talent.

A woman stood at a clothesline with her lithe arms stretched up, hanging a sheet that billowed around her slim body. Her long hair waved in the wind, and a slight smile played on her lips as if she was thoroughly enjoying the task or thinking of something happy. More sketches of the woman followed. Her sitting at a sewing machine. Standing at a stove. Playing with the dog and two cute boys. Even though they were young, Chloe easily recognized the boys as Grayson's brothers. Which meant that the woman had to be Grayson's mother. A woman who had died of cancer just like Chloe's mom had.

A sharp pang of pain and regret surfaced for a brief moment before Chloe pushed it down deep and closed the sketchpad. She'd started to put it back in the drawer when she noticed the smudged inscription on the cover. Holding it close, she read the words.

"To my sweet Graysie, Never stop creating. Love, Mom."

Suddenly everything became crystal clear. This was why Grayson was so obsessed with painting. He viewed this as his mother's last request. A last request he could no longer fulfill.

Again Chloe wondered what had caused his problem. Whatever it was, it had to have happened in Paris. He had been painting fine before he left. In fact for most of their road trip, he'd tried to talk her into posing for him.

She paused with her hand on the knob of the nightstand drawer as a thought struck her. A thought she quickly rejected. Her refusal couldn't possibly be responsible for his painting drought. He didn't even like her that much. No, his problem had no doubt started with some French beauty.

After she finished cleaning the room, Chloe was starving.

Since there was no way to get out the door, she opened the window. The bedroom was on the second floor. She could probably figure out a way to get down, but then how would she get back in? Above her the balcony caught her attention. The night before, Grayson hadn't locked the sliding balcony door after he'd checked on his seagull. Which meant that there was a good chance it was still unlocked. She calculated the distance between the decorative ledge that ran along the exterior of the wall and the balcony. It would be dangerous, but she had always enjoyed danger.

It didn't take her long to remove the screen and pull Grayson's painting stool over to the open window. If she could inch along the ledge to the balcony, she figured she could grab the metal railing and pull herself up. Unfortunately, the pulling-herself-up part was harder than she'd thought. She was struggling to get a good grip on the railing when her feet slipped off the ledge, and she was left dangling. The feel of cold air on her butt cheeks had her wishing that she'd taken the time to put on some jeans. Especially when she seemed to have an audience.

"Doris!" The yell almost made her lose her hold on the balcony railing. "There's another woman trying to jump off the neighbor's house and splatter her brains on the pavement."

The image of her brains being splattered on the pavement gave Chloe the strength she needed to pull her body higher and get her foot between the bars. A few seconds later, she was standing on the balcony, looking into the beady eyes of a seagull. Figuring it wasn't the seagull who had spoken, she glanced at the balcony next door. A little old man stood there as naked as the day he was born. Chloe averted her eyes, but it was too late. The image of the shriveled dangling thing was seared in her brain.

"So did Gary break your heart?" the man asked. "Is that why you want to kill yourself?"

"Grayson!" A woman came hurrying out the open balcony doors, and Chloe couldn't help it. She looked. The little old woman was as naked and wrinkly as the little old man, her breasts drooping almost to her sagging stomach. "Our neighbor's name is Grayson, Hammond, not Gary." She turned to Chloe and smiled. "And this beautiful young lady doesn't look like she's trying to kill herself."

"Well, she was. But she must've changed her mind."

Chloe kept her eyes on the seagull, which was shredding the bamboo plant in the ceramic pot in the corner. "I wasn't trying to kill myself," she said. "I was just…practicing my rock climbing." It was a pathetic lie, but one the old couple seemed to buy.

"We used to love to rock climb," the woman said. "But as we've gotten older, we've had to give it up. Although we are going to go zip-lining on our Mexican vacation—naked, of course."

While Chloe tried to get over the image of that, the old guy spoke.

"Mexicans embrace nudity much better than Americans. Although Gary doesn't seem to mind nudity, since he paints naked women. So are you modeling for him or just shagging him?"

There was something about his bluntness that made Chloe laugh and give up on trying to keep her eyes averted. If the old people were okay with their nudity, she figured she could be. "No, I'm not shagging Grayson."

"Do you want to?"

She rolled her eyes. "Even if I did, that's none of your business."

He grinned and exchanged looks with his wife. "Sassy little thing, isn't she? Reminds me of you, Doris, when I first met you."

Doris leaned over and gave the man a kiss on his wrinkled cheek. "But my sass didn't stand a chance against your charm."

The old man seemed to puff up with pride. "I was a charming son of a gun, wasn't I? Of course, I wasn't as charming as the Beaumont boys. First, the oldest one charmed Olivia right out of her power suit, then the middle one charmed my granddaughter right out of her uptight shell."

"You're Eden's grandparents?" The words were out before Chloe could stop them.

The woman's alert eyes snapped over to her. "So you know Eden?"

Chloe would've preferred to stay anonymous. The fewer people who knew she was there, the better. But there was no help for it now. She could only hope that the Huckabees left to go naked zip-lining before they could tell anyone.

"Yes," she said. "I'm Chloe."

Doris's eyes widened. "The one who stayed with my daughter in Grover Beach after your boyfriend beat you up?"

Chloe felt her face flush. "That would be me."

Doris flapped her hand. "Well, that's nothing to be ashamed of, dear. We all make mistakes when we're young. Just make sure not to make the same mistake again." She smiled. "And living with Grayson is a step in the right direction. I have never met a young man who is so respectful and kind. Did you know he offered to water Hammond's geraniums while we're in Mexico?" She looked at the brightly colored blooms in the planter that ran along the balcony. "Although I'm wondering if we shouldn't repot these and take them inside now that autumn is here."

Chloe studied the flowers. "If they were geraniums, I'd say that you could keep them outside for a few more months. True geraniums are frost-hardy perennials. But those happen to be pelargoniums—a flower that most nurseries will sell as geraniums. And they need more care in colder temperatures, so I wouldn't recommend keeping them outside longer than a few more weeks."

Hammond squinted at her. "So you garden?"

"A little."

"Well, it sounds like more than a little," Doris said. "It's nice to know that we have a flower expert living next door."

"I'm not living—" Chloe broke off when she heard a car pull into the driveway. She peeked over the balcony expecting to see Grayson's sports car. Instead it was a gold Lexus. She quickly stepped back out of sight and made her excuses in a hushed voice. "Well, it looks like I have company, so I better go." She turned to the sliding glass door and was relieved to find it unlocked. But before she stepped inside, Doris stopped her.

"I'll just drop our house key by later—along with some of my special brownies as a thank-you for taking care of the flowers. Grayson loves my brownies."

A car door slammed, so Chloe only nodded before she slipped inside and closed the door. The doorbell rang seconds later. Since she had no intention of answering the door, she walked into the kitchen and searched for something to eat. There wasn't much. Obviously Grayson wasn't a cook. She had just pulled a cartoon of eggs from the refrigerator when she heard the sound of a key being placed in a lock, followed quickly by the sound of the door opening and the click of heels on the wooden floor of the entryway.

Chloe didn't know why she felt surprised that a woman had a key to Grayson's house. Was it Natalia or another supermodel? Or maybe the woman from Paris who had screwed up his painting mojo? Chloe probably should've hidden, but curiosity got the best of her. Especially when the clicks were followed by the sound of a dead bolt being slid back. And since her entire savings were in her duffel bag, Chloe didn't hesitate to head for the stairs. But instead of finding a beautiful supermodel, she found an attractive middle-aged woman going through the paintings leaning against the bedroom wall.

She stepped into the room. "Can I help you?"

The woman straightened and sent her a haughty look. "Oh. I didn't realize that this was cleaning day." She flapped a manicured hand and went back to looking at the paintings. "Well, go about your business. I just need to grab a few things."

Chloe really should've let the woman think that she was the cleaning lady. It would've made everything so much easier. But there was something about her arrogance that didn't sit well. "Who are you?"

The woman turned, and her gaze landed on Chloe's bare legs beneath the T-shirt. "Ahh, I see my mistake. You're not the cleaning lady. Which explains why Grayson was in no hurry for me to drop by the house without him."

Chloe crossed her arms. "So if he didn't want you dropping by, why did you? And how do you have a key?"

The woman's eyebrow hiked up. "I have a key from when my daughter lived here."

"You're Olivia's mother?" Geez, was everyone related?

"Yes. And I'm Michael Beaumont's widow. And Deacon

Beaumont's mother-in-law. And Michael Paris Beaumont's grandmother."

Well, crap. Chloe dropped her stubborn stance. "I'm sorry. You should've told me that sooner."

Mrs. Beaumont went back to looking at the paintings. "A woman should always familiarize herself with a man's family. Especially if she's looking to become part of it."

"I don't want to be part of Grayson's family."

Mrs. Beaumont lifted her head and studied her. "So you're modeling for him?" Since it seemed like a good-enough excuse for being there, Chloe nodded. The information seemed to please Mrs. Beaumont. "Well, it's good to know that he's working on something else." She waved a hand at the paintings she'd been looking at. "Because these certainly aren't going to be enough for the charity benefit. He'll need to get busy on painting more immediately."

"Good luck with that."

Mrs. Beaumont's eyebrow lifted again. It was like it was attached to the woman's frown. Her lips went down, and her eyebrow went up. "And just what do you mean by that remark?"

"Nothing." Chloe changed the subject. "So what charity benefit are these for?"

"The American Cancer Society."

"I guess that makes sense given that Grayson's mother died of cancer too." She hadn't intended to attach the *too*. It just sorta popped out. She hoped that Mrs. Beaumont wouldn't catch it. She should've known better.

"Too? Your mother died of cancer?"

Chloe shrugged. "Lots of people die of cancer."

"Which is exactly why this charity event needs to be a success." Mrs. Beaumont's gaze sharpened as she gave Chloe a thorough once-over. "And I think I've just figured out how to make it one. How far along is Grayson's painting of you?"

"Umm...not very."

"Well, we'll have to do something about that, now won't we?" Mrs. Beaumont's chin lifted. "I have decided that your painting, my dear, is going to be the focal point of the charity benefit. The fact that your mother died of cancer as well will tug at people's heartstrings...and their wallets." As if that were the end of the conversation, she breezed past Chloe on her way to the front door.

"Wait a minute!" Chloe followed her. "I'm sorry, but I can't help you out with the benefit."

Mrs. Beaumont stopped. She was a head shorter than Chloe, which didn't explain why she could still look down her nose. "If you're worried about your name being released with your nude picture, don't be. Your name will be kept a secret. People don't need to know who you are. They just need to know that you have lost a loved one to cancer."

"That's not it," Chloe said. "I'm leaving town in a few days."

Mrs. Beaumont studied her as if she were a smashed bug on a windshield. "That will not do. Whatever he's paying you to pose, I'll pay you double."

Double? If Mrs. Beaumont paid her double the money and Grayson paid her too, she would have plenty to relocate. And if Grayson didn't paint her face and Mrs. Beaumont didn't release her name, then no one would know who she was. Of course there was still one little problem standing in her way. A problem that Mrs. Beaumont would have to find out about sooner or later.

"I'm afraid that Grayson has painter's block," she blurted out. "He can't even paint an apple."

Mrs. Beaumont blinked as if Chloe were talking Madison's pig Latin. "Painter's block? Don't be ridiculous. I've never heard of such a thing. And of course he can't paint an apple. There's only one thing that inspires Grayson." She sent Chloe a pointed look. "And since you're only here for a few days, my dear, I suggest you strip as soon as he walks in that door."

$\mathscr{C}$HAPTER EIGHT

After he'd ticked off Miles, Natalia, and Deirdre in the morning, Grayson's afternoon didn't improve. He accidentally hung up on one of the stockholders when he tried to put her on hold. Knocked over his cup of coffee and spilled it all over Deacon's desk, including some important documents. And totally spaced out in a meeting and couldn't ask one intelligent question. The morning he blamed on himself. The afternoon he blamed on Chloe.

He couldn't stop thinking about her. Or more like thinking about the wrath she was going to unleash on him when he got home. He had little doubt that she'd spent the day planning revenge. And when he walked through the door of his bedroom, he expected her to let him have it. Which was probably why, after he left the office, he postponed going home by stopping by to see his new nephew.

Deacon and Olivia had a beautiful house in Pacific Heights. Since Grayson didn't want to risk his Bugatti's getting hit on the narrow, hilly streets, he pulled into the driveway on the side of the house and entered through the kitchen door. The housekeeper was standing at the stove and jumped in surprise when she saw him, dropping her wooden spoon.

Grayson quickly walked over and picked it up. "Sorry, Lucia, I didn't mean to startle you." He handed her the spoon. "What are you cooking? It smells delicious." He didn't know if she would understand the question. Lucia was from Peru and still struggled with the language. He was surprised when she not only understood but responded in English.

"Soup for mister and missus." She placed the spoon in the sink and grabbed another one from the utensil container next to the stove. "You want?"

He smiled. "You've been studying."

Her face flushed. "The missus, she pay for my tutor." Her brow wrinkled with concentration. "Would you like some soup, Mr. Gray-son?"

"I would love some, but could you make it to go? I can't stay long." He glanced at the doorway. "So where is everyone?"

"Upstairs with the sweet one."

"Is he sleeping? Maybe I should come back later."

Lucia shook her head. "You no worry about that, Mr. Grayson. He sleep most the day and stay up most the night." She grinned. "Much to Daddy's trouble."

The housekeeper's word choice might be wrong, but Grayson had no problem understanding what she meant. He laughed. "So I guess little Mikey isn't following my big brother's plan?"

Lucia held up her thumb and forefinger. "Not even little."

"This should be interesting." Grayson headed through the kitchen to the stairs that led up to the bedrooms. He peeked into Deacon and Olivia's room and found his sister-in-law sprawled across the huge bed as if she had just fallen onto it and passed out. She was wearing a wrinkled pair of pajamas, and one house slipper dangled from the foot that hung off the bed.

Grayson walked in and removed her slipper before placing the edge of the down comforter over her. Then he went in search of his brother. He found Deacon in the next room trying to quiet his fussing son. He appeared as exhausted as Olivia. His hair was mussed, as if he'd been running his fingers through it, and it looked like he hadn't shaved in days.

"Now that will be quite enough, Michael Paris," Deacon said in the same stern voice he used with French Kiss employees...and his brothers. "You've been fed, burped, and diapered exactly like it says in the book. It's time to go to sleep, young man." Mikey minded almost as well as Nash did. Instead of stopping, his fussing grew louder.

Grayson bit back a grin as he rested a shoulder on the doorjamb. "Somehow I don't think he's listening."

Deacon turned around. "Holy hell, Gray, you scared the sh—"—he glanced at Mikey—"the shoot out of me. And close the door, would you? I don't want to wake Olivia. She was up all night."

Grayson walked into the room, pulling the door closed behind him. "From the looks of things, she wasn't the only one up all night. You look like hell, Deke."

His brother glared at him as he jostled Michael on his shoulder. "Shut up and hand me that Binky."

"The what?"

"The pacifier."

Grayson looked around the room at all the baby paraphernalia. "You're going to have to be more specific."

"The blue nipple-looking thing on the diaper table."

"Gotcha." Grayson walked over and had started to grab it when Deacon yelled.

"Don't touch the nipple, you idiot! It's sterilized."

Using just the tips of his fingers, Grayson grabbed the plastic ring of the pacifier and carried it to Deacon, who quickly stuck it in the baby's mouth. It worked for about two seconds before Mikey spit it out and continued to cry. Both Deacon and Grayson stared at the pacifier on the floor.

"So I guess it's not sterilized anymore," Grayson said.

"No shit, Sherlock."

"You mean *shoot*, don't you? No shoot, Sherlock." When Deacon mad-dogged him, Grayson figured he'd teased his brother enough. Especially when Deacon looked like he had been put through their grandmother's old washing machine wringer. "Here," he said as he held out his hands, "let me see if I can quiet the little guy."

Deacon hesitated for only a second before he pointed to a bottle of hand sanitizer on the dresser. Once Grayson had disinfected his hands, Deacon handed the baby over. "Be careful. You have to support his head."

"I got him. So you can let go now."

"Don't hold him like a football. You have to cradle him like a watermelon."

Grayson adjusted Michael in the crook of his arm. "Okay, Deke. Relax, man. I'm not going to drop my nephew on his head. That would be something that Nash would do. And quit hovering. You're freaking Mikey out even more."

To get away from his domineering brother, Grayson walked to the window and tried to quiet his nephew by bouncing him. It seemed to work. Mikey's cries stopped, although Grayson wasn't sure if it was due to the bouncing or the view outside the window. Mikey's eyes seemed to be focused on the garden that twilight had painted with strokes of ultramarine, cerulean blue, and cobalt violet. It was an overwhelmingly beautiful sight that needed to be captured on canvas. It was too bad that Grayson could no longer capture anything.

"What happened?" Deacon hurried over.

Grayson looked down at the wrinkled face peeking from the swaddled blanket. "I'm not sure, but I think he likes gardens."

"Gardens?" Deacon picked up a book that sat on a table by the rocker and thumbed through it. "This didn't say anything about babies liking those."

"Maybe every baby is different. You, Nash, and I are all different." He glanced down at Mikey. "Hey, I think he's going to sleep. Should I put him in his crib?"

"No!" Deacon hissed in a whisper. "That's what started him crying the last time. Just keep doing what you're doing."

Grayson continued to bounce. "For how long?"

"For as long as he's sleeping." Deacon slumped down in the rocking chair. "But don't worry. It never seems to be more than ten minutes." He released his breath and leaned his head back. "So fill me in on what's going on at the office. I saw the *ET* piece, and you handled it well. You answered the question about being handcuffed with just enough detail to satisfy people's curiosity, but not enough to make them think that you were hiding anything. And once the camera panned over to Madison and Natalia, no one cared about you anyway."

"Thanks a lot."

"It's true. Those two models are worth their weight in underwear. And speaking of Madison and Natalia, I want them front and center in the new catalog. Miles took some great shots of them that should work."

This was the point where Grayson should have mentioned that he'd pissed off both Miles and Natalia. Instead he left that piece of information out and skirted the subject.

"I'm not really feeling the photos that Miles took. I want something edgier—especially for my collections."

Deacon opened his eyes. "Edgier?" He thought for a moment before he nodded. "Okay, I'll leave that up to you. I'll have enough to worry about when I get back in a few days."

"Are you sure you'll be ready to come back to work in a few days?" Grayson glanced down at his sleeping nephew.

"Mikey is going to be fine. He just needs to figure things out."

Somehow Grayson didn't think it was Mikey who needed to figure things out as much as his father, but he kept that to himself. He bounced the baby for a few more minutes before he glanced at the cow-jumping-over-the-moon clock on the wall.

"I better get going, Deke." He turned to hand the baby off to his brother and discovered Deacon fast asleep in the rocker.

If Chloe hadn't been locked in his bedroom, Grayson might've continued to hold the kid and let his brother sleep. But he'd delayed dealing with her wrath long enough. So he carried Mikey to his crib and tried to lay him down. But as soon as his nephew's cheek touched the sheet, he started crying, waking up not only his father but also his mother.

During the ensuing chaos, Grayson slipped out of the room. Not more than fifteen minutes later, he was entering his house with a Tupperware container of Lucia's spicy chicken soup. He should've stopped by the grocery store for some bread to go with it. And some smooth peanut butter and chocolate milk. His paltry offering of soup probably wasn't going to go over very well.

Loosening his tie, he climbed the stairs and prepared for

battle. He froze on the landing when he noticed his bedroom door was open. One glance told him that Chloe was
gone...and that his room was spotless. Which annoyed him
almost as much as her being gone.

"What the hell?" he said.

"What the hell is right."

He glanced up and saw Chloe's head peeking over the
steel-and-glass railing of the staircase.

"What the hell kind of jailer are you, leaving me nothing
but a few measly crackers and crappy crunchy peanut butter?" she asked.

Grayson didn't know if he felt relief or regret that she was
still in the house. He climbed the stairs and found her standing at the top. She wore an oversize T-shirt, her legs bare and
her painted toes curled over the top step like ten tiny black
piano keys. Since she stood on the top stair, their lips were
even. Although why he noticed that he couldn't have said.

"So did you climb out the window or jimmy the lock?"
he asked.

"How would I jimmy a dead bolt?" She nodded at the
container in his hand. "So is that all you brought me for dinner? What are you trying to do? Starve me to death?"

He glanced up at the ceiling. "Okay, so when is the
bucket of hot tar going to drop on me?"

"You are such a wussy, Gray," she tossed over her shoulder as she turned and walked away.

It wasn't the *wussy* part as much as his shortened name
that made him tense. Only his family called him Gray. Only
the people who cared about him. And Chloe did not care
about him.

He jerked off his tie as he climbed the stairs. She was
seated at the breakfast bar with her chin cupped in her hand.
Those big brown eyes followed him as he tossed his tie on

the back of the couch and walked into the kitchen. He tried to ignore her as he pulled a bowl from the cupboard, but it was hard when she wouldn't shut up.

"Please don't worry about fixing anything for me. I already made myself an omelet. You're out of eggs, by the way. And sardines."

He turned. "You ate Jonathan's sardines?"

"Oops." She made a face. "I didn't realize those were for your pet. Although he probably wouldn't have eaten them anyway. He was too busy destroying your bamboo plant on the balcony. Not that it was a big loss. It was a bad choice for your small balcony. I would recommend a golden creeping Jenny potted with some Japanese pieris."

He poured some soup out of the container and into his bowl. "Let me guess, you know plants as well as you know how to cut hair." He put the bowl of soup in the microwave and slammed the door a little harder than necessary before hitting the minute button. Then he turned to Chloe. "So why didn't you leave?"

She shrugged. "I started thinking about Eden's honeymoon. And I don't really want to ruin it. So I guess I'll stay until she gets back. It's the least I can do, since she gave me a place to stay after I left Zac." She looked down at her finger, which was tracing a vein of the granite countertop. "And since you're the one who took me to her parents' house, I guess I owe you too."

"You owe me nothing."

She lifted her gaze and smiled. "Good. Because I hate to owe people. And speaking of owing…Olivia's mother came by and wasn't real thrilled with the selection of paintings."

Grayson stared at her in disbelief. "You let Deirdre go through my paintings?"

"What was I supposed to do when she had a key and let

herself in? Kick her out? She's your brother's mother-in-law, for God's sake. Besides, she had to find out sometime that you lost your ability to paint."

His eyes widened. "You told her that?"

"Don't worry. She refused to believe that you've lost your painting mojo."

Up until that point, he'd done a pretty good job of keeping his anger in check. But no more. He took two steps closer, his voice ringing off the ceiling. "I did not lose my painting mojo!"

She completely ignored his anger and slipped off the barstool, then casually strolled over to a kitchen drawer. Obviously she'd spent most of the day going through his things because she had to open only one before she found what she wanted. She pulled out the sketchpad and one of his mechanical pencils.

"Then go ahead and sketch something." She held them out. "The coffeemaker. The light fixture. Me." She flapped the sketchpad. "Draw anything."

Just looking at the sketchpad and pencil made cold sweat bead up on his forehead. And it pissed him off to no end that she knew exactly how terrified he was.

"Fuck you." He pushed past her and walked out of the room. He took the stairs two at a time and got real satisfaction from slamming his bedroom door. He stripped off his shirt and dropped it to the floor, kicked his shoes at the closet, then took off his pants and left them puddled by the bed. He had just jerked the neatly made covers back when the door opened and Chloe walked in with his bowl of soup.

"Didn't anyone ever teach you to knock before you enter someone's room?" he asked as he climbed beneath the sheets.

"I thought this was my room." She sat down on the bed

and started eating his soup. *His soup.* "This is amazing. You should really try it."

He punched a pillow and adjusted it behind his back. "I was wrong. You shouldn't stay until Eden and Nash get back. You should leave now."

"Too late," she said. "You wanted me as a guest, you got me. So what do you think caused your problem?"

"I'm not talking about this."

"If you don't talk about it, you'll never fix it." She held out a spoonful of soup. "Hurry and take a bite before it drips on the sheets."

He should've ignored the spoonful of soup. Unfortunately, he was hungry. He leaned in and took the offering. The soup *was* good. "You want to talk," he said. "Let's talk about why you dated a guy who liked to use you as a punching bag."

She fed him another bite of soup. "It's no secret that I have a thing for abusive relationships. But at least I'm working on my problems. I haven't been with a jerky guy for six months—if you don't count the last twenty-four hours."

"Like I believe that. What about the guy at the bar?" He took the bowl from her and continued to eat.

"You mean Jeff? He's not a jerk. He's an FBI agent. Besides, we're just friends."

"That's not what he wants."

"Well, that's all I want. I'm through with guys for a while." She scooted farther onto the bed and crossed her legs pretzel-style, flashing him a peek of sexy black panties that had him choking on his soup.

She patted him on the back. "See, I knew you were hungry. Slow down or you're going to choke to death." Once he caught his breath, she continued. "So tell me when you first noticed that you couldn't paint."

He should've gotten up and left the room. He didn't need Chloe examining his problem. Unfortunately, she would be able to examine more than just his problem if he got up. He had one hell of a boner.

"There wasn't any certain moment," he said. "I just woke up one morning and couldn't do it." No longer hungry, at least for soup, he lowered the spoon to the bowl and set both on his nightstand.

"This was when you were in Paris?"

"No. I haven't been able to paint since we went to the catalog shoot in Fiji."

She looked surprised. "You mean you haven't painted for six months?"

"Six months, fifteen days, and twelve hours to be exact. Now if you're through psychoanalyzing me, I'd like to go to sleep." He scooted down in the bed and tucked the covers around him. He quickly sat up again when he noticed his hard-on tenting the blankets. Luckily, Chloe was too wrapped up in her therapy.

"Maybe it was something you ate in Fiji," she said. "They served us some crazy fish at the resort—maybe you got mercury poisoning. Or maybe the cabin pressure in the plane screwed with your inner ear, which then affected the right side of your brain—or is it the left side that's creative? I always get those two mixed up."

"It wasn't the cabin pressure or the seafood. Maybe I'm just blocked—like a writer."

She thought for a moment before she hopped up from the bed. "Then we need to unblock you." She walked to the closet and came out with his camera. "Take some pictures of me."

He snorted. "And have you call me a pervert? No, thanks."

"That was when you were sneaking around taking pictures of me in my bikini."

"I wasn't sneaking. And you signed the release form fast enough when I offered to pay you cash for the picture."

"True, but you took it without my permission. Now you have my full consent, although I'll expect you to delete them as soon as we're through. This is just an exercise to get you unblocked."

"Taking pictures with a camera isn't the same as painting, Chloe."

"No, but it's a start. It might get your creative juices flowing." She tossed him the camera, and if he didn't want his six-thousand-dollar Nikon busted, he had no choice but to catch it. It felt foreign in his hands, but not as foreign as a pencil or a paintbrush.

"This isn't going to work," he said.

"Of course it's not going to work. I have on too many clothes."

Grayson watched in horror as Chloe slipped the T-shirt over her head and dropped it to the floor.

CHAPTER NINE

It wasn't like Chloe was standing in front of Grayson buck-naked. The black bra-and-panty set Madison had given her wasn't even as skimpy as some of her bikinis. And yet she couldn't seem to help the flush of embarrassment as Grayson's violet eyes ran over her.

Did he think she was too skinny? Too flat-chested? Too slim-hipped? Did he think the tattoo on her hip bone was cheap? Did he notice the scars on her knees from being a clumsy kid and that her second toes were longer than her big toes? To someone who had photographed and painted the most beautiful women in the world, Chloe must be a major disappointment. If he was disappointed, he didn't show it. His face gave nothing away. He just sat studying her as his chest slowly rose and fell with each breath.

This was the first time she'd seen Grayson without a shirt. Even in Fiji he had worn a T-shirt with his board shorts. At the time she'd thought he was embarrassed about his body. Now she realized that he had nothing to be embarrassed about.

Grayson had the type of body that women drooled over and men wished they'd been blessed with. His bones were long, and his muscles lean—although they seemed to bunch in all the right places. Like his biceps. His shoulders. And the hard pectoral muscles that flexed beneath her gaze. Suddenly her flush had nothing to do with standing before him in her underwear and everything to do with the hot spring of desire that welled up inside her.

A click pulled her gaze away from his muscled chest to the camera he held to his face. When he lowered it, his expression was hard and unyielding.

"There. I took a picture. Now get out."

If not for Mrs. Beaumont's offer, Chloe might've given up. She really didn't need the aggravation. Unfortunately, what she did need was money. She placed a hand on her hip. "That's it? You aren't even going to give it the old college try?"

"What do you know about the old college try?"

The words stung, and she really wanted to come back with a scalding reply. Instead she kept her cool. "We're not talking about me. We're talking about you. Now are you going to make an attempt at getting over your painter's block or am I going to need to take more clothes off—"

"Fine! You want a photographer, you'll get a photographer." Jerking back the covers, he got out of bed and walked to his dresser, where he put down the camera long enough to open a drawer.

He continued to rant and rave, but Chloe wasn't listening. She couldn't hear anything over the loud pounding of desire in her ears. In nothing but a pair of tight white boxer briefs, Grayson was more than just hot. He was molten. Or maybe the sight of the impressive bulge stretching the seam in the front and the nice butt stretching the white cotton in the back had just made her feel molten. Sort of like her insides had turned to magma and were waiting to erupt.

It took his slipping on a pair of ripped, faded jeans for her brain to function again. Although it wasn't functioning very fast. Not when he still looked so good. The jeans molded to his butt and legs, and his back muscles flexed as he picked up his cell phone and tapped the screen. Hard-core rap music came from the speaker on the nightstand, but not loud enough that she couldn't hear his commands.

"Get on the bed."

"Excuse me?"

He sent her an exasperated look as he moved a floor lamp closer to the bed and turned it on. "If we're going to do this, then you need to follow directions. Now get on the bed. I want you on your stomach with your head by the headboard and your ass toward me." He grabbed the covers and jerked them to the floor.

"I don't think...," she started, but he cut her off.

"It's not your job to think. Just take orders."

After Zac she had sworn that she would never take orders from a boyfriend again. But Grayson wasn't her boyfriend. At the moment he was her photographer—soon to be her employer if she could get him to paint her. So she crawled onto the mattress and tried to follow his instructions. Unfortunately, she had never modeled before and didn't have a clue how to arrange her arms and legs. She ended up keeping her arms at her sides and her legs together...like a circus performer getting ready to be shot out of a cannon.

She heard an exasperated groan before the mattress sagged and a pair of lean, muscled thighs in ripped jeans straddled her. Pinned, she could do nothing but lie there as he rearranged her limbs with hands that felt as hot as the spot between her legs. His fingers encircled her wrists and lifted her arms so they curved around her head. He leaned in and spoke against her ear, his breath hot and spicy. "Close your eyes and don't move a muscle."

He didn't have to worry. She had no muscle. She was just a puddle of tingly sensations. Fortunately, he released her wrists and got off. Although a second later his hand was back, leaving a trail of heat as he bent one knee and angled her leg to the side until she felt completely exposed. There was a pause, and just the thought of him looking at her made Chloe feel vulnerable and...anticipatory. Which was crazy. She was not having sex with Grayson Beaumont. Not only because he didn't like her but also because she was taking a break from men. All men. But mostly arrogant bad boys. And even though he hadn't been a bad boy, Grayson was a bad boy now.

A very, very bad boy.

Her breath hitched when he slipped a warm finger inside the elastic edge of her panties and tugged. He did the same to the other side, leaving her with exposed butt cheeks and a satiny wedgie that deliciously abraded the heated spot between her legs. She bit her lip to keep from groaning and waited for his next touch...actually craved it. But instead there was another long stretch of silence.

"Is something wrong?" she croaked out in a voice she didn't recognize.

"Nothing," he said. "You're perfect—I mean the pose. The pose is perfect."

Before she could think too much about his words, he got off the bed. Only a second later there was a camera click, followed by a succession of staccato clicks.

"Roll to your back," he ordered. She did and found him standing on the bed, looking down at her with an intensity that left her breathless. "Knee bent. Hands over your head.

That's it. Keep your eyelids half closed and lips slightly parted." His gaze lowered to her mouth, and she could almost feel those indigo orbs lasering right through her. "Wet your lips," he said, his voice softer and huskier. Her tongue flicked out. He studied her, his long lashes half covering his eyes. "More."

She swept her tongue over her top lip before pulling her bottom lip into her mouth and sucking on it gently. Grayson didn't move. Not a muscle. His entire attention seemed to be riveted on her mouth. Then the hand that wasn't holding the camera twitched. The movement seemed to snap both of them out of their trances, and he lifted the camera to his eye and snapped off numerous shots.

"Stand up," he ordered. She was surprised by how quickly she complied. The desire strumming through her body had really messed with her head. "Hold on to the headboard with your back arched and ass out. Glance over your right shoulder...the other right."

She switched shoulders and forced a smile, even though she didn't feel like smiling. She felt like reaching orgasm. It had been over six months since she'd had sex, and she hadn't realized how much she missed it until now.

"No smile," he said. "Think of something sexy and let your lips relax naturally."

It wasn't hard to do. The "something sexy" was standing on the bed right behind her. Grayson looked sexier than anything Chloe could ever dream up in her head. His jeans hung low, showing off the white waistband of his boxer briefs and the muscles of his stomach. He didn't have an obvious six-pack, but there was enough definition to make Chloe want to run her tongue over each dip and hard ridge.

"Good," he said as he crouched down. "That's exactly what I wanted. Now turn around and lean against the headboard with your right leg stretched out and your left slightly bent." He turned the camera and clicked off some more shots. "Head thrown back and looking at the ceiling."

There was a staccato of clicks before a long stretch of silence that had Chloe lowering her head. Grayson had gotten off the bed and was rummaging through the chest of drawers. When he found what he wanted, he turned and strode toward her. Or more like stalked. He jumped to the bed like a tiger after its prey, and within seconds was standing in front of her, his naked chest filling her entire vision.

She fought with the desire to lean in and capture one of his quarter-size brown nipples in her mouth. Would he taste as good as he looked? While she was lost in her fantasy, something cold touched her shoulder. She started and glanced down to see a dab of purple paint.

"What—" she started to ask, but the word ended on a hiss of air when Grayson smeared the paint over the top of one breast and across her collarbone to the opposite shoulder. Seconds later, another dab—this one a shimmery silver— was smeared in the opposite direction. After that it was a free-for-all of paint dabs and smears. Her arms. Her stomach. Her legs. Even her cheeks got a streak of purple and silver.

Chloe didn't object. She couldn't. Not when her insides quivered and her thighs clenched with every single stroke of his hot fingers against her skin. By the time he finished, she was a trembling mass of need while Grayson seemed completely unaffected. He jumped off the bed, wiped his hands on the dress shirt he'd left on the floor, then grabbed the camera and started issuing orders again. But this time he punctuated every order with words of praise. And Chloe had always been a sucker for praise.

"Perfect. That's exactly what I wanted." Click. Click. Click.

"Yes, wet those lips. I love the pout." Click. Click. Click.

"You're beautiful. Absolutely beautiful." Click. Click. Click.

"More, baby. Give me more."

She gave him more. Fueled by his praise, she primped and posed to the seductive thump of the rap music, not for the camera but for Grayson. It was Grayson she wanted to please. And when her bra strap slipped off her shoulder, she didn't pull it back up. She left it there, even leaned so her breast swelled over the cup.

Click. Click. Click. "Yes, baby. That's what I want. Perfect. You're so damned perfect."

She pushed down the cup and revealed her entire breast, then dipped her finger in the still-wet paint and streaked it across her naked breast. The touch of her finger on her hardened nipple caused her breath to halt, and she tipped her head back and released a deep throaty moan. When it ended, she noticed two things: The camera clicks had stopped. And Grayson's heavy breathing could be heard over the rap music.

She opened her eyes, and her gaze locked with his. His eyes seemed to burn like gas flames as his chest rose and fell with each rapid breath. She didn't know how long they stared at each other before he dropped the camera and stepped up to the mattress. In two strides he had her in his arms and was devouring her lips with his. And Grayson knew how to devour. Chloe felt totally consumed by the lush pull of his lips and the seductive lure of his tongue.

As with his photography, he demanded her full cooperation, and she gave it. His tongue teased hers into a mating dance of tangled heat and slick strokes. His teeth nipped her bottom lip, and she responded with a nip of her own. But for all his demands, she never felt forced. Even when his hands slid over her butt cheeks and yanked her closer, his hard chest pressing into her breasts and his even harder fly pressing into the spot between her legs.

The explosion of sensation that rocketed from the point where his hard-on met her throbbing clitoris had them both moaning in each other's mouths. Chloe was seconds away from reaching orgasm. Something she very much wanted to reach. Unfortunately, before she could, Grayson's cell phone rang.

His hands tightened on her butt cheeks for a brief second before he released her and stepped back. His eyes were still heavy lidded, but his facial expression was one of disbelief.

"Fuck," he said.

The word snapped her out of her sexual fog, and she had to agree. What the fuck had she been thinking? She was leaving. The last thing she needed was to get involved with Grayson. And if his phone hadn't rung, they would've been heating up the sheets right now. She ignored the stab of disappointment and tried to come up with something to say that would make light of the situation. When she noticed the streaks of paint she'd left on his chest and the fly of his jeans, she found one.

"Who would've thought that I'd end up painting you?" she teased in a breathy voice.

He didn't seem to get the humor. Without even a hint of a smile, he got off the bed and walked into the bathroom, slamming the door behind him.

She should've left well enough alone. But she couldn't. There was very little time left before the benefit, and very little time left before word got out that she was staying with Grayson. Which meant she couldn't let emotions get in the way of his painting her. They had made some progress tonight. She wasn't about to let a little desire—okay, a lot of desire—keep her from the money she needed.

Pushing up her bra strap, she hopped off the bed and tapped on the bathroom door. "Grayson?" When he didn't answer, she turned the knob and walked right in. He stood at the vanity with his hands on either side of the sink, and his hard gaze pinned her in the reflection of the mirror.

"Obviously I'm going to have to start locking doors," he said dryly.

She closed the lid of the toilet and sat down, trying to keep her eyes away from the bulge in the front of his jeans. "Okay, so I think that went pretty well. All it took was a little prompting, and you immediately got back into the swing of things."

He turned to face her. "Is that what you call it? Getting into the swing of things?"

Her cheeks heated. "I was talking about the photo shoot."

He stared at her for a moment before he grabbed a hand towel from the rack and turned on the faucet to wet it. "You can take a shower—in the other bathroom. Then get dressed. I'm taking you back to your apartment."

It wasn't want she'd expected to hear. She couldn't go back to her apartment. She needed to stay here and get Grayson to paint her.

"But what about Eden?" she said. "You don't want to ruin your brother's honeymoon, do you?"

"I don't care if you leave town anymore. I want you gone."

Since she had no other choice, she told the truth. "I can't go back to my apartment."

Grayson stopped wiping the paint off his face and turned to her. "Why not? Is someone after you? Is it Zac? Did he get out of jail?"

"No. It's not Zac." She paused. "It's someone else."

He studied her. "So that's why you were in such a hurry to leave San Francisco? You're running from this guy?" When she didn't answer, he released his breath and tossed the towel in the sink. "Fine. But for the rest of your stay, there will be no more photo shoots." He pointed a finger at her. "And definitely no more getting into the swing of things."

CHAPTER TEN

*T*here were mistakes, and then there were monumental mistakes. Letting Chloe talk him into photographing her had been a monumental mistake. Or maybe the mistake had been kissing her. Because up until that point, everything had been going pretty well. For the first time in months, Grayson had had an image of what he wanted to create and a medium to create it with. But taking photographs hadn't been enough. His hand had twitched with the desire to paint.

Which was how Chloe had become his blank canvas.

And what was mind-boggling was that she'd let him. She hadn't uttered one word of refusal as he streaked paint from her head to her cute little black-painted toes. Gone was the feisty, belligerent girl who didn't agree with him on anything, and in her place was a compliant, sexy woman who gave him everything.

Even a kiss that blew his head off.

Unable to stop himself, Grayson switched over from the sales reports he'd been looking at on his laptop to the photographs he'd downloaded from his camera the night before. It was about the hundredth time he'd pulled them up. They were still as good as they had been five minutes ago. No, not just good, but damn good. As he had always known, Chloe was the ultimate model.

In each frame her big brown eyes projected innocence while her body projected a sexy toughness that was more than just appealing. It was captivating...and edgy. The bright paint on the wall accented her black bra and panties, while the purple and silver paint on her body accented Chloe's dark hair and eyes and her tattoo. But as much as Grayson loved these pictures, he loved the last set even more.

In these her eyes were no longer innocent. They held a passion that spoke of hungry kisses and tangled limbs. Harsh groans and hard thrusts. Unrestrained lust and uncontrollable release. Grayson's cock hardened beneath his fly, and he clenched his hands into fists. Hands that still tingled with the memory of holding Chloe's firm butt cheeks as he searched for release.

Of course her passion hadn't been for him. Her passion had come from the sexy underwear and the thrill of being worshipped by a camera. Grayson had seen it happen before with models. Once you made a woman feel beautiful, she would give you whatever you wanted. Ego seemed to be directly connected to the libido. Even the models he had painted had offered him sex on more than one occasion. He hadn't taken them up on it. He had never wanted to use his art to manipulate women...until now.

"Grayson?"

Samuel's voice broke through his thoughts, and he pulled his gaze away from the pictures of Chloe to find the head designer walking into his office. The man was as immaculately dressed as always, with his tie perfectly knotted and not a gray hair out of place. Which had Grayson self-consciously straightening his loose tie and combing his fingers through his mussed hair before he rose to shake the man's hand.

"What's up?" he asked. "I thought we had our meeting at one."

Samuel glanced at his watch. "It is one."

Grayson tried to hide his shock and annoyance that he'd spent the entire morning mooning over Chloe's pictures. He smiled as he sat back down. "I guess time slips away when you're having fun."

Samuel sat in a chair across from him. "And are you having fun?"

It was hard to lie to a man Grayson respected as much as he respected Samuel. "Not yet. I'll be glad when Deacon and Nash get back."

A smile eased the corners of Samuel's mouth before disappearing as quickly as it had come. Samuel had never been much of a smiler. "Somehow I don't think Nash is in a hurry to get back. And as for Deacon, Deirdre called the house this morning, and I think *chaos* is too mild a word to describe what is going on over there."

Grayson nodded. "I stopped by yesterday, and it does seem like my new nephew has stirred things up."

Before Samuel could reply, Kelly walked in. She lifted a white deli bag, her spangled Hello Kitty bracelet flashing in the afternoon sun that shone through the window. "Even though you said you weren't hungry, I took the liberty of ordering you lunch." She set the bag down on his desk and pulled out a takeout container. "I thought a bowl of soup might put a smile on that handsome face of yours."

An image of Chloe feeding him soup flashed through

Grayson's mind, and he shook his head. "Thanks, but I'm really not hungry."

Kelly sent him a perturbed look. "If you're going to work as hard as you have been, you need food." She glanced at Samuel. "Tell him, Mr. Sawyer."

Samuel cleared his throat. "I don't think that's in my job description, Ms. Melvin."

Kelly huffed. "Well, it's in my job description to take care of my boss." She pushed the container of soup toward him. "Now eat!" She turned and flounced out of the office.

After the door closed, Grayson shook his head. "I never realized that my brother had two wives."

"It sounds like she's just worried about you." Samuel steepled his fingers against his chin. "And so is Deirdre. She told me that you think you've lost your ability to create."

Grayson's hand twitched, but now with the strong desire to wrap it around Chloe's throat. She'd had no business telling Deirdre Beaumont about his problem. Now it looked like it would be spread all over the company. He didn't care about the employees finding out, but he did care about his brothers. His inability to paint would worry them, and they had enough to worry about between their new baby and new marriage.

He sat back and looked at Samuel. "I would appreciate it if you wouldn't repeat that information."

Samuel nodded. "I'm not much for gossip, Grayson. Although I've found that secrets always have a tendency to get out." He hesitated for a moment before continuing. "So if I might ask, what makes you think you can't paint?"

"If you got a look at my last few paintings, you wouldn't have to ask. They're crap." He got up and walked to the floor-to-ceiling windows. "I can't even paint a damned apple."

Samuel joined him at the window. "I went through a creative dry spell once. I couldn't sketch a line without hating it...and myself."

Grayson glanced at him. "So how did you fix it?"

"I decided to just draw and not look at the finished product. So that way I couldn't judge myself too harshly. When I finished one design, I'd turn the page and start another. Most of them were crap, but I continued to draw until my mind relaxed enough to let my instinct take over." Samuel reached out and patted Grayson's shoulder. "It's there. You haven't lost it. Just give it some time."

It was surprising how much Grayson wanted to believe him. "I hope you're right. Painting is my life. Without it I'm nothing."

Samuel's eyes registered surprise. "If you'll pardon me, that's the biggest pile of bullshit I've ever heard. Painting isn't who you are, Grayson. It's what you do. If I never design another piece of lingerie in my life, I'll still be Samuel Sawyer. Just like you will always be Grayson Beaumont—with or without the painting."

"But what if I don't like the Grayson Beaumont who doesn't paint?"

"Then it's up to you to make that man worth liking."

"And if I don't know how?"

Samuel looked around. "I think you're doing a pretty good job so far. Not many men would be willing to take on the responsibilities of an entire company—especially creative men who would much rather be in a studio than an office."

He followed Samuel's gaze. "Right now I have no desire to be in my studio. Besides, I owe Nash and Deacon much more than just a few days of work."

"I heard that they helped raise you after your mother died."

"Not helped. They did raise me."

"That must've been hard," Samuel said as he stared out at the view.

Grayson nodded. "It was hard on Nash and Deacon."

Samuel turned to him. "I wasn't talking about them. I was talking about you. It must've been hard to be raised by two older brothers who couldn't understand the sensitivity of an artist."

"I'm not sensitive."

The look in Samuel's eyes was one of understanding. "All artists are sensitive, Grayson. Without sensitivity to the world around us, we'd have no need to create."

Turning back to the window, Grayson studied the view of the bay and allowed his brain to absorb Samuel's words. Of course he was wrong. Beaumonts weren't sensitive. With the life they'd had, they couldn't be.

Needing to change the subject, Grayson headed back to his desk. "I wanted to show you the catalog pictures and get your opinion before I piss off Miles any more than I already have." He sat down and tapped his laptop, not recalling Chloe's pictures until they popped up. Before he could click to another screen, Samuel moved behind him.

"Wait. That's the woman from the elevator—the one with the duck bouquet. I thought she didn't model." He leaned over Grayson's shoulder to get a closer look. "So is this the cover for the new catalog? It's brilliant. The woman encapsulates your new collection to a T—belligerent youth all wrapped up in sexy innocence."

Grayson frowned. That was Chloe. Belligerent, sexy innocence. It was a deadly combination. "I'm not planning on using the picture for the cover."

"Of course not. The bare breast wouldn't work. But the concept is perfect to attract younger women."

"Younger women?" Deirdre swept into the room, causing Grayson to get to his feet. Today she was dressed in a black-and-lime-green tennis dress with matching visor and tennis shoes. Most women would look cute in the outfit. Deirdre just looked more intimidating—like she could backhand you across the room with her Spalding. She moved around the desk and gave Samuel a kiss on the cheek. "Don't you even think about turning me in for a younger model, Samuel Sawyer, or I'll mess up your underwear drawer—no more starched and wrinkle-free Calvins for you."

Her gaze landed on the laptop. "Ahh, wonderful. I see that Chloe lit a fire under you." She lifted an eyebrow at Grayson. "So when can I expect the painting that is going to make my charity event a huge success?"

"Chloe?" Samuel looked at him. "This is the same woman Deirdre told me about? The woman who is living with you?"

"She's not living with me," Grayson snapped a little too loudly.

Deirdre's eyebrow hiked even higher. "Then what was she doing at your house wearing nothing but a skimpy T-shirt?"

Since there was no way he was going to go into the details of his kidnapping with Deirdre, he sat down and ran a hand through his hair. "Okay, so she's living with me, but I'm not painting her. I'll paint someone else."

"I don't want someone else. I want Chloe. Her mother died of cancer, so it only makes sense that she's your model."

He lifted his head and looked at Deirdre. "Chloe's mother died of cancer? How did you find that out?"

"She told me," Deirdre said. "Although she's as talkative as you are, Grayson. Now, when will the painting be ready for me to pick up? And don't give me any of that painter's block nonsense. If you truly have a problem, I'll call my therapist right now and get you in for an appointment." She pulled a cell phone out of her purse. "And I'll call Deacon and tell him to come in to work—"

"Fine!" Grayson threw up his hands. "I'll paint Chloe for the benefit, but I can't guarantee that it won't be a pile of crap."

Deirdre smiled and lowered her phone. "Haven't you realized by now that wealthy people love to buy art—crap or not? It makes us feel so wonderfully superior." She waved a hand. "Now I must be off. I have a tennis lesson at three." She kissed Samuel and tugged his tie loose from its perfect knot. "Better."

After she left, Samuel straightened his tie. "That woman is a force to be reckoned with. Which is why I fell in love with her. There's never a dull moment." He leaned closer. "Now show me the rest of Chloe's pictures."

Once Samuel saw them, he was convinced that they needed to use one for the cover of French Kiss's winter catalog. And the more Grayson looked at them, the more he had to agree. There was only one problem.

Chloe.

She wouldn't want her face on the cover of a catalog. He'd had a hard-enough time convincing her to let him use the one he had taken in Fiji, in which the hat covered her entire face. Again he wondered whom she was hiding from. Did it have something to do with her mother's death?

Kelly's tap on the door brought him out of his thoughts. She walked in and took one look at the untouched container of soup before sending him a hard look. "You do realize that gaunt, skinny men will not sell underwear. That's what gaunt, skinny runway models are for." She walked over to his desk and handed him a folder. "And speaking of runway models, Natalia wanted me to give you this."

"What is it?"

"Her resignation."

Grayson sat straight up. "Her what?" He opened the folder and quickly scanned the barely legible letter. "But I don't get it. Why would she do something like this? I thought she loved modeling."

Kelly examined the tiny little cat decals on her fingernails. "Well, I might have an idea of why she quit. Of course, I'm not saying a word to a man who won't even taste the soup I brought him."

Grayson narrowed his eyes at her. "I'll eat the soup. Now spit it out."

She dropped her hand and leaned closer. "Well, from what I hear, she loves modeling, but she loves something else more."

"What?"

"You." Since all Grayson could do was stare at her in confusion, Kelly continued. "It seems she has a major crush on you, and after the kiss in the elevator, she thinks you have one on her too. And the only thing that's keeping you two apart is the fact that you won't date employees." She nodded at the resignation. "And now she's not an employee."

Grayson sat back and covered his face with a hand.

"I wouldn't worry about it," Kelly said. "I'm sure she'll come back once she figures out you're living with a woman."

He lowered his hand. Obviously Deirdre liked to gossip as much as Kelly. He started to deny it, but then stopped. Maybe Kelly was right. If Natalia heard he was living with someone, she would stop this foolishness and come back to work. Hopefully before Deacon found out and killed him.

"And I'm afraid I have something else you need to deal

with," Kelly said. "It seems that a tenant in the apartment building that Nash owns has disappeared. A Mr. Garcia called and is all up in arms about it and wanted Nash to come and check on her." She handed him a key. "I told him that Nash was out of town, but that you'd stop by."

"I don't have time to stop by and check on some—" He paused. "These are the apartments where Eden lived?"

"The same. In fact, the tenant that disappeared lived in her same apartment."

Finally, here was something Grayson could handle without screwing it up. "Call Mr. Garcia back and tell him that he has nothing to worry about. The young lady who lived there has moved out."

Kelly held out her hand for the key. "Great, after I call Mr. Garcia, I'll let the building manager know that he can start looking for another tenant."

Grayson probably should've handed her back the key and let her make the call. He sincerely doubted that Eden could talk Chloe into staying. Especially when she was obviously running from someone. The question of whom had his hand closing around the key. "I think you should wait on making that call until I've checked out the apartment and made sure she's gone."

Since he had a full schedule, he wasn't able to use the key until later that day. He opened the door to the apartment to find it as neat and clean as his room after Chloe straightened it. Or more like neat and sterile. There were no knickknacks, pictures, or girlie trinkets that might give him a clue about her past or why she was running. The closet was empty, and the drawers held only lingerie. He thought of the nightshirt she'd packed in her duffel. He still hadn't seen her wear it. But it was there, while she'd left this much prettier lingerie. Why?

Finding no answers, he locked up the apartment and pocketed the key. On the way out, he ran into a man with a dog.

"Pardon me," Grayson said as he held the door open for the man.

The man eyed him warily on the way in. "You new to the building?"

"No, sir. My brother owns it." He held out his hand. "Grayson Beaumont."

The man shook hands as his little dog sniffed around Grayson's shoes. "So you're Nash's brother. I'm Rudy Garcia." He squinted at him. "So what are you going to do about Chloe? Your secretary called me and told me that she'd moved out, but I still think there is something fishy going on. Especially when men keep showing up asking about her."

Grayson allowed the door to close. "What men?"

"The cop that came by the other day." Mr. Garcia nodded at the door. "And now that blond guy in the red sporty car was asking about her."

Grayson remembered seeing the red Porsche when he pulled up, although he hadn't paid any attention to who was inside. He would now. "You're right. That does sound fishy. I think I'll just go have a chat with him and find out what's going on."

Mr. Garcia nodded. "You want me to come with you?"

"No. I think I can handle it." He pulled open the door and stepped out. The car was still there, except now the blond guy was leaning against it, watching the front of the building. When he saw Grayson, he lifted a hand in greeting.

"Excuse me. Do you live here?"

Grayson came down the steps. "Nope. Just visiting a friend." He nodded at the car. "Nice. Three point eight six-cylinder engine?"

"Yeah." The man impatiently pulled out his cell phone. "Look, I was wondering if you've seen this girl." He handed Grayson the phone. If not for the eyes, Grayson wouldn't have recognized the laughing teenager with the long blond hair. But those big brown emotion-filled eyes gave her away. It was hard not to react.

"She does look familiar," he said. "What's her name?"

"Selena. Selena Cameron."

CHAPTER ELEVEN

Something had happened. Something that had turned Grayson from an angry roommate to a pensive one. He sat across from her at the breakfast bar answering her attempts at conversation with feeble replies as he picked at the roasted chicken he'd brought home from the grocery store.

"Something wrong with the chicken?" she asked. "Mine was good."

"It's fine."

"Thanks for getting everything on my list, including Fritos and chocolate milk."

"No problem."

"So when are Nash and Eden coming back?"

"Soon."

Chloe rolled her eyes. "Geez, Grayson, I realize that last night turned out kind of weird, but get over it. It was only a kiss." Okay, so that was an understatement. If it had been only a kiss, she wouldn't have spent the entire day thinking about it and fantasizing about what would've transpired if his phone hadn't rung.

His eyes darkened. "That kiss shouldn't have happened."

"I agree," she said. "But if I had a dime for every time I did something that I shouldn't have done, I'd be as rich as you are." She got up and pulled his sketchpad and pencil out of the drawer. "Now tonight I think we should move on to sketching. Especially since the photo session went so well." She paused. "You erased those pictures, right?"

Instead of answering he stared at the sketchpad and pencil she held out as if they were going to bite him. So she set them on the counter and slid them over to him. "Quit being such a wuss. Now where do you want me?" She grabbed the hem of the T-shirt. She got it only halfway up before he stopped her.

"Keep your clothes on."

She pulled the shirt back down. "I don't think that Deirdre Beaumont wants a painting of a woman in a T-shirt and yoga pants, but you're the boss. So you want to go to your bedroom?"

"No!" When she startled at his abrupt answer, he blushed and nodded at the breakfast counter. "Here is fine."

She studied his red face for a moment. She found his blush endearing. It reminded her of the Grayson she'd first met, the soft-spoken artist who blushed often when she was around. Again she wondered what had changed him. Paris? His inability to paint? Or maybe just life?

Life had certainly changed her. Before her mother passed away, she had been a happy child who laughed often. Now she was a grumpy woman who rarely smiled. Although lately she had found more to smile about.

"Okay," she said. "But let me clean up first." She picked up their dinner plates and utensils and carried them to the sink. While she was rinsing them and placing them in the dishwasher, she noticed the Tupperware container on the counter. Mrs. Huckabee had dropped it off with her house key that morning as a thank-you for taking care of Mr. Huckabee's flowers. As soon as Chloe finished with the dishes, she opened the container to find thick, chocolaty brownies.

"Do you want some dessert?" she called over her shoulder.

"What I want is to get this over with."

"Suit yourself." Chloe took out a brownie and bit into it. It was as chocolaty and delicious as it looked. On the way back to the breakfast counter, she took a few more bites. "You're missing out. These brownies Mrs. Huckabee brought over are—"

Grayson whirled around on his barstool. "Don't eat that!"

She froze for a second before she popped the last of the brownie into her mouth. "Geez, Grayson. It's not like I ate the last one." She turned back to get him one, and herself another, but before she could open the container, he grabbed it from her. While she watched in horror, he opened the bottom cupboard door and dumped the brownies into the trash.

"Have you lost your mind?" she asked. "Those were amazing."

"Of course they were. They're magic."

It took her a moment to comprehend what he was saying. Then she burst out laughing. "Magic? You think that Eden's grandma puts pot in her brownies?" When he didn't join in, she sobered. "Okay, I get that you're nervous about drawing, and it's making you a little crazy. But I don't think you have anything to worry about. All you need to do is relax and let your natural instincts take over. In fact..." She walked to the wine fridge and opened it. She pulled out the racks and checked the labels, bypassing any Napa wines and settling on a merlot from Oregon. After taking a corkscrew from the drawer, she uncorked the bottle and poured him a glass.

"You shouldn't drink with Mrs. Huckabee's brownies," he said.

Even after all these years, she couldn't help swirling and sniffing before she handed it to him. "It's not for me. I hate wine. It's to relax you."

"I guess Zac was a connoisseur of wine," he said as he accepted the glass.

"No. Tequila." She carried the bottle over and set it on the coffee table before she walked back to Grayson. She handed him the sketchpad and pencil, then pulled him over to the swivel chair across from the couch. "Sit," she ordered.

He sent her a hard look before he complied. "It's not going to work. I can't draw."

"You can't if you don't try." She picked up his phone from the breakfast bar and tapped his radio app, then searched until she found the artists she wanted. When the perfectly harmonized voices came through the speakers, she glanced up to find Grayson watching her with a quizzical expression. "The Ten Tenors," she said. "They're very relaxing." She set the phone on the counter. "So how do you want me to pose, O Gifted One?"

"It doesn't matter." After only one sip, he set the glass of wine on the coffee table and flipped open his sketchpad. He held his pencil with so much tension that it was almost painful to watch.

Wanting to ease that tension, she sat down on the couch and spoke softly. "Just draw anything. It doesn't have to be me."

His gaze lifted. He studied her for a long moment before his hand moved. Once he'd drawn one line, he drew another...then another, until the pencil was sweeping over the paper as if it had a will of its own. His strokes weren't smooth or fluid, but at least he was drawing, his eyes flickering from her to the sketchpad and then back again.

With nothing else to do, Chloe just sat there and stared at the glass of wine. When she had swirled it earlier, the legs of the wine had slid slowly down the sides of the glass. It would be a sweet, high-alcohol wine. She would bet that a late-harvest grape had been used. But without tasting, she couldn't be sure.

Oh, what the hell. She picked up the glass and took a sip. She thought it would taste as bitter as her memories. Instead the richness burst upon her tongue and brought tears to her eyes. She swallowed the sip and took another, this one going down smooth and perfect. Definitely late harvest. And subtly different from Napa wines. Which was probably why she was enjoying it so much. Or maybe she had just outgrown her fear of the past and mellowed.

She felt mellow. Like if the balcony doors were open, she could float right out into the star-filled night. Suddenly hungry, she wondered what stars would taste like. Probably like the sugar cookies she used to make with her father—fragile, light, and sweet as they melted on your tongue. Her father had loved baking as much as he had loved wine. Every holiday she had helped him make the sugar cookies. He'd let her unwrap the butter sticks and crack each egg, never once getting mad if she got some shell in the batter. Of course that was when he'd still been her father. It should've been a sad thought, but instead it made her giggle. Once she started giggling, she couldn't seem to stop.

She expected Grayson to comment, but he seemed to be too enthralled with his drawing. Something had happened while she was wine tasting because he seemed more relaxed. Now his entire attention was focused on his sketchpad. His pencil flew, his hand like a conductor's during the most technical of symphonies. It was mesmerizing. But not as mesmerizing as Grayson himself. He had changed out of his suit when he got home and now wore a soft, well-washed T-shirt and ripped jeans. His hair was mussed, and the scruff on his jaw dark and sexy. But what was even sexier was the intensity in his eyes as he drew. She now knew why women were drawn to artists—it was the desire to have that intensity focused on them.

"You're hot." She didn't realize she'd said the words until he glanced up in surprise. She should've felt embarrassed, but she didn't. She just felt happy. Like she wanted to give the entire world a great big hug. Which made her wonder if he wasn't right. Maybe Mrs. Huckabee did put some magic in her brownies. She giggled and poured herself some more wine, fascinated by the way the burgundy liquid looked as it spilled into the glass. When she glanced up, Grayson was watching her.

"So don't get a big head over it," she said. "You're hot, but you have a bad attitude and could use a haircut." She curled up on the couch with her legs pretzeled and took a sip of wine. "I could give you one if you want."

He went back to sketching. "No, thanks. Especially if your bangs are an example. Why did you change the color from blond?"

She giggled and took a sip of wine. Oregon made some kick-ass wine. The flavor seemed to burst in a kaleidoscope of flavors. She could almost imagine each little taste bud absorbing it and doing a happy dance. Which had a very weird effect on her tongue. It loosened it.

"Because that blond, frivolous little princess who liked frilly pink dresses and pretty purple rooms died. She died when the queen got sick and the truth came out."

Grayson stopped drawing and looked at her. "And what truth is that?"

"The truth is that I'm not a little princess at all. I'm just an orphaned bastard who hates pink and purple."

"Which is why you wear black?"

"Black goes with my personality. Didn't you know that I'm very dark and crabby?" She would've poured herself some more wine if Grayson hadn't gotten up and taken the bottle from her. He set it and the sketchpad down on the breakfast bar before joining her on the couch. He was close. Much too close. She could see all the different shades of his eyes—from the deepest indigo to the lightest lavender.

"I don't think you have a dark personality," he said. "I think your personality goes with the wall you painted in my room—bright, bold, colorful." He paused for only a second before he continued. "I think you choose to wear black because you're still mourning your mother."

She looked away from his intense eyes, no longer wanting his gaze directed at her. No longer feeling like she wanted to hug the whole world. "Who told you?"

"Deirdre mentioned that your mother had died of cancer, which is why she's so insistent about having a painting of you for the charity event. So when did your mom die?"

Chloe leaned back on the couch and stared up at the ceiling. "I was fifteen."

"Then you remember her."

She nodded. "Almost every second I had with her. She was witty and beautiful and the best hostess. People loved to attend her parties. She always knew exactly what to wear, what to serve, what to say to make people feel right at home." She paused. "When she was gone, there was no home."

"Is that why you ran away, Chloe? Because your mother died?"

"No. I ran away because I discovered that my castle was made of nothing but a little girl's fantasies. Fantasies that evaporated when she was forced to grow up." She stared at the bottle of wine. "And you? What was your mother like?"

He hesitated before he replied. "I wish I knew." He leaned his head back on the cushion next to hers and stared at the ceiling. "While my brothers have all these memories, I don't have any. Not a damned one. I look at pictures, or the drawings I did of her, and hope that they'll trigger some memory. But it's like looking at a stranger." He ran a hand through his hair and gripped it tightly, as if trying to pull all the memories from his brain.

Ironically she wished for the reverse. She wished she could shove all the memories back inside and never think of them again.

"I'm sorry," she said.

He released his hair and nodded. "Me too. The only things I know about my mother are what I've heard from my brothers and father. She loved to draw, to sew, and to sing Bruce Springsteen."

"My mom loved eighties movies," Chloe said. "I don't know how many times I had to watch *Sixteen Candles*—a hundred, at least. For my birthday, my dad would always bake two cakes. One for my party, and one for my mom and me. When everyone else had gone to sleep, we'd climb up on the dining room table and sit cross-legged with nothing but the glowing candles on the cake between us. 'Happy Birthday, Lena,' she'd say, 'Make a wish.' I'd always wish for something stupid. A new horse. A trip to Disneyland." She squeezed her eyes tighter. "I never once wished that she would always be there. Not once." She swallowed hard. "My bad."

Chloe didn't expect him to say anything. There was nothing to say. And that was the good thing about Grayson. He wasn't an empty talker who filled space with nonsense. So they just sat there, listening to the tenors sing like a choir of angels. After a time Grayson reached out and took her hand, interlocking their fingers so their palms touched. And that was all he did. He just held her hand tightly in his, as if he needed the human touch as much as she did. She didn't know how long they sat like that. Long enough for the memories to not feel as painful as they once had.

Finally she opened her eyes and turned her head to find his face only inches away. His eyes were open, the violet depths beckoning like a garden on a bright summer day. Emotions swelled inside her. But not lust. These emotions were deeper, more intense. So intense that they took her breath away. And intense emotions had always been her downfall. She quickly sat up and searched for anything to break the spell Grayson had woven. She was relieved when she spotted the seagull sitting in the planter on the balcony.

"Jonathan Livingston roosts here at night?" she asked.

Grayson sat up. "Not usually. Usually he only shows up in the mornings for his sardines."

She quickly got to her feet. "Well, he looks like he's tucked in for the night. And speaking of being tucked in"— she picked up her wineglass—"I think I'll head to bed." She had started to take the glass to the kitchen when she noticed Grayson's sketchpad sitting on the counter. Unable to stop herself, she picked it up.

The drawing took her breath away. Not because of the talent behind each stroke, but because of the girl who looked back at her. A fifteen-year-old girl who Chloe had forgotten existed. Gone were the somber features and the eyes that reflected pain, and in their place was a bright smile and eyes that reflected happiness. How had Grayson seen this girl? Was she still there deep down inside? Chloe wanted to believe it.

Having no words to express what she felt at that moment, she set the sketchpad and glass on the counter and turned toward the stairs. She had almost reached them when Grayson spoke.

"Good night, Princess Lena."

With tears clogging her throat, she answered.

"Good night, Graysie."

CHAPTER TWELVE

"Where the hell are you, Grayson?" Deacon's voice came through the speakers of the Bugatti loud and clear.

Grayson glanced at his GPS and realized that he wasn't quite sure. He was somewhere in Napa Valley. Although that wasn't something he wanted Deacon to know. Especially when Grayson was supposed to be at the office.

"I'm running a little late this morning," he said.

"That's one of the first rules of business, Gray—a late boss means late employees." There was a pause, and Grayson could hear faint crying in the background. "In fact, maybe I need to come back to work."

"Absolutely not, Deke. You planned to stay home a couple weeks with Olivia and Michael, and you need to stick to it. I've got everything under control." It was a bald-faced lie. He had nothing under control, and driving around Napa Valley only proved it. He had no business nosing into Chloe's personal life when he should be at French Kiss smoothing Miles's ruffled feathers and getting Natalia to come back to work so they could pull together the catalog. Not that he hadn't tried to get Natalia to come back. He had called her just that morning and explained that he wasn't going to date her whether she worked for French Kiss or not. The obstinate model wasn't getting it. She was convinced that he was fighting his true desires. And he was fighting his true desires. But they had nothing to do with Natalia.

Maybe that was why he'd come on this wild-goose chase. Once he solved the puzzle that was Chloe, he could forget about her and move on with this life. Not that he had much of a life without his painting. He glanced at the navigation system and took a left as the green arrow indicated.

"So you haven't had any problems at work?" Deacon asked.

"Just the usual," he hedged. "Now would you stop worrying and concentrate on your family?"

"You're right," Deacon said. "Maybe if I focus on getting Michael on a schedule, things would be going a little smoother."

"I gather that my nephew is still keeping you up at night."

A tired sigh came through the speakers. "He started sleeping great during the day, but at night all he wants to do is eat and poop."

"He sounds like Jonathan Livingston. The stupid bird has decided to take up permanent residence on the planter on the balcony. Maybe I shouldn't be feeding him. Maybe we've made him too domesticated."

"It's too late now. Olivia will not be happy if you starve Jonathan. And don't compare my son to a stupid bird. Michael is much smarter. Although his poops do resemble the stuff Jonathan used to drop on Olivia's balcony rug."

"You're kidding, right?"

"I wish I was. I swear it's the nastiest stuff I've ever seen."

"After Nash and I moved in, we got rid of the rug, and now I just hose off the balcony. Maybe you could do the same with Michael." There was a pause, as if Deacon was considering it. "I was joking, Deke."

"Yeah…right. Speaking of your house, Olivia's mom mentioned stopping by to see your paintings. What's this I hear about a woman living with you? Why didn't you tell me you were in a serious relationship?"

"Because I'm not in a serious relationship," he said. "She's a friend of Madison's that needed a place to stay for a few days." Grayson realized the holes in the lie when Deacon fired off his next question.

"Why isn't she staying with Madison?"

He scrambled for a good answer and decided to stay as close to the truth as possible. "Because her ex-boyfriend is abusive and Madison's is the first place he'll look." It turned out to be the perfect response. Deacon had always had a soft spot for a woman in trouble.

"Well, it's nice that you're helping her out, Gray. And if she needs a lawyer to get a restraining order on the asshole, you can ask Jason to give you a reference."

"Deacon!" Olivia's voice came through the speakers amid even louder baby wailing.

"I have to go," Deacon said. "But I'll call you later. I want to hear about the holiday catalog and what we'll be using for the cover. We used Madison for the fall catalog so I'm thinking Natalia."

Grayson cringed. "Umm…maybe we should use one of the newer models—you know, a fresh face."

The crying got even louder. "We'll have to talk about it later."

Once Deacon hung up, Grayson realized that he had

missed a turn. He made a U-turn and then took a left. This road was dirt and not exactly meant for a low-riding sports car. Luckily, he had to drive only a short distance before the sign for the vineyard appeared.

Casa Selena.

He had spent the night Googling the name Selena Cameron and any other words that might pull up pictures of Chloe. Remembering the expert way Chloe had opened the bottle of wine, he'd added "wine" to his search and hit pay dirt.

Unfortunately, the Selena Cameron he'd found pictures of was an older woman who had started a vineyard in Napa Valley. It seemed too much of a coincidence to ignore. He realized his mistake when the winery came into view. The massive Spanish-style stone structure that sat on the hill looked more like a medieval castle than a winery. There was no way in hell that anyone would run away from this fairy tale.

Grayson thought about turning around, but since he had come all this way, he might as well check it out. He parked in the visitors' parking lot, then got out and walked along a pebbled pathway that led through a beautiful flower garden. He stopped where the path divided, unsure of what direction to go in.

"If you're lookin' for the tasting room, it's to the right."

Grayson turned to see an old man in baggy cargo pants and a tattered plaid shirt standing amid the flowers like the Scarecrow in *The Wizard of Oz*.

"This way?" Grayson pointed.

The man squinted beneath a straw cowboy hat that looked like it had been run over by a semitruck—repeatedly. "That would be the way."

Grayson nodded his thanks before heading down the path

to the tasting room. He pushed open the large oak door to find a sunlit room with a bar on one side and on the other a bank of windows that looked out over the valley. An older touristy couple was standing at the bar, tasting the wine a young woman in a white shirt and red apron poured.

"This is our Chardonnay," the young woman said. "A medium-bodied wine with delicate notes of apple and pear and a hint of oak."

The woman, who was wearing a hot pink sun hat, took a sip and nodded. "Yes, I do taste the oak." She looked at the man. "Don't you taste the oak, Harry?"

The man downed the wine in one swig. "Yep, Milly, tastes like an entire forest of oak." He set the glass down with a loud clink before addressing the server. "You wouldn't have a beer, would you, sweetheart?"

Milly swatted his arm. "Can you act civil for one second, Harry? And considering I spent our last vacation touring the Milwaukee breweries with you, it's the least you can do."

"Fine," Harry grouched. "But do you think I could get more than a thimbleful next time?"

"Of course," the server said politely. "But we charge by the glass. A tasting is all that's included in the tour package. Would you like a glass of Chardonnay? Or perhaps the pinot grigio you tasted earlier?" She had bent to pull another bottle of wine from beneath the bar when she noticed Grayson standing by the door. "Are you here for wine tasting or the tour?"

Grayson walked to the bar. "Just a tasting." He smiled at the couple. "Enjoying your vacation?"

"Not yet," Harry grumbled, and got another swat for his trouble.

"Don't pay him any attention," Milly said. "We're having

a wonderful time." Her gaze took in Grayson's suit, and she swatted her husband yet again. "I told you that we should've dressed nicer, Harry."

Grayson tasted one wine with the couple before their tour started. Once they were gone, he attempted to get some information out of the young woman. "So this must be a fun job. How long have you worked here?"

"The last two years. The Camerons are real nice about working around my college schedule."

"So you know the owners?"

"The younger Cameron mostly. Mr. Cameron doesn't deal with the tasting room as much as with the production." She uncorked another bottle of wine.

"This is Robert Cameron we're talking about?"

"No. Robert is retired, and his wife, Selena, passed away. Davis Cameron, their son, is the one who runs the vineyards now, along with his youngest nephew." She poured him a splash of wine. "This is our Syrah. It's a full-bodied wine with blackberry and peppery tones."

Grayson took a drink. Like Harry, he would've much preferred a beer. "So how many children does Davis have?"

"None that I know of, which is why his nephew works with him and will probably inherit the winery." She pointed to the wall behind the bar, which was filled with awards and a variety of pictures that ranged from the cattle ranch the place had once been to the castle-like structure and winery it was today. In the midst of these photographs was a framed picture of two men standing in front of a stack of wine barrels.

"That's Davis Cameron and his nephew Cain."

Grayson examined the picture, but neither man looked like Chloe. Feeling foolish for coming all this way for nothing, Grayson pulled out his wallet. "Thanks for the wine. I'll take a case of the Syrah and Chardonnay. I'm assuming you ship?"

After he'd paid and given his address, he headed back out the way he'd come. But before he could reach the parking lot, the gardener stopped him.

"So what did you think of the wine?"

Grayson turned and found the old man kneeling in the flowers, his aged hands deep in the dark soil. He should've just said the wine was good and been on his way. But there was something about the man that reminded him of his own grandfather, and Grandpa Beaumont had had zero respect for a man who couldn't tell the truth.

"I'm afraid I'm not much of a wine drinker," he said.

The man laughed. "Well, that makes two of us. I never did understand why my Selena loved it so much. Of course, I could never understand how she could fall in love with an old cowpoke like me either."

Grayson stared at the man. "You're Robert Cameron?"

The man chuckled again. "On my gardening days, I'm sure it's hard to believe." He brushed off his hands, then used the hoe next to him to climb to his feet. "Robert Cameron. I'd shake hands, but I wouldn't want to dirty that nice suit."

Grayson held out his hand. "I've never worried about a little dirt." He shook the man's hand. "Grayson Beaumont. It's nice to meet you, Mr. Cameron."

"Just call me Bob." He squinted beneath the brim of his hat. "Beaumont? Last month I read an article about a Deacon Beaumont in *Forbes* magazine. Any relation?"

Obviously the man did more than garden. "My brother."

"So you're one of the undergarment billionaires, are you?"

Grayson laughed. "I prefer that to *panty billionaire*."

A smile creased Bob's face. "Well, either way, it's intriguing." He stepped out on the path. "Come on, Grayson Beaumont. I'll get you something more refreshing than a glass of wine."

Grayson really should've made his excuses. He didn't have any more time to waste on this foolish trip. But he couldn't bring himself to be rude, so he followed Bob along the left side of the path, down some stone steps, and through the tidy rows of grapevines to a much smaller house set back in a cluster of pecan trees.

"This was our first home. Once Davis built his castle, he gave this to the winemaker he'd brought over from Italy." He shook his head. "The biggest mistake of his life." He rested the hoe that he had used as a walking stick against the side of the house, then hooked his cowboy hat on it. "Davis wanted to burn the entire house down after Beth passed away, but I wouldn't let him. Jealousy can make a man do foolish things."

Burning down a house seemed a little extreme, and Grayson had to wonder what kind of jealousy would spur the action.

Bob opened the door. "Come on in, but wipe your feet first. I don't want grape stains on my carpet."

Grayson thoroughly wiped his feet on the mat, then followed the man inside. The living room was spacious and looked like an older person lived there. Throw blankets covered all the furniture, including the recliner that sat in front of a flat-screen television. Next to the recliner was a TV tray filled with prescription bottles and over-the-counter pain relievers.

Bob bypassed the chair and shuffled into the sprawling kitchen. Grayson followed him and took a seat at the table, which was positioned in front of a bay window with a perfect view of the vineyards. He enjoyed the view as Bob washed his hands and then dried them on the dish towel hooked over the oven handle. "You hungry? Rosa brought me some enchiladas last night for dinner, and there's plenty left over. Can't get the fool woman to realize that I can't eat spicy foods without getting heartburn."

"No, thank you." Grayson glanced at the clock on the wall. "I don't have much time."

"Time is a tough taskmaster. Although when you don't have a lot of it left, you wonder what all the hurry was about." Bob took two glasses out of a cupboard. He filled each one with ice from the freezer, followed by lemonade from the pitcher he took out of the refrigerator. Before he brought them to the table, he poured a healthy dose of whiskey in each.

"My daddy used to call this a 'Sour Horse's Ass.' I never understood why until I got drunk as a skunk on them. If you're not careful, they can turn you into one hell of a horse's ass." He handed a glass to Grayson before lifting it in a toast. "To youth and good women—both slip away much too fast." He took a drink before he eased down in the chair across from Grayson.

Grayson took one sip, and his eyes watered. "I was sorry to hear about your wife. From the article I read online, she was the one who started the vineyard."

Bob stared out the window at the rows of grapevines. "She loved everything about life—family, good food, and great wine. When oil prices cratered and my oil company was close to bankruptcy, she talked me into moving here to the land she'd inherited from her family. She had a dream, and she stuck with it until it succeeded. Selena McAlister was as smart as she was beautiful."

The glass almost slipped out of Grayson's hand. He caught it in time, but still splashed some on his pant legs. Bob's eyes narrowed, and for a second Grayson worried that he had caught the slip. But then he leaned over and grabbed the dish towel off the oven handle and tossed it to Grayson.

"Blot it with that," he said. "It won't stain, but you don't want to go to work looking like you wet yourself."

Grayson blotted his pants and tried to get more information without giving anything away. "Selena is a beautiful name." He set the towel on the table and picked up his drink. "Did you have a daughter to pass it down to?"

Bob shook his head. "Selena sure wished for one, but God only blessed us with two sons. One we lost in a plane crash more than twenty years ago, and the other one runs the business with my grandson."

"I saw a picture of your son and grandson in the tasting room. So you just have the one grandchild?"

Bob got up and poured himself another splash of whiskey—without the lemonade this time. He took a deep drink before turning back around. "I have two grandsons, both from my late son. Cain runs the winery with Davis, probably because he's the only one who can put up with Davis's pigheadedness. The other, Gavin, runs my oil company. "

If Grayson hadn't been worried about giving Chloe's whereabouts away, he would've just come out and asked Bob if he had a granddaughter. But there was a reason Chloe had run away, and until he found out what that reason was, he wasn't about to put her in danger. And since it looked as if Bob wasn't going to volunteer that information, it was probably time for him to go.

"Well, thanks for the lemonade, but I really should get back to San Francisco." He stood and took his glass to the sink. When he turned, he noticed the picture of the vineyard hanging on the wall. Which gave him an idea. "Could I use your bathroom before I go?"

Bob pointed. "Just down the hall, second door to your right."

The hallway was long and, as he'd hoped, lined with photographs. The first pictures were of Bob's sons, a variety of high school football, soccer, and graduation photos. The next were more recent pictures of the grandsons. But at the very end were pictures of a blond girl that proved this hadn't been a wild-goose chase after all.

Chloe's expressive brown eyes stared back at him from a chubby baby's face. An adorable toddler's. A pigtailed little girl's. And a laughing teenager's. The last picture was of the entire Cameron family. Grayson quickly recognized a younger Bob standing next to his wife. His sons stood on either side with their wives, two boys stood in front of their mother and father, and Chloe stood in front of hers.

"Lost your way again?"

Grayson turned to see Bob standing at the end of the hallway. His eyes were steady and piercing. He hesitated for only a second before he asked, "So you want to explain what you're really doing here, Grayson Beaumont?"

"I was just looking at your pictures."

Bob shook his head. "I think we both need to quit the flimflam and get to the truth. I didn't invite you here to quench your thirst. I invited you here to find out why a billionaire would show up at a winery during the workweek. Especially when he doesn't like wine."

Grayson didn't want to lie to the old guy. But he also couldn't tell him the truth. Not when he didn't have all the facts.

"Thank you for the lemonade, sir," he said, "but I really need to be going."

Bob studied him for a long moment before he stepped out of the way. Grayson walked past him and out the door. He was almost to the steps that led to the winery when Bob called out to him.

"Grayson!" When he turned, Bob was standing in the doorway of the house, somehow looking years older than he had before. "Please bring her home."

CHAPTER THIRTEEN

I think it's only fair that you know that I don't like you. You have no personality. You're obstinate. And you stink." Chloe stopped watering the Huckabees' flowers and stared at the seagull sitting in the ceramic pot on the balcony next door. "So if you don't want to eat your sardines, then don't eat your sardines. It makes no difference to me one way or the other." She moved to the next planter and tipped the watering pot. "The only reason I even opened the can is because Grayson seems to like you and is worried because you won't eat and all you want to do is sit there in that pot looking stupid. And it wasn't very nice of you to bite the hand that feeds you. Grayson was only trying to see if you were injured."

Just the thought of the incident had Chloe smiling. Grayson had been trying to check out Jonathan's wing when the bird had snapped at him. Grayson had jumped back so quickly that he'd tripped over the coffee table, and his expression when he landed on his butt had made her laugh until she cried. She'd expected his ego to be bruised, but Grayson had only joined in with her laughter. Obviously their nightly sketching sessions had loosened him up. He no longer scowled as much as he used to. And he wasn't nearly as hostile. In fact he'd started to act like the Grayson she'd first met—except not as quiet.

In the last few days, he'd finally opened up and talked. Not a lot, but enough for Chloe to discover the man beneath the handsome face. From their nightly conversations, she was able to piece together a clearer picture of Grayson. He was a loving son who deeply mourned his mother. An insecure youngest sibling who worried about measuring up to his brothers. A talented artist who worshipped the female body. And a sincerely kind man who cared about a stubborn seagull who refused to eat. Well, Jonathan Livingston wasn't going to die on her watch.

"Okay, Jonny." She glared across the balcony at the bird. "By the time I finish watering Mr. Huckabee's plants and get back over there, if you haven't eaten those sardines, I'm going to shove them straight down your throat—"

"That I've got to see."

The voice had Chloe dropping the watering can. She turned just as Eden stepped out onto the balcony looking suntanned and happy. She didn't hesitate for a second before she pulled Chloe into a bone-crushing hug. Which had Chloe feeling guilty. She didn't deserve Eden's love. Not after she'd ignored her and skipped her wedding.

As always, the guilt had her snapping. "Why don't you just scare the crap out of me, Eden?"

Eden laughed. "Sorry, but I didn't exactly expect you to be on my grandparents' balcony. I expected you to be locked in Grayson's house."

Chloe eyes widened. "I knew it! You and Madison were

behind the kidnapping. I thought as much when Madison refused to answer my calls."

"I told her not to. She can be talked into doing anything for her friends and would've released you if you'd asked. And the kidnapping wasn't my idea, but I was totally willing to support the plan if it kept you here until I got back." Eden grinned as she picked up the watering can and handed it to Chloe. "And from the looks of things, you seem to be enjoying your captivity. Did my pops con you into watering his plants while they are in Mexico?"

"Your grandmother was the one who asked. Although she was nice enough to pay me with marijuana brownies. Why didn't you tell me that your grandparents are stoners?"

"It's not exactly something I'm proud of. You didn't eat one, did you?"

"What do you think?"

Eden shook her head. "Of course you ate one. You and Madison will eat anything chocolate. So what happened?"

Something had happened. She had started to like Grayson more than she should. But she couldn't tell Eden that. "Nothing happened, but I would like you to explain how you ended up being so uptight with your hippy grandparents and yoga-loving mother."

Eden shrugged. "I'm sure they've asked the same question. And speaking of my mother, she was very upset when she heard that you were leaving San Francisco. She had high hopes that you would go to college after she helped you get your GED."

"What would I do in college?" Chloe refilled the watering can from the outside spigot and continued watering.

"How about study horticulture? Then you could buy a greenhouse and sell flowers to every vendor in northern California. I'd be willing to invest."

It was an intriguing idea. One that Chloe might look into once she was in England. But not here. "I'm not staying in California."

Eden didn't look shocked as much as exasperated. "You can't tell me that you're still planning on leaving."

Chloe was still planning on it, and sooner rather than later. She had promised to stay until Eden got back. Well, Eden was back. Which meant that all she needed to do was get Grayson to paint her so she could get her money from Deirdre Beaumont.

"Okay." Chloe stepped around Eden. "I won't tell you."

"Chloe!" Eden grabbed her arm and turned her around. "That is such bullshit. And I'm not letting you go until you give me three good reasons for leaving. And I'm not talking about the crap you gave Madison about being young and needing excitement. San Francisco is one of the most exciting cities in the world."

This was the reason Chloe hadn't wanted to tell Eden she was leaving. The woman was as stubborn as the day was long. Or maybe as stubborn as Chloe.

"Look, it's nice that you like me and want me to stay," she said. "But I don't need three reasons for leaving. I only need one...because I want to." She placed the watering can by the spigot. "Lock up when you leave."

She should've known that it wouldn't be that easy. Eden caught up with her at the front door. "I don't believe you for a second," she said as she stepped outside and waited for Chloe to lock the door with the key Mrs. Huckabee had given her. "You don't really want to leave. You love San Francisco. This is your home. Where all your friends are."

Chloe pocketed the key and walked the twenty or so feet to Grayson's front door. "We're not friends, Eden. I didn't even come to your wedding. What kind of friend is that?"

"The kind who has been hurt badly in the past and is afraid of opening her heart," Eden said.

Chloe rolled her eyes. "I hope your book isn't as dramatic as you are. And I'm not afraid of opening my heart. I opened it to Zac."

Eden sent her a smug look. "I'll have you know that my editor loves my dramatic prose. And the only reason you felt comfortable loving Zac is because he didn't love you back. You're not afraid of loving people, Chloe. You're afraid of people loving you. If they love you, then you feel like you owe them something—something you don't think you can give."

Eden was right. There was a responsibility that came with someone loving you. And Chloe had to live with enough guilt. She didn't need any more.

She pulled her hand free. "It doesn't matter, Eden. I'm still leaving—" She broke off when she looked over Eden's shoulder and saw Grayson standing not more than a few feet away. The last couple of days, his eyes had sparkled with humor. Today his eyes were direct and solemn as they studied Chloe.

"Grayson!" Eden walked over and gave him a hug. "I'm glad you're here. You can help me talk some sense into Chloe and keep her from leaving."

Grayson continued to look at Chloe as he spoke. "I promised you that I'd keep her here until you got back. I did that." Without another word he brushed past Chloe and disappeared inside the house. It was hard not to feel annoyed. He could've at least acted a little disappointed that she was leaving. Of course, why should he feel disappointed? He'd kept her here only so she wouldn't ruin Eden and Nash's honeymoon. Now that they were back, he probably couldn't wait to get rid of her.

"Poor guy," Eden said. "He's been working overtime since Nash and Deacon took off. And then I placed you on his doorstep. That couldn't be fun."

"Thanks a lot."

Eden sent her a dubious look. "As if you don't know that you're a pain in the butt." She glanced at her watch. "I have to go. I've got a meeting with my literary agent."

"When does your book come out?"

"Not for months. I'm working on revisions now and then I want you to read it and tell me what you think. Which is just another reason why you can't leave."

"You can always send me your book."

Eden shook her head. "Oh no, I'm not falling for that one. Once you're gone, we'll never hear from you again." She held out her pinkie finger. "Which is why I want you to pinkie swear that you won't leave until we've talked."

Knowing that Eden wouldn't leave until she got the promise, Chloe rolled her eyes and hooked her pinkie with Eden's as she crossed the fingers of her other hand behind her back. "Fine. I pinkie swear that I won't go anywhere until you get back. Now get out of here before you're late."

She waited for Eden to climb back into her car before she headed inside to search for Grayson. The faster he did the painting, the faster she could go. She found him sitting on the balcony trying to get Jonathan to eat a sardine by waving it in front of him. The bird didn't even look at the fish. He just sat in the pot with his eyes closed.

"I thought you learned your lesson yesterday. The bird doesn't mind biting the hand that feeds him." She sat down in a chair. "So when did you get home? I didn't hear that growling beast of a car pull into the garage."

"I took the trolley to work today." He placed the sardine back in the can and, without another word, got up and walked back inside. It was obvious that he wasn't in a talking mood, and she should have taken the hint and given him some space. Instead she followed him downstairs to his bedroom. After the first night, Chloe had moved into the guest room. Which explained the messy condition of the room.

"Did anyone ever tell you that you're a slob, Grayson?" She sat down on his mussed bed and crossed her legs pretzel-style. "What are you doing home so early?"

"Nash is back at work." He disappeared inside the walk-in closet.

"That should be a relief," she called. "Now you don't have to be there so much."

A few moments later, he appeared in the doorway of the closet in ripped jeans and his dress shirt, now unbuttoned. It was hard to keep her eyes away from the thin strip of hard chest and firm abs. But his next words pulled her attention to his face. "Why did you pinkie swear to Eden? We both know that you're not going to say goodbye."

It didn't surprise her that he'd overheard her talking to Eden. She and Eden had been standing right under the balcony. "Goodbyes are overrated," she said. "No one wants tears and sadness to be the last memory they have of someone."

"That's bullshit." He jerked off his shirt and dropped it to the floor. "My dad thought I was too young to see my mother the night she died so I didn't get to say goodbye. And I'm still pissed at him for that. People need to say goodbye. They need closure—or at least the opportunity to tell the people leaving how much they're going to be missed. But you aren't going to let anyone do that, are you? You're just going to run off in the middle of the night like a chickenshit."

Chloe's anger rose to the surface, and she jumped from the bed. "I'm not a chickenshit!" She paused. "You're going to miss me?"

He ignored the question as he walked to the dresser and pulled out a T-shirt. "I don't know what you'd call it. It seems pretty chickenshit to me. When are you going to stop running and face your problems head on?"

"Oh, let's talk about facing problems, shall we? You can't even pick up a paintbrush without hyperventilating. All you've done for the last three nights is doodle—and I've peeked at your sketches, Graysie, and they stink!" It was a lie. They didn't stink. They were amazing. But she was hoping the statement would make him want to prove her wrong. And it did exactly that.

His eyes widened for a second before they narrowed. "You want to see me pick up a paintbrush? Fine!" He dropped the T-shirt and headed to the chest of drawers where he kept his paints. He chose numerous tubes and brushes before placing them on the table next to the easel. Unsure of what to do, Chloe just stood there and watched as he opened each tube of paint and dabbed some on the palette before mixing them with something that looked like a little gardening trowel.

When he glanced up, he lifted an eyebrow. "What are you waiting for? Get naked."

It was weird. Five days ago she would've stripped for him without any compunction whatsoever. But after getting to know him, she now felt suddenly shy.

"Right now?" She fidgeted with the hem of her T-shirt. "I mean, don't you need to do some warm-up exercises first? A few finger flexes. Some more drawings of me...with my clothes on."

"I'm as warmed up as I'll ever be." He cocked his head. "What's the problem? I thought you wanted to do this. Have you changed your mind?"

"No. No, I didn't change my mind." She took a deep breath and slowly released it before she pulled off her T-shirt and shimmied out of her jeans. She wore another one of the bra-and-panty sets that Madison had given her. This one a deep maroon with a black satin ribbon laced through the eyelet material.

When she'd posed for Grayson before in her underwear, she hadn't felt the least bit bashful—probably because he'd been hidden behind a camera. But now he wasn't hidden behind a camera. He was just sitting there on the stool next to the easel and canvas, his gaze running over her with an intensity that made a blush heat her body from the top of her head to the tips of her toes. And she couldn't seem to get the rest of her clothes off.

Grayson must've figured it out because, after picking out a canvas and placing it on the easel, he walked to the door. "By the time I get back, I want you naked and on the bed. And if you need to go to the bathroom, do it now. You won't be moving much in the next couple hours."

Once he was gone, she didn't hesitate to take off her underwear and dive on the bed. She was completely covered with the sheet when he walked back in with a bottle of wine. He poured her a glass and handed it to her.

"There's no need to be nervous," he said. "All you have to do is lie there. I'll do the rest."

"I'm not nervous." She took the glass and gulped it down in four swallows, then held it out for more.

His eyebrow hiked before he refilled the glass, then he walked to the dresser and picked up his phone. And while he was choosing the music, Chloe took another sip of the excellent cabernet. It didn't seem to help. She almost jumped out of her skin when the music came on, even though it was the soothing voices of the Ten Tenors.

He turned, his eyes smoldering.

"Take off the sheet, Chloe."

CHAPTER FOURTEEN

Holding the sheet to her breasts, Chloe downed the last of the wine and set the glass on the nightstand. With shaky hands she slowly inched the sheet down, but stopped before she revealed her nipples. "You probably realized the other night that my body isn't exactly model-perfect. I have small breasts... and bony hip bones... and knobby knees—"

In a single motion, Grayson grabbed the sheet and jerked it to the floor.

"Hey!" Chloe tried to cover the most embarrassing parts, but he had already turned and was walking to the easel.

"Keep one pillow and toss the rest to the floor."

She did what he asked, but used the last pillow to hide behind. Grayson was so busy preparing his paints and canvas that it took him a few minutes to notice. When he did, his eyebrow cocked.

"My mistake," he said. "Get rid of the pillow."

She glared at him and threw it, hoping to smack him in the head. Instead it dropped before it even reached the easel. With nothing else to hide behind, she was forced to accept the situation, although she couldn't help the blush that seemed to cover every inch of her body. If Grayson noticed, he didn't comment. His eyes were intense as he studied her.

Did he find her as attractive as she found him? Or did he like more voluptuous women like Madison? She glanced at her slim hips and noticed the tattoo to the left of her hip bone. When she was sixteen, the Chinese symbol had seemed cool. Now it looked ugly and immature. She covered it with her hand.

"What does it mean?" Grayson asked.

She glanced over to him. " 'Brave.' "

A smile flirted with his lips. "Then be brave enough to show it off." She lowered her hand, but as soon as she did, he started ordering her around. "Lie on your side facing me…that's it. Place your hand on the mattress…higher so I can see your breasts. Lower your knee a little…more. Can you move your hip back?" He studied her for a moment before he tossed down the pencil. "No. This isn't right."

Before she could feel completely inadequate as far as naked models go, he walked over and started arranging the blankets and pillows on the floor. He covered them with a quilt, then stepped to the bed and scooped Chloe into his arms. She had a brief tingle of hard chest against soft breast before he lowered her to the floor and knelt next to her, arranging her limbs like she was his own personal Gumby doll.

With his hot hands touching her feet, her calves, the sensitive skin on the backs of her knees, her bones turned to butter. As he adjusted and readjusted, she could do nothing but drink him in. The dark whiskers on his jaw. The small indentation at the base of his throat. The strong horizontal ridges of his collarbones. The heart-shaped birthmark on his shoulder. The tempting hard planes of his pectoral muscles as he lifted her legs—

Chloe sucked in her breath as he adjusted a pillow beneath her hips and his fingers brushed her butt cheeks. She had barely gotten over the jolt of the touch when he manacled her wrists and stretched her arms above her head, leaning so close that she could smell the cabernet scent of his breath. So close that she could count his thick lashes and the indigo flecks in the irises of his eyes.

Once he had her where he wanted her, he leaned back and gave her one more heated once-over before getting to his feet. "Don't move," he ordered. "Stay right where you are."

He didn't have to worry. Her body was nothing but a melted puddle of wax. She couldn't have moved if she'd wanted to. Every one of her senses seemed to be relaxed and, at the same time, on high alert. She no longer felt embarrassed. Stretched out on the floor in front of him, she just felt sexy. The feeling only intensified as he took a seat and started to draw.

He sketched on the canvas with the fluidity and skill of a man who knew exactly what he was doing. Exactly what he wanted. It seemed like only seconds had passed when he tossed down his pencil and picked up his brush. The way he painted was twice as sensuous as the way he drew. The brush was like an extension of his hand, and the canvas her body. Wherever his hot gaze landed, she felt the stroke of his brush. Her feet. Her legs. Her breasts. Her warm center. Time seemed to stand still and, at the same time, race forward. And all she could do was lie there and watch as he worshipped her like no man had ever worshipped her. He made her feel beautiful. Breathtaking. And wicked.

She now understood what it meant to be "captured on canvas." With every brushstroke he captured her mind, body, and soul. She was no longer Chloe McAlister... or even Selena Cameron. Right now she was Grayson's. For all eternity she wanted to be...

"Grayson's."

She didn't realize she had spoken until his hand halted in mid-brushstroke. His gaze found hers, and she lost herself in the depths of the bluish-purple flames as he dropped the brush and slowly rose from the stool. He walked toward her. Or more like stalked. She definitely felt like prey as he stood at her feet and looked down at her with hungry eyes. She could've lowered her arms—it was obvious that the painting session was over—but she didn't. Instead she remained perfectly still. A willing sacrifice on the altar of Grayson.

"Are you sure you want this?" he asked.

She nodded, then watched as he flicked open the fly of his jeans, then slowly lowered his zipper. While he painted, she'd thought he viewed her as a subject rather than a woman, but the rigid penis that popped out said otherwise. The sight of his tangible passion had a moan slipping from her lips. A second later his jeans and boxers were off and kicked to the side.

"Spread your legs," he ordered. When she complied, he knelt on the quilt between them, his hard thighs brushing the insides of hers. With the pillow beneath her hips, she was completely exposed to his view. But she didn't feel embarrassed. Only needy. The need intensified when his gaze devoured her. "You are so fuckin' beautiful."

He reached out as if his finger were a paintbrush and stroked her from the top of her moist center to the bottom and back again. When his fingertip flicked against her clitoris, it was all she needed to send her toppling into an orgasm. She didn't realize how pumped with desire she had been until it exploded in a shower of white-hot release.

"Gray!" she heard herself yell as her hips lifted against his finger and her legs stiffened around his thighs.

"Fuck," he said before he lifted her hips even higher and plunged inside. The deep stretch had her desire resurfacing, but before things could get even hotter, he stopped and spoke between his teeth. "Please tell me you're on birth control, Chloe."

Before she could finish shaking her head, he had withdrawn and was gone. She heard drawers opening and slamming, then the thump of hurried footsteps out of the room, followed only a second later by, "Thank you, Nash!" He came striding back into the room, and she didn't even have time to admire his body before he was kneeling between her legs. He lifted her hips and, in one deep thrust, entered her. The look on his face catapulted her right back into a haze of desire. He looked as if he had just found heaven. His eyes were closed and his head thrown back, all his muscles tight and straining for release. A hiss came through his teeth before he pulled out and thrust again. And again. And again.

His lovemaking wasn't gentle or hesitant. It was raw and commanding. His hands gripped her hips as he drove into her and took complete possession. By the fifth stroke, she was mindless. By the eighth, she had her feet on the floor and was meeting him thrust for thrust. And at the tenth, she toppled over the edge once more and gave up ownership of her body to him. "Gray!"

His hands tightened on her hips as he thrust one last time with a loud groan. She felt his body relax as he slid over her. With his arms holding most of his weight, he pressed his face into her neck and released his breath on a sigh of contentment.

"That was so damned good."

She smiled and closed her eyes, too satisfied to say anything.

He lifted his head. "Chloe?" She opened her eyes to find him staring at her with a knotted brow. "It was good, right? I mean it was good for you?"

The insecure question was so unlike Grayson that she couldn't help teasing him. "No, it was awful. Three orgasms are standard—two just merely okay."

She expected him to laugh. Instead he looked even more concerned. "Okay?"

She would've confessed the truth if she hadn't gotten a cramp in her neck. Not a little cramp, but a clawing fist of a cramp that radiated down her spine. She tried to grab at the painful spot, but couldn't with Grayson in the way. "Get off," she yelled. As soon as he complied, she rolled to her side and grabbed her neck.

"What is it?" Grayson asked.

"A cramp. A bad cramp."

Kneeling over her, he pushed her fingers out of the way and started to massage her neck. "Give it a second. It will go away. You probably just posed in one position for too long."

"Ya think?" she said sarcastically, maybe a little too sarcastically, because Grayson stopped massaging and left. She tried to lift her head to see where he'd gone, but it hurt too much. "I'm sorry," she yelled. "I get a little nasty when I'm in pain."

"That's putting it mildly." Grayson reappeared and lifted her into his arms.

"What are you doing?" she asked. "I can't go to the hospital. They ask a lot of questions at a hospital."

"You don't need to go to the hospital. You need some heat." He carried her into the bathroom and straight into the tiled shower stall, where blissfully hot water was already spraying from the showerhead. He set her on her feet, then directed the nozzle until it hit the cramping spot on her neck. Within seconds the muscles released and the pain lessened. She enjoyed the hot spray of water for a few minutes before she lifted her head and scraped back her wet hair.

Grayson stood at the back of the shower looking like the cover of an erotic romance novel with water beading and dripping down his smooth skin and tight muscles.

"Are you all right?" he asked.

Rather than stare at him in rabid lust, she reached for the soap and started washing her body. "I guess posing followed by floor sex was too much for my muscles to handle."

There was a moment of silence before he spoke. "Even if the sex was just okay?"

She bit back a smile. "Maybe *okay* wasn't the right word. It was nice."

"Nice?"

"Very nice." She dipped her head under the water to rinse off, then almost choked when strong hands closed around her waist. "What are you doing?" she sputtered as he pulled her out of the spray and into his arms.

"Going for a better grade." He lowered his head and kissed her. And Grayson's kisses were as amazing as his lovemaking. He kissed like he painted, his lips and tongue stroking a picture of heat and passion that had her entire body trembling. She could've continued to kiss him forever, but he pulled back with a nip on her lower lip. "So tell me what you want, Chloe. Exactly what you want."

At that moment all she wanted was another taste of his lips. "Kiss me," she whispered as her hands curled around his neck.

But instead of kissing her mouth, he kissed her chin. "Here?" When she shook her head, he moved lower, tracing her neck with lips that seemed hotter than the spray of water on her back. "What about here?" Again she shook her head. He moved up to her ear and nibbled on her lobe. "Here?" A fresh wave of tingles skittered through her as he moved lower, trailing kisses over one shoulder, along her collarbone, then down the center of her rib cage. Her nipples hardened just from the sight of his dark head nestled between her breasts. "Here?" His breath brushed her skin like warm syrup as he moved to the rigid nipple of one breast. "Or maybe here?"

She expected a gentle kiss like the ones he'd given the rest of her body. Instead his lips delivered a hot, wet pull that had her fingers burrowing into his wet hair.

"Please, Grayson," she said on a groan.

"Aww, here." His breath chilled the wetness of her nipple before he continued the sweet torture, but this time he used the edges of his bottom teeth until she gasped. He did the same to her other breast until it was as pebbled and hard. Then he knelt in front of her and kissed his way down her stomach to the spot between her legs.

The heat of his mouth had her knees buckling. His grip tightened on her waist before she could melt to the floor, and he moved her to the bench, where he spread her legs and continued his deep, intimate kisses. He didn't flick his tongue as much as swirl it. Around and around her clitoris in slow circles that made her dizzy without her even moving. It felt amazingly good, but as her body tightened and her desire heightened, she needed more.

"Faster," she breathed as her hips lifted and her fingers tightened in his hair. "Harder." He took instruction well, and within seconds she was spiraling into an orgasm. Since she had yelled out her last two, she tried to keep quiet. But it was no use. The feelings were too intense, too amazing, to keep inside. "Yesss! Yes!" She rode the wave until the last tingle, then allowed her muscles and bones to melt back against the shower wall.

"So was that just nice?"

She opened her eyes to find Grayson still kneeling in front of her. His hair hung in damp ringlets, and droplets of water beaded his shoulders, where her feet rested. When had she put her feet there? She might've been embarrassed if she hadn't felt so content. She left them there and sent him a lazy smile. "It was amazing."

He looked like he had just won the spelling bee. "Really? You're not just saying that so you don't hurt my feelings?"

She rolled her eyes. "Everyone knows how much I worry about hurting people's feelings." She lifted her foot and tapped the tip of his nose with her big toe. "For someone who has bedded hundreds of simpering models, you certainly are insecure."

He grabbed her foot and kissed the bottom, his tongue flicking out and leaving a heated trail along her sole. "Who told you that I've bedded hundreds of women?"

"No one had to tell me. If you make other women you paint feel the way you made me, it just makes sense."

He lifted his head, and his eyes drilled right through her. "How do I make you feel, Chloe?"

She didn't know why she suddenly felt scared. Maybe because she didn't want to examine the way he made her feel too closely. It was past sexual attraction. Past anything she had ever felt with another man. But she couldn't tell him that. Not when she was leaving. So instead of answering, she leaned forward and kissed him. She kissed him with everything she had. With all the feelings he'd made her feel. With all the goodbyes she'd never said. She kissed him like she was going to stay with him forever.

Without breaking the kiss, he stood and pulled her up with him. He made love to her against the shower wall. This time much more slowly than before. She didn't think she could come again, but he proved her wrong.

When they were both spent, he turned off the shower and dried her off before carrying her to his bed. He tucked a pillow under her head and tossed the quilt over her before he snuggled against her back. The warmth of his body spooned around her made her feel warm and secure, and she closed her eyes and drifted to sleep. Or almost to sleep. She was in that place between wakefulness and dreamland when he whispered, "You're wrong, Chloe. You're the only woman I can't resist."

CHAPTER FIFTEEN

*G*rayson woke at dawn with two feelings.

Contentment.

And inspiration.

It took only a quick glance down at the woman snuggled against him to know where both feelings had come from. While she was standoffish when she was awake, in sleep Chloe was a cuddle bug. Her bed-head rested on his chest, her arm was slung over his rib cage, her leg was hooked over his thigh, and her foot had found its way beneath his calf. But as content as her possessiveness made him feel, the inspiration would not let him lie there for long. He had to paint. And he had to paint now.

Carefully he removed each limb and eased out from under her before he headed to the canvas on the easel. The painting was good. Damned good. Better than anything he'd done before. She hadn't wanted him to paint her face, but it was her face that made the painting. The soft, parted lips. The flaring nostrils. The dark, velvety eyes filled with passion. Just looking at the painting made him want to go back to bed and make love to her, but he ignored his desire and sat down to work.

It felt like he had been painting for only a moment when an annoying chiming interrupted his focus. He glanced at the clock on the nightstand and realized he'd been painting for over two hours. He also realized that the chiming was the doorbell. He would've ignored it and kept working if the annoying person hadn't started knocking—or more like pounding. Not wanting whoever it was to wake up Chloe, he grabbed a pair of jeans and pulled them on as he headed to the door.

When he saw Nash standing there, Grayson remembered that he had made plans to run with his brother.

"What the hell, Gray?" Nash said. "You were supposed to meet me at the park a good forty minutes ago. And when you didn't answer your phone, I thought something had happened."

"Sorry," Grayson said. "I had my phone on mute while I was painting."

Nash lost the pissed look. "So you're painting again? Well, it's about damned time."

"You knew I couldn't paint?"

"Of course I knew. Unlike Deacon, my head isn't completely lost in the business cloud." He brushed past Grayson. "Do you have some Advil? I've got jet lag to beat all jet lags." He headed straight for Grayson's bedroom.

"Wait, Nash." Grayson tried to stop him, but as usual his big brother paid absolutely no attention to him. Although he did come to a sudden halt when he reached the doorway.

Grayson moved next to him. Chloe was still asleep, but now she lay on her stomach with one arm and foot dangling off the edge of the bed and her face pressed into a pillow.

Something about seeing her in his bed made Grayson exceedingly happy. Wanting her to stay there, he glanced at Nash and pressed a finger to his lips before pointing to the stairs. Nash didn't even wait until they reached the top before he started quizzing him.

"So you want to explain what's going on?"

Grayson walked into the kitchen and opened the cupboard where he kept the Advil. He pulled out the bottle and tossed it to Nash, who had followed him into the kitchen. "I'm surprised that Eden didn't tell you."

Nash uncapped the bottle and shook out some tablets. "She told me that you were keeping her here until she got back, but she didn't mention that you were bedding her."

Grayson could've denied it and said that Chloe was just using his bedroom, but he had never lied to his brother and wouldn't start now. Nor would he kiss and tell. "That's none of your business." He opened the refrigerator and grabbed two power drinks, handing one to Nash.

Nash tossed the pills in his mouth and took the bottle, unscrewing the lid and downing half of it in two gulps. When he lowered the bottle, his gaze was intent. "You're right. It's not my business. But I hope like hell that you used a condom because that girl has been around the block a time or two."

Grayson stopped unscrewing the cap of his drink. "Shut up, Nash."

"Don't stick your head in the sand, little brother. You know as well as I do that her boyfriend was a pimp and he was using her as a wh—"

He quickly reached out and grabbed Nash by the front of his shirt. "Don't you fuckin' say it. Do you hear me? Don't you dare fuckin' say it."

Normally Nash would've already had Grayson in a

headlock, but this morning he just stared at him. "Jesus, Gray. Please tell me that you haven't fallen for Chloe."

It took a real effort to release Nash's shirt. "Hell, no. She just doesn't deserve to be called that. She wasn't one of Zac's escorts."

A look passed over Nash's face before he nodded. "Okay. Believe what you want to believe. Just wear a condom. And promise me that you won't get infatuated with her. Not only is she young, Gray, but she also has some problems. Otherwise she wouldn't have run away from home and lived on the streets."

"Maybe it wasn't her that had the problems. Maybe she had a good reason for running away."

Nash set the bottle down and rested back against the counter. "Is that what she told you?"

Grayson glanced at the stairway. He didn't want Chloe eavesdropping on their conversation, but he really needed to talk with someone about what he'd learned. And since Nash had always been his confidant, he seemed like the obvious choice. "Her real name is Selena Cameron. Her family has a vineyard in Napa Valley."

Nash came away from the counter. "Davis Cameron's vineyards—Casa Selena?"

"You know her father?"

"Not personally, but I know of him. And the Cameron family doesn't just own vineyards. They own oil wells."

"I thought those went dry."

"They did, but I guess Davis's nephew came up with a way to get the natural gas out of them that works better than fracking. Gavin Cameron patented the machinery he uses and is now worth billions. And you're telling me that Chloe is related to him?"

"Would you keep it down?" Grayson said as he glanced

at the stairs again. "And yes, that's exactly what I'm telling you. When I went there, I met Davis's dad and I saw a picture of Chloe with the family."

Nash shook his head. "But why would Chloe leave a family like the Camerons? From what I hear, they're good people."

"You can't always believe what you hear. People believed the worst about you, and they were wrong."

"I wouldn't say that, little brother. Until I met Eden, I was pretty screwed up. But I'll concede the point that there must be a reason Chloe ran away." He glanced at the stairs. "And since you're being so quiet, I'm going to assume that she doesn't know you talked with her family."

Grayson should've told her that he'd met her grandfather, but something had stopped him. More than likely fear that his snooping would piss her off and she'd leave. He wasn't ready for her to leave. At least not yet. "No, I haven't talked with her about it. I was hoping to find out more before I did."

Again Nash studied him with concern. "Maybe you should just leave it alone, Gray. Sometimes people need to keep their secrets." He picked up his power drink and finished it off. "So are we running or what?"

Since Grayson couldn't keep his thoughts from the woman tucked in his bed, he shook his head. "You go on without me. I'll meet you at the office."

Nash hesitated for only a moment before he headed for the stairs. "I would tell you to be careful, baby brother. But somehow I don't think you're going to listen."

Once he was gone, Grayson walked down the stairs to his bedroom. Regardless of what he'd told Nash, he didn't want to go to the office. Nor did he want to paint. He wanted to crawl back in bed with Chloe. Unfortunately, when he got there, she was no longer in bed and the bathroom door was closed. He stripped out of his jeans and climbed in bed to wait. He had just stuffed a pillow behind his head when the door opened and she walked out. He had hoped she would still be naked. Instead she wore one of his dress shirts. She looked sexy as hell. She also looked grumpy.

He bit back a smile. "Good morning." All he got for a reply was an annoyed squint. Which made him laugh. "What happened to the cheery person who made me coffee yesterday?"

"She's sore from posing for a tyrant who wouldn't let her move." She glanced at the window. "What time is it?"

"Almost nine."

"So you're not going to work?"

"I was thinking about spending the day in bed." He held out a hand. "Wanna join me?"

A look entered her eyes, and this time he had no trouble reading the longing. Unfortunately, it was followed by firm resolve. "Sorry, but I called Madison and she's coming to pick me up."

Just that quickly Grayson's happy mood fizzled. He sat up. "You're leaving?"

She searched around the floor for her clothes, refusing to look at him. "Of course I'm leaving. I was always leaving. You didn't think that just because we had...I mean, it was amazing, but..."

The *but* took away any joy he had gotten out of *amazing*. He had told Nash that he wasn't falling for Chloe. And he wasn't. He wasn't that stupid. But he hadn't thought she would just leave after the night they'd had together. It had meant something. Or at least it had meant something to him.

"I didn't think anything." He swung his legs over the edge of the bed and walked into the bathroom, slamming the door behind him. He turned on the shower and stepped in without waiting for it to warm up, then braced his hands on the wall and tried to gain control over his anger.

He had no right to be angry. Chloe had never made any promises. And he didn't want any promises. In fact he should be glad that she was going. He'd gotten everything he wanted from her—sex and Deirdre's damn painting. But if that was so, then why did he feel as if the skin had been stripped from his bones, leaving him feeling exposed and raw?

"Shit!" He punched the wall before he shut off the water and got out. He toweled off then jerked open the door. She wasn't in the bedroom, and he quickly grabbed his jeans from the floor and put them on before heading to the guest bedroom. When he didn't find her there either, the raw hurt turned to desperate panic.

He took the stairs two at a time up to the living area, giving the space only a quick glance before he hurried down the stairs and out the front door. He ran into the street, loose asphalt biting into the soles of his feet. He glanced both ways as the panic turned to despair. She wasn't just leaving. She was gone. He tipped his head back and wanted to yell at the cloudless skies. Instead he just stood there and tried to breathe until her voice drifted down to him from above.

"Shouldn't you be spouting off some beautiful words about me looking as bright as the sun?"

He glanced behind him. Chloe stood on the balcony still dressed in his button-down shirt. The stiff collar framed her teasing smile. "I mean you're standing under my balcony and your name is Romeo."

He moved closer. "I'm afraid that I've never been good at beautiful words."

Her smile faded. "You don't need to be. Your paintings speak more beautifully than any words ever could."

"You saw the painting?"

She nodded. "You painted my face." It wasn't an accusation as much as a statement.

"I had to." When a few moments passed and she didn't reply, he said what he should've said at the very beginning. "Stay."

Even from a distance, he could see the grip of her hands on the railing and the flicker of uncertainty in her eyes. She studied him for a moment longer before she motioned with her hand. "Come up here. There's something you've got to see."

Grayson was more than a little apprehensive about what he would find. As unpredictable as Chloe was, it could be anything. Hopefully, she hadn't slashed his painting to smithereens. But it wasn't his painting that she pointed to when he reached the balcony. It was the planter and the three speckled teal-colored eggs sitting in a nest of twigs, newspaper, and what appeared to be a shredded Snickers candy bar wrapper.

"I think these explain what's been wrong with your seagull," she said.

He stared at the eggs. "Jonathan laid those?"

"Not Jonathan as much as Josephine. Your male bird is really a female."

Feeling a little drained from his emotional morning, he sat down on the couch and rubbed his temples. "And I thought it was bad enough when he was crapping all over the place. Now I have to worry about hatching baby seagulls."

Chloe laughed. "Relax, Grayson. It's not like you'll have to deliver them. Josephine will be back." She sat down next to him, so close that her bare thigh pressed against his. She ran her fingers through the hair at the back of his neck, leaving a trail of heat that made his scalp tingle. "You still need a haircut." She paused so long that he finally turned to look at her. Her eyes held sadness. Part of him hated to see it there, but the other part liked knowing that this wasn't easy for her either.

"I've been thinking," she said. "Maybe I could stay for a little while longer. Just long enough to trim your hair." She glanced at the planter. "And see some eggs hatch." She looked back at him. "And pose for a painting that doesn't show my face." She pointed a finger. "Because if you think you're giving that one to Deirdre for public auction, Grayson Beaumont, you can think again."

Grayson didn't know why he suddenly felt as if the sun had just come out from behind a dark gray cloud. Maybe because she had accurately pointed out the reason behind his raw emotions. And it had nothing to do with falling for Chloe. It had to do with his painting. She was the one who had brought him out of his painting funk. Which meant that she was the only one who could make sure it didn't return.

Getting to his feet, he scooped her into his arms.

She didn't protest. Instead she hooked her hands around his neck as he carried her into the house and down the stairs. "Let me guess. You need to paint."

That was his intention. But once Grayson had her naked, painting came later.

Much, much later.

CHAPTER SIXTEEN

 his is such great fun!" Madison looked like she was about to burst from happiness as she picked up a slice of pizza from the takeout box on the balcony coffee table. "I'm so glad you decided to stay, Chloe. I can't tell you how much I've missed our girl time."

Since Chloe was feeling pretty happy herself, it was hard to be mad at Madison and Eden for stopping by unexpectedly. It was a beautiful fall day. The sun was shining. Josephine Livingston Seagull was nesting contentedly on her eggs after having eaten two cans of sardines. And Eden and Madison had brought pizza... and three new bottles of nail polish. Bubbly Pink for Madison. Just Peachy for Eden. And Purple Rage for Chloe. Not that Chloe liked purple. Okay, so maybe it was growing on her. It no longer reminded her of squashed grapes. In fact, once she had the polish on her big toe, all she could think about was Grayson's eyes and the way they looked when he painted her, or kissed her, or made love to her.

Made love to her? No, no, no. She and Grayson didn't make love. They had sex. Just sex.

She quickly screwed the cap back on the bottle of polish and exchanged it for Madison's pink polish. She opened the bottle and covered the purple she'd already painted on her big toe. Since the polish was still wet, it turned a lighter purple that looked even more like Grayson's eyes. She recapped the bottle and wiped the polish off with a napkin, leaving a smudged bruise of color. She frowned at it.

"I don't know why you wanted to try it," Madison said as she took the bottle back. "You've never liked pink. You're much more Purple Rage." She tipped her head and studied Chloe. "Although today you don't look as angry. In fact, you do look all Bubbly Pink."

Eden stopped painting her toenails and lifted her gaze to Chloe. "She's right. You look happy. This wouldn't have anything to do with your decision to stay, would it?"

"I'm not staying."

The look Eden sent her was dubious. "Really?" She glanced in through the open balcony door. "Well, it certainly looks like you're planning on staying. Aren't those Chips Ahoy! in the cupboard? And isn't that your favorite chocolate milk in the refrigerator? Not to mention the picture of me, you, and Madison at the marathon on Grayson's nightstand?"

While Chloe was trying to get over the fact that Eden had been snooping through the house when she was supposedly going to the bathroom, Madison asked a very good question. "Why is that picture on Grayson's nightstand? Did you give it to him?"

"No, I did not give it to him," Chloe snapped before her eyes narrowed on Eden. "I'm surprised you aren't still a reporter, with all the snooping you enjoy doing."

Eden only shrugged and went back to painting her toenails. "I prefer fiction writing to nonfiction. And it didn't take all that much investigating to figure out that you're nesting."

Her eyes widened. "What?"

"Nesting." Eden dipped the brush in the bottle of polish. "Not like Josephine, I'm not saying you're pregnant. All I'm saying is that you've made Grayson's house your home."

"Grayson and Chloe?" Madison looked surprised for just a second before a smile bloomed on her face. "O-o-oh, that would be so sweet. Then you and Eden would be in-laws."

Until that point Chloe had been only slightly stunned. Now she felt as if she'd been hit with Miley Cyrus's wrecking ball. Marry Grayson? She sat up so fast that her knee hit the coffee table, almost knocking over her glass of Chardonnay. Which wouldn't have been a great loss. She had always preferred reds to whites.

"Have you lost your mind!" she said so loudly that she startled Josephine. The bird ruffled her feathers and glared at her, so Chloe continued in a softer voice, "Grayson and I would never get married. We're just—"

"Don't tell me that you're just having sex," Eden said. "Because that doesn't explain why you're playing house."

"I'm not playing house."

"I don't know what you'd call it. You clean, you cook, you just got finished telling us that the scratches on your arms are from planting roses in the garden. You're playing house with Grayson whether you are willing to accept it or not." She cleaned polish from the edge of her toenail with her finger.

Madison smiled weakly at Chloe. "She does have a point. But don't worry, sweetie, you're not alone. Every model at French Kiss wants to marry Grayson. That's the reason Natalia resigned. She thought, if she wasn't his employee, Grayson would date her—especially after he came back from Paris looking so lost and hot." Her eyes scrunched in thought. "But come to think of it, he hasn't looked so lost lately. Now he looks as happy as you do."

Wanting to put an end to this train of conversation, Chloe jumped in. "Okay, so we both look happy. Good sex can do that to a person."

Eden nodded. "She does have a point." A dreamy expression settled over her features. "The other night, Nash did this thing with his—"

"Please," Chloe said, "I do not want to hear the details of your sex life."

"I want to hear about Eden's sex life," Madison said as she picked up the last slice of pizza. "Of course, I'm going to get to read about it soon enough when her book comes out."

"That's just a misconception that romance writers write about their own sex lives," Eden said. "My book is purely fiction . . . okay, well, there is that one part where my hero has my heroine pushed up against the shower wall—"

"Enough," Chloe cut in.

"You are such a party pooper, Chloe," Madison said. "The least you could do for a friend who hasn't had sex in forever is tell her about your sex life."

"It's your own fault. When are you going to stop hanging out with those old guys and start dating someone who doesn't need Viagra and a resuscitator to make love?"

Madison shrugged. "As soon as I find a man as sweet and caring as my Georgie, Freddie, and Harry." She stared at the slice of pizza for a few seconds before shoving it at Chloe. "Here, eat this so I won't. You wouldn't believe how fat I looked in the pictures from the catalog shoot."

"You did not," Eden said as she closed her bottle of polish. "Nash showed them to me, and you looked amazing. So did Chloe."

Chloe stopped with the slice of pizza halfway to her mouth. "Me? What are you talking about, Eden? I wasn't at the catalog shoot."

Eden studied the paint on her big toe. "Of course you weren't. I was just thinking about how amazing you looked on the last catalog cover. Why is it that you don't want to model for French Kiss again?"

"Because I'm not the model type." Chloe took a bite of pizza.

"I didn't think I was the model type either," Madison said, "but then Grayson convinced me that I was beautiful and would make a perfect model. He has that way about him."

It was true. Grayson had made Chloe feel beautiful as well. She had gotten so used to Zac's backhanded compliments that she'd forgotten what it felt like to be appreciated by a man. Grayson knew how to appreciate women. Not just their bodies, but also their minds. While Zac had paid little attention to what Chloe said, Grayson really listened. And maybe that's why she wasn't in any hurry to leave. That and the great sex.

The sound of a car pulling into the driveway had Madison getting up and peeking over the balcony. "It's UPS. I just love the way those guys look in their little Boy Scout shorts. Ooo, it looks like you've got a big package. I'll get it." She hurried through the open sliding door with a click of high heels.

When she was gone, Eden took up the conversation. "So what's the real reason you don't want to model? Are you hiding from someone?" Her eyes narrowed. "The cops? The Mafia? Are you in a witness protection program?"

Chloe rolled her eyes. "Maybe I just don't want to sell my soul to the Beaumonts."

Eden smiled slyly as she reached for her wineglass. "Hmm? Are you sure you haven't already done that?"

The question made Chloe instantly defensive. "I have not sold my soul to anyone! I'm just staying here until Grayson finishes his painting for Deirdre's benefit." It was a lie. Both the first painting and the one for the benefit were finished. Which didn't explain why she was still there and hadn't pressed Grayson or Deirdre for the money they owed her. She glanced over at Josephine. The eggs. She was waiting for the eggs to hatch. That was all.

"Don't blow a gasket, Chloe," Eden said. "I'm glad you're still here. And Nash is thrilled that Grayson is painting again. He's been concerned about Grayson for the last six months—ever since he stopped sketching and then suddenly wanted to go to Paris."

"So Nash doesn't know what caused his painting slump either?"

Eden shook her head. "But I have a theory."

"You have a theory on everything."

"It comes from being a newspaper reporter. When searching for a cutting-edge story, you come up with a theory and then try to prove it with facts. I usually look for one common denominator."

"And what is the common denominator for Grayson losing his painting mojo?" She took a big bite of pizza.

"You."

Chloe choked, and it took Eden giving her a hard thump on the back to get the chunk of pizza unstuck from her throat. It flew out of her mouth and across the balcony just as Madison stepped out the door.

"The UPS man was no Boy Scout," she said. "Once he got over the shock of a French Kiss model answering the door, he asked if I wanted to see his package." She looked between Eden and Chloe. "So what were you guys talking about while I was gone that made Chloe toss her pizza?"

Before Eden could answer, Chloe spoke up. "Nothing. We weren't talking about anything." She reached for the bottle of wine. White or not, she needed a drink. Unfortunately, the bottle was empty.

"No worries," Madison said. "That was what you got delivered. Two entire cases of wine." She headed back inside.

As soon as she was gone, Chloe turned to Eden. "That is the craziest theory I've ever heard. How could I be responsible for his painting block?"

"Think about it. He stopped sketching and painting when you showed up. And he didn't start up again until he kidnapped you."

"That's just a coincidence. Nothing more."

Eden smiled. "Maybe, but somehow I don't think so."

"I chose the Syrah." Madison stepped out the door with a bottle of wine. "Just because I love the name. Sy-rah. It sounds like an Arabian princess." She filled Chloe's glass and handed it to her before filling both hers and Eden's.

Eden picked up her glass and held it up in a toast. "To Chloe staying in San Francisco." Her eyes twinkled. "And Grayson getting over his painting slump." She clicked their glasses before she took a sip. "Mmm, this is delicious. Where's it from?"

"A winery in Napa." Madison took a sip. "Casa Selena."

The glass slipped from Chloe's numb fingers and crashed on the balcony floor.

CHAPTER SEVENTEEN

"What are you doing here, Deke?" Grayson asked when Deacon came striding into his office at one o'clock in the afternoon.

Nash, who had just been going over some sales reports with Grayson, answered for him. "I would say he's come to take over the reins." He grinned. "You look like hell, big brother."

It was an accurate statement. With the dark circles under his eyes and the lines of fatigue on his face, Deacon did look like hell. He also looked annoyed that Grayson was sitting in his chair. Since Grayson was more than happy to hand over the reins to his brother, he quickly got up and joined Nash on the other side of the desk.

"What's that on your suit?" Nash asked.

Deacon didn't even glance at the yellowish stain on the lapel of his gray suit jacket. "Baby spit-up. I burped Michael before I left."

"You get on me and Grayson for wearing jeans to the office, but it's okay to wear baby puke?"

"As the CEO of this company, I can wear anything I like. But if it offends your delicate sensibilities, Nash, I'll take it off." Deacon slipped out of the jacket and hooked it on the back of his chair. When he turned around, Grayson couldn't help smiling at the dark wet spots on the front of his purple dress shirt.

"Please tell me that's water," Nash said.

Deacon followed his gaze. "You could say that. Once the diaper comes off, Mikey thinks it's time to let loose." He took a seat and looked at Grayson. "So do you want to explain what's happened while I've been gone, Gray? I got two calls at home this morning. One from Miles, who was in tears because you questioned his creative genius and are not using his pictures for the catalog, and one from Natalia, who was in tears because you won't date her...even after she no longer works for French Kiss." His face hardened. "And why are you smiling about our top model resigning only weeks before the fashion show?"

Grayson wasn't smiling because Natalia had resigned. He was smiling because he was happy. Happier than he'd been in years. Of course, he couldn't tell his brother why. Unfortunately, Nash had no problem telling Deacon.

"He's smiling because he finally had sex."

Deacon lifted an eyebrow at Grayson. "With Natalia?"

Before Grayson could answer, Nash did. "No. With Chloe."

"Is this the same Chloe who posed for the pictures Samuel thinks we should use for the cover of the catalog?"

Grayson stopped mad-dogging Nash and turned to Deacon. "Samuel sent you pictures of Chloe?"

Deacon nodded. "And they're quite good. Although I think they might be too edgy for the cover."

It looked like Samuel had learned a few deviant tricks

from Deirdre—like helping himself to Grayson's art when he wasn't around. Grayson wanted to kick himself for leaving his laptop alone with the wily old guy. "Samuel had no business copying those pictures," he said. "They aren't for publication."

Deacon looked confused. "But I thought this Chloe is the same girl that you're painting for Deirdre's benefit. So why wouldn't you want her modeling for us if she models for you? Or are you feeling possessive over this woman?"

Leave it to his brother to come up with the perfect word for the way Grayson felt. He was possessive of Chloe. He wanted to possess her body. He wanted to possess her mind. And he wanted to possess her soul. And since Grayson had never felt this intensely about anyone in his life, it was more than a little disturbing.

While he was trying to figure out how to answer Deacon, Kelly peeked in. "Sorry to interrupt, but your father is on line one."

Deacon nodded. "Thanks, Kelly." He waited until she left before he pushed a button on his phone. "What's up, Dad?"

"I told your secretary to contact me when all my boys were back. I wanted you all together when I give you the news."

"If you bought that fishing boat you were telling me about," Deacon said, "I'm going to be pissed. You don't need another boat, Dad."

"This isn't about the boat. Although that boat is twice as nice as the one I have and a steal of a deal. And it sure would come in handy when I take Mikey fishing."

Deacon glanced at Grayson and Nash and shook his head in exasperation. "He's still a little too young for fishing, Dad."

"Well, it won't be long. So you should really reconsider

giving me the money for the boat. In fact, it would make a great wedding present."

For a moment Grayson thought he had misunderstood. But when he looked at his brothers' surprised faces, he realized he hadn't. Talk about a sucker punch. Grayson felt like he was down for the count.

"What's the matter, boys?" his dad said. "Cat got your tongues? Aren't you going to congratulate your old man?"

Deacon recovered first. "Is this one of your jokes, Dad?"

"You should know that your old dad doesn't joke about marriage. I've decided to tie the knot."

"With who?" Deacon asked.

"My neighbor, Suzanne."

"The one you were fighting with?" Nash asked.

"That's the one. Turns out all that piss and vinegar was just her way of protecting her heart. And as she pointed out, all my carousing has been my way of protecting mine."

All three of the Beaumont boys sat stunned. But his brothers couldn't be as stunned as Grayson was. His happy feeling had long since faded, and now all he felt was a hurt so deep that he couldn't seem to catch his breath. His father had one wife. Just one. A perfect wife he had repeatedly said couldn't be replaced. And now he was replacing her. It wasn't right. Donny John held most of the memories of Althea Beaumont. If he remarried, those memories would be lost. Then there would be nothing left of Grayson's mother.

"No!" His voice resounded off the high ceiling, and Nash and Deacon looked at him as if he'd lost it. And Grayson had lost it. But he didn't care. He had spent his entire life going along with what his father and brothers had wanted, but he refused to go along with this. He refused to let his mother slip away completely.

He moved closer to the phone's speaker. "You want to

fool around with some neighbor lady, you go right ahead. But you're not marrying her. Do you hear me? You're damned well not going to marry anyone!"

Without another word he turned and walked out of the office. Kelly sat at her desk with her mouth in a perfect O, but he didn't acknowledge her. Or any other person he passed on his way to the parking garage. He needed one thing at the moment. He needed to paint.

It didn't take him long to drive to his house. Once there he parked in the garage and looked for Chloe. He found her in the bedroom. He didn't even glance at what she was doing before he headed to his easel.

"Get naked," he said as he grabbed a brush and paints.

"What is the matter with you? You can't just waltz in and start ordering me—"

He turned to her. "Please, Chloe. I need you."

She studied him for only a second before she reached for the hem of her shirt. Grayson didn't know how long he painted. But when he finally set down his brush, his fingers cramped, evening light filled the room, and Chloe was sleeping. Painting her had taken away the brunt of his pain, but he still felt like there was a hole in his chest. He could think of only one way to fill it.

Wiping his hands on a rag, he took off his clothes and joined her on the bed. He didn't touch. He just looked. Her hair had grown, and her crooked bangs now hung over her eyebrows. He brushed them back, and her eyes opened. Most people thought brown a boring color, but they hadn't seen Chloe's eyes. They were the color of rich, fertile soil. Of decadent dark chocolate. Of freshly brewed coffee. And the emotions that flickered through them only added to their depth.

"So I guess your day was as bad as mine," she said in a sleep-husky voice.

For a man who had trouble expressing himself, words spilled easily from his mouth. "My dad is getting remarried. He just called the office and dropped the bomb like it wasn't any big deal—like him getting married was something we should've expected."

"And how did you want him to tell you?"

He stopped touching her and fell to his back, staring up at the ceiling. "I didn't want him to tell me. He shouldn't be getting married. He will never love her like he loved my mother."

Chloe cuddled next to him, resting her head on his chest. "Of course he won't." Her fingers ran along his collarbone in a slow brush that was soothing and hypnotic. "From what you've told me, he adored your mother. There's no way that anyone could replace her."

"Exactly. He just needs to realize that."

"Hmm?" Her fingers stroked the center of his chest. "Or maybe he isn't trying to replace her. Maybe he's just tired of being alone."

He pulled back so he could look in her eyes. "Is that why you stayed with me? You were just tired of being alone?"

"I stayed because I can't seem to tell you no." She looked away to study her hand that was drawing circles on his chest. "But I have to go. My past has finally caught up with me." Her hand stopped moving. "My family owns a winery in Napa. Casa Selena. Today two cases of wine were delivered from there. It's my father's way of letting me know that he found me."

At that point Grayson should've told her the truth about going to Casa Selena and meeting her grandfather. And if she were a calm, collected woman, he would've. But Chloe wasn't calm, and she wasn't collected. She was a hot tempered woman who would be ticked that he'd meddled in

her life. And when she got angry, her first response was to
run. He couldn't let her do that.

His hands tightened around her as he pressed his lips to
her forehead. "Tell me, Chloe. Tell me what you're running
from."

He expected her to hedge the question. Instead she hesitated only a moment before she spoke. "Most people think
runaways leave because of abuse—physical, sexual, mental.
But that wasn't me. I had a perfect life. I had a beautiful
mother who loved me. And a father who thought I hung
the moon. I thought he not only hung the moon but he also
made it. He was this bigger-than-life man who everyone respected and loved, and I was his little princess. A princess she
showered with frilly pink dresses and ponies and anything
my heart desired. But all I really desired was for my life to
never change. Unfortunately, that wasn't something he could
give me."

Grayson felt a hot tear hit his chest before she continued.
"My mom kept the secret of her cancer from me for months.
And she kept the secret of her affair with the vintner for fif-
teen years."

The pieces of the puzzle started to fall into place. No
wonder Davis Cameron had wanted to burn down the vintner's house. But that didn't explain why Chloe had left.

"I understand you were upset," he said. "But why would
that make you run away from home?"

Chloe lifted her head and looked at him, her eyes swim-
ming with heartbreaking tears. "Because he isn't my father.
I guess my mom was having trouble getting pregnant, and
instead of going to a fertility doctor, she decided to go to
the vintner and see if he could make babies as well as he
made wine." She must've read Grayson's shock because she
nodded. "I know, and I can only imagine how shocked my

father felt when he heard my mother's deathbed confession. For months after my mom died, he couldn't look at me. And I understood perfectly. Why would he want to look at someone who reminded him of his wife's betrayal?" Her shoulders lifted in a pathetic shrug. "So I figured it would be best for everyone if he didn't have to."

"Oh, Chloe." Grayson pulled her close. "I'm so sorry. And your biological father? Does he know about you?"

She nodded against his chest. "I contacted him after I ran away. I had this dream about living in an Italian villa, but he wasn't exactly thrilled with the news. He took the number of the Chinese restaurant where I was working, but he never called."

Grayson rubbed her back. "Then that's his loss." He paused before he continued. "But it seems to me that you have a father who wants to see you. Otherwise he wouldn't be looking for you so hard."

"Because he thinks that he can forgive me. And maybe he can. Maybe it's me that can't forgive." Another hot tear dripped to his chest. "You told me that you hurt because you couldn't remember your mother and the happy times. Well, I remember the happy times. I remember feeling loved and adored. And maybe I don't want to go back and have those memories shattered. Maybe I want to hang on to the image of that perfect family."

He understood completely. That was exactly what he was trying to hold on to. The image of a perfect family. But after listening to Chloe's story, he had to wonder if there was such a thing.

"Maybe there are no perfect families," he said. "Maybe it's the expectation of perfection that destroys families. Maybe if we just accepted things the way they are, we would all be much happier."

She lifted her head. "If you're trying to say that I need to face my father, then you can just forget it, Grayson Beaumont. I'm not ready for that, and I don't think I ever will be."

"I'm not saying that at all. All I'm saying is that you need to stop running from who you are, Chloe."

"And what if it's too painful to accept who I am?"

"Then we'll take it slow. When I couldn't paint, you started me off with photographs, then eased me into painting. Let's start you off with one truth at a time." He held out his hand. "Hi, I'm Grayson Romeo Beaumont. What's your name?"

She stared at his hand for so long that he thought he'd lost her. But finally she took it in hers and held tightly. "Hi, I'm Selena Elizabeth Cameron, but you can call me Chloe."

CHAPTER EIGHTEEN

*G*rayson *was* the Woman Whisperer. There was no other explanation for why Chloe was driving through the sun-dappled vineyards of Napa on the way to a place she'd sworn she'd never return to.

"This isn't the frickin' Daytona, Gray," she snapped.

He shot her a quick glance, then reached over and took her hand, giving it a light squeeze. He was dressed casually today in a white linen shirt, jeans, and loafers. Aviator sunglasses shielded his pretty eyes from view, but looked sexy with his tan and stubbly jaw. He had his window down, and the wind played with the shortened strands of his hair.

The haircut she'd given him had turned out as uneven as her bangs. And yet he hadn't said one word of complaint— probably because he was partly to blame for the uneven strands. The entire time she'd been cutting his hair, he hadn't been able to keep his hands off her. In turn, she'd completely lost her focus. But she had no problem focusing now as they drew closer and closer to Casa Selena. Every nerve in her body seemed to be on high alert.

"You okay?" he asked.

She suddenly realized that she had his hand in a death grip. She released it and smoothed out her black dress. "Of course I'm okay. I'm not the one driving like a maniac."

He glanced down at the speedometer. "I'm going four miles under the speed limit."

"Oh." She looked away, feeling like a complete idiot. "I guess these expensive sports cars just make you feel like you're going faster."

Instead of laughing at her ridiculous statement, he took her hand again and pressed his lips to her knuckles. "We don't have to go, you know? We can just take a leisurely drive and head back to San Francisco without ever stopping."

A part of her wanted to jump on the plan, but the other part knew that if she didn't face her father now, she never would. And Grayson was right. She wasn't an insecure, frightened teenager. She was an independent, strong woman who, instead of running from her past, needed to face it.

"No, we're going to Casa Selena." She glanced at him. "And cut the reverse psychology crap."

He lowered her hand, and a quirky smile curved his lips. "That obvious, huh?"

She rolled her eyes before she looked out the window.

The grape leaves had started turning gold and red, and in their straight diagonal rows they resembled one of her grandmother's fall afghans thrown over the rolling hills. They looked exactly as they had looked the morning she'd run away. It seemed like a lifetime ago and, at the same time, only yesterday. Before her mind could travel back to

bad memories, a ringing cut through the classical song playing on the radio. Grayson quickly answered, sounding all
business.

"Beaumont."

The voice that came through the speakers wasn't busi-
nesslike at all. "Gar-a-son, you have been a very naughty
boy."

Chloe didn't know what ticked her off more—the annoying way the woman said his name or the fact that Grayson's
face turned a bright, guilty red...like he had been a very
naughty boy.

He shot a quick glance over at Chloe. "Look, this is a bad
time, Natalia. Could I call you back?"

"No, Gar-a-son, you may not call me back. It is time to
stop with this cat-and-mouse game and finally reveal our
true feelings for each other."

Chloe crossed her arms and glared at Grayson. "Yes, by
all means. I'd love to hear what your true feelings are."

"Who is that?" Natalia's voice no longer purred. "Is that
another woman—"

Grayson pushed the button on his steering wheel and cut
the voice off. "Sorry," he said sheepishly. "So what were we
talking about?"

Chloe lifted an eyebrow. "We weren't talking."

"No?" He looked around. "I thought we were talking
about what a gorgeous day it is."

Chloe had never been the jealous type, but the swell of
anger felt a lot like a green-eyed monster. Why she had
thought she was the only woman in Grayson's life, she
didn't know. He was a Beaumont, after all. Every woman
with a television or access to a shopping mall or the Internet
was in love with him. Why should she think that she was the
only one having sex with him?

"If you don't mind, Gar-a-son," she said in the worst Russian accent ever, "I'd like you to stop the car so I can get out."

He glanced over. "Don't be ridiculous, Chloe. She means nothing to me."

"Did you paint her?" The blush on his cheeks deepened, and Chloe's own cheeks flamed. But not with guilt. Without another word she lifted the handle and opened the door while they were still moving.

"Shit!" Grayson quickly slowed to the side of the road and grabbed her arm. "Would you stop overreacting and listen to me for a second? There is nothing going on between me and Natalia."

Chloe pulled her arm away. "Then explain the kiss in the elevator. And we both know what happens when you paint women naked."

"That's only happened with you."

She snorted. "Right. And you expect me to believe that?"

Grayson studied her for a moment before he released his breath. He leaned his head back on the leather seat. "You're right. It does seem a little far-fetched. But it's the truth. I've never had sex with a model before you." He stared out the windshield as his face grew even redder. "In fact, I've never had sex with anyone before you."

It took her a moment to process his words. "You mean you were a...virgin?"

His Adam's apple slid up and down in a swallow that was just as endearing as the blush on his cheeks. "Yes."

Just like that the green-eyed monster shriveled up, to be replaced by a buoyant feeling that left Chloe speechless.

"Yeah," Grayson said. "I get it. It's weird. Especially since I'm a Beaumont. People just assume I go around having sex with every girl I meet. After all, that's what my father did. And while Deacon and Nash were selective, they didn't hold on to their virginity much past puberty."

Chloe finally found her voice. "So why did you?"

He continued to stare straight ahead. "I'm not sure. When I was younger, I was just scared to death of women—something that comes from growing up around all males. But in high school, I got over my fear. I started dating Mary Jane Fuller, who had snuck more than one boy into her bedroom after her parents went to sleep. Unfortunately, when she stripped for me, I was so enraptured by her body that I grabbed a pencil and notebook from her nightstand and started sketching. She didn't seem to mind. But once I finished, she was sound asleep. So I left my drawing and slipped out the window."

"And the other women who modeled for you? Why didn't you ... ?"

"Because then my paintings wouldn't be art. They'd just be cheap paintings of women I'd used."

"So am I just a woman you used?"

He turned to look at her, his eyes sincere. "No. You're special, Chloe. As much as I wanted to keep away from you, I couldn't."

At that moment, with the sun shining through the golden leaves overhead and the vineyards glowing red, Chloe fell head over heels in love. And the wonderful, consuming feeling was nothing like what she'd felt for Zac. This feeling was as pure and honest as Grayson.

Unfortunately, she could never let him know how she felt. He deserved someone just as wholesome and pure. Someone who didn't have Chloe's sordid past. But that didn't mean she wasn't honored to be his first. Or that she wasn't going to keep him for just a little while longer.

She sent him a smile. "You're pretty special yourself."

He leaned in and kissed her. It was a soft kiss, nothing compared to the ones he gave her at night when they were tucked between his sheets, but the tenderness of his lips touched her much more deeply.

He put the car in gear and pulled back onto the road while she snuggled down in the seat and smiled with contentment.

But when they turned off on the road to Casa Selena, all the contentment drained right out of her. She had never experienced a panic attack before, but now she knew exactly what one felt like. As the beautiful stone house and winery came into view, she couldn't seem to catch her breath, and her heart started beating so rapidly that it felt like it was about to jump from her chest.

She must've made some sound because Grayson glanced over and quickly read her panic. He took her hand in his much warmer one as he pulled into the visitors' parking lot. He cut the engine and then turned to her.

"Breathe, Chloe," he instructed in a soothing voice. "That's right, baby. Just take one deep breath...good...now release it slowly and take another...perfect...you've got this." He drew circles with his thumb on the inside of her wrist. Just that simple touch caused the frozen fear to thaw and her breathing to regulate. He waited a few minutes before he spoke. "Are you okay?"

She nodded. "I just want to get it over with."

He released her and quickly got out, coming around to open her door. When she stepped out, he drew her into his arms and whispered against her ear, "I'll be right there beside you, and any time you want to leave, all you have to do is say the word."

Unable to speak around her fear, she let him take her hand and walk her down the path. The garden was as beautiful and well tended as she remembered. The beauty of the flowers her grandmother had planted and her grandfather had lovingly taken care of since his wife's death calmed her just as much as the tight grip of Grayson's hand. When they got to the fork in the path, she was able to take the lead. "This way."

When she was a child, the front door of her home had always looked so huge. Gavin and Cain had liked to tease her with stories about its once belonging to a child-eating giant who would one day come back to get it. But as she stood in front of the solid oak, it didn't look as big as she remembered. Still, it took a moment for her to get up the courage to press the doorbell. Grayson squeezed her hand just as the door was opened.

Chloe didn't recognize the Hispanic woman who stood there.

"I'm sorry," the woman said, "but this is the main house. The tasting room is in the other direction." She sent an apologetic smile to Chloe before she started to close the door.

Chloe stepped closer. "Is Davis Cameron here?"

The woman stopped closing the door and studied her more intently. "I know you." Her face brightened. "You are his daughter, Selena. The one in all the pictures." She clapped her hands to her ample breasts. "Praise the saints. I've been praying for your return. Maybe your papa can be happy now."

Tears formed in Chloe's eyes, and she tried to keep her voice from quavering. "Do you know where he is?"

"He's in the tank room, but perhaps I should call—"

"No need to call," she said. "I know the way."

The tank room was located behind the tasting room. It was an airy room with high, barnlike ceilings that housed huge stainless steel tanks. The tanks held the juice from the grapes after they had been harvested, crushed, and pressed. Being held in the temperature-controlled tanks was the first stage of fermentation, before the wine was placed in oak barrels in the cellar for the second stage.

Chloe had never cared for the tank room. With the sun shining in the high windows and reflecting off the stainless steel, it had always seemed too bright and industrial for her tastes. Even now she shielded her eyes with her hand as she and Grayson stepped inside. A young man in a cable-knit sweater stood by one of the tanks, examining the gauges. When he noticed them, he approached. It wasn't until he got closer that she recognized her cousin. Cain had been a skinny, gangly kid when last she saw him. He and his brother had spent a few weeks every summer in Napa, but it was Cain who had fallen in love with the winery. She was glad he had returned to help her father.

"I'm sorry, but this area isn't open to visitors..." Cain paused, and his eyes widened. "Lena?" In a blink he picked her up and swirled her around. "I can't believe it. I thought you weren't ever coming back." He set her on her feet and gave her a thorough once-over. "What happened to your hair?"

"I could ask the same about you," she teased as she ruffled his close-cut hair. "When you left for college, your hair was to your shoulders."

He ran a hand through the mussed strands. "I guess six years—" He paused, and his expression darkened. "Six years, Lena. Do you know how worried everyone has been? In fact, I should take you over my knee and paddle your butt for the hell you've put us through."

Grayson stepped up and placed an arm around her waist. "I don't think that's a good idea."

Cain turned to him. "Who are you?"

Before fists could fly, Chloe quickly stepped between them and made the introductions. "Cain, this is Grayson Beaumont. He drove me out from San Francisco."

Cain's attention returned to her. "So that's where you've been. The private detective Uncle Davis hired said as much, and I should've believed him. You always hid right next to base when we played hide-and-seek so you could tag before the seeker." His eyebrows lifted. "Now the question is, why didn't you tag home earlier?"

She would've answered if the door at the far end of the tank room hadn't opened and her father hadn't walked in. Like her, he shielded his eyes with a hand. And she knew she had only a few seconds before his eyes adjusted and he saw her.

"I'll tell you all about it later," she said. "For now, could you show Grayson around while I talk to...Davis?"

Cain stared at her for a moment before he released an exasperated huff. "You always did have me wrapped around your little finger." He sent her a pointed look. "But then you're explaining why you left without a word, followed by me giving you a major ass-chewing." The words held no threat when he pulled her into his arms for a tight hug. "Damn, it's good to see you." He motioned for Grayson to follow him. "Come on, Beaumont, I'll teach you about wine."

Grayson's hand tightened on her waist. "Are you sure you don't want me to stay?"

"I'm a big girl. I guess it's time I started acting like one." She noticed the uneven strands of hair that had fallen over his forehead and brushed them back. "I need to even these out."

A slow smile spread across his face. "I'll look forward to it." He brushed a kiss over her lips before he followed Cain out the door.

For some reason Grayson's kiss gave her the courage to face her father. He had lowered his hand and was now studying her with open curiosity. The sight of his aged face and graying hair made tears clog her throat. But while his physical appearance had changed, his eyes hadn't. As soon as they recognized her, they filled with undeniable love. At the sight, the truth finally dawned.

Her father wasn't some Italian vintner who'd had one night with her mother. Her father was the man standing in front of her. A man who had taught her how to bake sugar cookies, ride a horse, and know when grapes had reached their peak and were ready for harvest. A man who had never stopped looking for her.

"Oh, Daddy." The words came out without thought, as if they'd been waiting six long years to be said.

They started toward each other at the same time and met in the middle of the tank room.

"Lena," he said as he pulled her into his arms. "Thank God."

Tears dripped from her lashes and splashed down her cheeks. "I've been so stupid," she sobbed. "I thought you hated me."

"Hate you? How could you think that?"

"Because it only makes sense. I'm the living proof of Mom's betrayal."

He chuckled, a sound she'd thought she'd never hear again. "You were always such a stubborn child. Once you got something in your head, you refused to let it go. But you're wrong, Lena. I never viewed you as anything but my daughter."

She drew back. "Then why did you stop talking to me?"

"I stopped talking to everyone. I was upset after your mother died. I loved her with all my heart and soul. Yes, I was shocked and disappointed, even angry, when she told me about her affair and that you weren't my child. But I quickly got over it when I realized that, if not for that night, I would never have you. You might not be my blood, Lena, but you are my daughter. And you will always be my daughter, Princess."

There was no way to describe the joy and relief she felt. Or the self-loathing. She'd been running for six years because she was terrified of losing her father's love just as she'd lost her mother's. But standing in her father's arms, she realized that she hadn't lost either.

Love transcends distance and even death.

CHAPTER NINETEEN

Cain Cameron was the type of man who didn't believe in beating around the bush. They had no more than stepped out the door when he turned to Grayson.

"So, Mr. Beaumont...would you like to explain how my cousin ended up with a panty billionaire?"

Grayson wasn't surprised that Cain knew who he was. Cain's grandfather had no doubt spilled the beans. Something Grayson wasn't about to do. "That's not my place. If Chloe wants you to know, I'm sure she'll tell you."

Cain studied him for a long moment before he headed for the tasting room. But they didn't stop to do some sampling. Instead they walked past the counter to a door at the back that looked as if it belonged on a hobbit house. Cain opened it to reveal a stone stairwell that led down. Before he started down the stairs, he turned to Grayson.

"You have family, Mr. Beaumont. So how would you feel if one of your brothers ran off for six years, then suddenly reappeared with some stranger? I think you'd have plenty of questions too."

"I would ask my brother. Not the stranger."

"If you knew Selena at all, you'd know that she doesn't like to share information. And I'm not asking you to tell any secrets. I'm just asking you how you met my cousin and what you are to her."

It was a good question. One that Grayson couldn't have answered if he'd wanted to. He didn't have a clue what he was to Chloe. He knew she liked him. He knew she enjoyed having sex with him. But he didn't know the extent of her feelings. All he knew was the extent of his. He cared for her. Much more than he should.

"We're friends," he finally said. "We met through a mutual friend."

"So she was doing all right—I mean she wasn't going hungry?"

When she had been living on the streets, Grayson had little doubt that Chloe had gone hungry. But he didn't think that was something Cain needed to know. Nor did he need to know about Zac. So he kept his answer simple. "She wasn't going hungry when I met her."

Cain's shoulders visibly relaxed. "Thank God. I couldn't get rid of this vision in my head of her living in a soggy cardboard box and eating people's leftovers out of a Dumpster." He shook his head. "She's just stubborn enough to do something like that even though all she had to do was ask and I would've sent her any amount she wanted."

"Chloe doesn't like to take handouts. Which probably has more to do with her pride."

Cain grinned. "A family trait."

Some of the tension seemed to ease between them, and Cain led the way down the long staircase. They had almost reached the bottom when he spoke. "I blame myself. I should've taken a semester off from college after her mom died. If I had been here, maybe things would've played out differently." He stopped at the bottom of the stairs and turned. "But I had my studies and my own grief to deal with—Chloe's mother was more of a mom to me and Gavin than our own mom. And Gavin was in Texas trying to revive Granddad's oil fields. It was a hard time for all of us, but mostly for Uncle Davis and Selena. They were the ones who had to stay here and deal with all the memories."

And the truth about Chloe's father. Grayson had to wonder if Cain knew about the affair with the vintner and that Chloe wasn't related to them by blood. Somehow he didn't think it would make a difference in how Cain felt about Chloe. There was obvious affection between the two.

Cain hooked his hands on his waist and studied the toes of his boots. "I just wish she had called me." He shook his head. "But I guess that's in the past. She's home now."

The word *home* struck a shaft of fear through Grayson and made him realize that, when he'd pushed Chloe to come to Napa, he hadn't really thought things through. Like the fact that once she reconciled with her family, she wouldn't want to come back to San Francisco with him. Which made his reply a little snappy. "She has a home."

Cain lifted his head and looked at Grayson. "I guess we'll have to see about that."

Grayson wasn't going to see about anything. Chloe belonged with him, and that's where she was going to stay. But he didn't need to get in an argument with Cain over it. He would need to save all his arguments for Chloe. Without a word he followed Cain into the cellar.

"If the grapes are the blood of the winery," Cain said, "this is the heart. A lot of wineries just ferment in the stainless steel tanks. But their wine lacks the smoothness and hint of vanilla that comes with using the barrels."

Grayson had no trouble reading the pride in Cain's eyes. And the wine cellar was impressive. While the barn-size tank room was filled with modern wine-making technology, the cellar was filled with wooden barrels that looked hundreds of years old. There were no windows or sunlight glinting off shiny stainless steel. The cellar was dark and dank and smelled like fermenting fruit. And still there was something captivating about the underground room. Something magical. Standing there was like traveling down a rabbit's hole, where everything was made from earth and stone and wood. The only things that weren't natural were the halogen lights strung along the ceiling, and even those weren't overly bright or intrusive. Their light shone softly off the aged wood of the huge wine barrels, giving them an almost mystical appearance.

Unable to stop himself, Grayson pulled out his cell phone and started snapping pictures. The curve of a cedar barrel. The wine spout that protruded at an imperfect angle. The smooth river rock of the walls and arched ceiling. When he had snapped off at least a dozen pictures, he glanced over to see Cain leaning against a barrel watching him.

"So I wondered which Beaumont you were. Now I know. You're the artist."

"I paint," he said as he placed his phone in his back pocket.

Cain straightened. "I believe I read somewhere that you enjoy painting nudes." It wasn't a question, and still Grayson nodded. All friendliness left Cain's face. "You've got exactly two seconds to say that you didn't coerce my little cousin into posing naked for you before I knock your lights out."

"You'll do no such thing, Cain Eli Cameron." Chloe appeared from the darkness of the stairwell. Grayson was more than a little relieved to see her. Not because he was worried about getting his lights knocked out, but because he'd been worried about leaving Chloe alone with her father. But from the looks of things, he'd worried needlessly. She looked fine. In fact she looked unbelievably happy. Which made him scared all over again.

"What I do is my business." She confronted Cain with the same feistiness that Grayson had come to admire...and that he feared losing. "I don't need you to fight my battles for me."

Cain continued to glare at Grayson. "Tell me that you didn't pose naked for this guy, Selena."

"It's Chloe. And once again, that's none of your business. Now quit glaring at Grayson and tell me where I can find Granddad. Dad said he was at the old house, but when I knocked, no one answered."

"He's there. He probably just fell asleep in his chair. Where's Davis? I'm surprised he let you out of his sight."

She smiled. "He's talking with the housekeeper about killing the fatted calf."

Cain laughed. "With Rosa, it will be more like the fatted chicken—although her green chile enchiladas are better than steak." He pulled out his phone. "I better call Gavin. He's in Texas at the moment, but he'll be happy and relieved to know that you're home."

Chloe hooked her arm through Grayson's and pulled him toward the stairs. "Come on, I want you to meet my grandfather."

Grayson should've told her on the way to Napa that he'd already met her grandfather, but he was afraid she would want to turn around. Now he struggled with how to tell her and not get her pissed. Before he could come up with the right words, Chloe spotted her grandfather in the garden.

"Granddad!" she yelled as she ran to the old guy and wrapped her arms around him in a bear hug. Grayson was surprised. He had never seen her show such open affection. It was obvious how much she loved her grandfather. And how much her grandfather loved her. His eyes instantly filled with tears as he pulled back and looked at her.

"And who might you be, young lady?" he said with a twinkle in his aged eyes. "I'm afraid that I don't recognize the face at all."

Chloe rested her head on his bony shoulder. "I'm sorry, Granddad. I shouldn't have stayed away so long."

"No, you shouldn't have." He patted her back. "But you're here now and that's all that matters." His alert gaze wandered over to Grayson. "So you brought your beau?"

Chloe stepped back and made the introductions. "This is Grayson Beaumont, Granddad."

Bob looked confused, and since the cat was about to be released from the bag, Grayson figured it would be best if he was the one to release it.

"Actually, we've already—"

Bob cut him off before he could finish. "Good to meet you, Mr. Beaumont." He walked over and shook Grayson's hand. "Now let's go on down to the house and get us some lemonade." He looked back at Chloe. "That's if you still like lemonade."

"I haven't had good lemonade since I left." Chloe claimed her grandfather's arm, and together they headed toward Bob's house. Cain and Grayson started to follow, but Bob stopped and addressed his grandson.

"I'm sure you've got business to attend to, Cain. You'll be able to catch up with Lena later."

Cain didn't look happy to be dismissed, but he didn't argue. "Yes, sir." He pointed a finger at Chloe. "Don't you dare disappear again." He turned and headed back to the tasting room.

Unlike the time before, Bob didn't make Horse's Asses. The straight lemonade was tart and a little too sweet for Grayson's taste, but he sat at the table and sipped it anyway as Chloe and her grandfather talked. She talked about her life after leaving the winery, but left out the more dramatic parts—living on the streets and Zac's abuse. Although Bob seemed to be pretty good at reading between the lines.

"Hmm?" he said. "That Chinese restaurant must've paid their employees pretty darn good for you to survive in San Francisco." He took a sip of lemonade as Chloe fidgeted with the edge of the tablecloth. "So how are you taking care of yourself now?"

She shot a quick glance over at Grayson before she answered. "I'm doing some modeling for French Kiss."

"Really?" Bob glanced at Grayson. "Is that how you two met each other?"

It wasn't exactly how they had met, but like Chloe, Grayson didn't think the old guy needed to hear about his granddaughter getting beaten up by a bully. "We met on a photo shoot in Fiji," he said.

Bob glanced between them. "Love at first sight?"

Chloe's face turned as red as the checks of the tablecloth. "It's not like that, Granddad. Grayson and I are just..." Her brow knotted as she searched for a word. Since Grayson had done the same thing when Cain had asked a similar question, he understood her confusion. Which didn't explain why he felt so annoyed when she came up with the same answer he had. "Friends," she said. "We're just friends."

"Ahh, friends." Bob smiled. "I remember me and Grandmother being just friends. It was some of the most enjoyable days of my life."

Chloe's face flamed even brighter as she quickly got up from her chair. "If you'll excuse me, I have to go to the bathroom."

Once she was gone, Bob's entire attention zeroed in on Grayson. "And what about you, son? Do you want my granddaughter as just a friend?"

He should've gone along with Chloe and what he'd told Cain, but for some reason he couldn't lie to the old guy. "No."

Bob leaned back in his chair and laughed. "Well, at least one of you isn't trying to blow smoke up my ass. I don't believe a word of what Selena told me about her life being all roses and sunbeams. But I'm not going to make a big scene over it either—sometimes the past is best left there. What I'm most concerned with is the present." He leaned forward and rested his arms on the table. "Has she found happiness?"

It was a question that Grayson wished he had the answer to. He knew he was happy. Happier than he'd ever been in his life. But he wasn't sure about Chloe. She was a hard person to read.

"I can't speak for Chloe, sir," he said. "But I can tell you that I'm going to make every effort to give her that happiness."

Bob's shoulders visibly relaxed. "Fair enough. Now explain to me why you didn't tell her that you've been here before."

Lying was never easy to explain. Suddenly Grayson felt like he was five again and trying to explain to his own grandfather why he'd stolen his pack of Dentyne gum and chewed every stick—then swallowed it.

He cleared his throat. "I was going to tell her but, as you know, Chloe has a temper and a tendency to overreact. And I worried if she found out I'd been at Casa Selena, she'd be so upset at me that she would refuse to come here. Thinking that her father knew where she was living pushed her to face him."

Bob's eyes narrowed in thought. "But she could've just run away again. Which makes me wonder if it had more to do with you. It sounds like she found a place she wants to stay."

"I certainly hope so, sir."

"You certainly hope what?"

They turned to find Chloe standing in the doorway. Bob quickly got to his feet. "He certainly hopes he can see some childhood pictures of you." He walked to a shelf in the living room and pulled down a photo album. "And it just so happens that I have a few."

They spent the next couple of hours talking about Chloe's childhood and looking at pictures. She had been as photogenic then as she was now. Although the picture of her with pimples and braces might've been the exception. Grayson had just leaned in for a closer look when the door opened and Davis Cameron walked in. Since they had yet to be introduced, Grayson immediately got to his feet and held out a hand.

"Grayson Beaumont, sir."

Davis studied him for a long moment before he took the offered hand. "It's nice to meet you, Grayson. I hope you'll stay for dinner."

Dinner was quite the feast. The housekeeper hadn't killed the fatted calf, but she'd come close. Platters and bowls of Mexican food filled the table. As instructed, Grayson sat on one side of Davis while Chloe sat on the other. Grayson expected him to ask some tough questions, but instead Davis seemed content just to have his daughter home. And Chloe looked just as content. Her eyes sparkled and her cheeks were flushed as she reminisced with her family. She looked even happier when Rosa brought out the chocolate cake with lit candles for dessert.

"Mr. Cameron baked this himself," the housekeeper said as she set it in front of Chloe.

Davis sent Chloe a bright smile. "I know it's not your birthday, but I figured I had some catching up to do."

Seeing the love and tears of joy in Chloe's eyes as she looked at her father, Grayson found that all the arguments he'd planned for why she needed to come home with him fizzled out. For now the best place for her was with her family.

So after eating a slice of cake, he made his excuses. "I should be getting back to San Francisco." He pushed back his chair, and was surprised when Chloe pushed back hers and spoke.

"I agree. It's time we went home."

There was no way to describe the relief he felt, and he couldn't help slipping an arm around her waist and brushing a kiss over her lips right there in front of her entire family. Neither Davis nor Bob looked surprised or argued. It was Cain who got to his feet.

"Oh no. You're not leaving yet. Gavin is on his way home and will be ticked if you aren't—"

"That's enough, Cain," Davis cut him off. "I'm sure Gavin will understand." He rose from his chair and came around the table to give Chloe a long hug. "But I hope you'll be back soon."

She hugged him close. "Very soon. I promise." She pulled back and smiled. "I love you, Daddy."

"I love you too, Selena." He grinned. "Sorry, but I'm much too old to start calling you a different name." After Chloe had hugged her grandfather and Cain, he walked them to the door and shook Grayson's hand. "Take good care of my girl."

"I will, sir."

Once outside, Grayson took Chloe's hand and headed for his car, but when they were halfway there she stopped and pulled him in the opposite direction. Through the dark they walked around her grandfather's house to the rows of vineyards that grew behind. While the other grapevines looked trimmed and manicured, these five rows grew wild and untouched.

"These are the first vines that my grandmother grew," she said as she walked between them, her hand reaching out to brush the turning leaves, which gleamed in the moonlight. "Even after the vineyard started making money, she tended these first vines herself. And after her death, Granddad refused to let anyone touch them."

"He must've loved her very much."

She nodded. "He did." She stopped at the end of the row and plucked a withered grape from the vine. She didn't eat it. She just held it in her palm and studied it. "I was so convinced that I was doing the right thing by leaving. But if I hadn't jumped to conclusions, I could've saved everyone so much heartache."

She dropped the raisin and turned to stare at the miles and miles of vineyards. She didn't cry, but the dejected slope of her shoulders spoke of her pain much more clearly than tears ever could. Having spent years dealing with his mother's death and his own doubts about his father's love, he understood her hurt. Understood that there was nothing he could say or do to fix the years with her family she'd lost.

So instead he moved behind her and encircled her waist with his arms. They stood like that until night and the cold settled around them.

Then he took her hand, and they went home.

CHAPTER TWENTY

"Are you going to sleep the day away, Chloe Cameron?"

The name had her eyes opening to the sunlight that shone through the window. She rolled to her back to find Grayson standing at the foot of the bed in a gray suit, with a sappy grin on his face. She sat up and stretched her arms over her head, the sheet slipping down to reveal her nightshirt. The word *Romeo's* glittered in the bright morning sun.

Grayson's gaze lowered, and his smile grew. "Did I tell you how much I like your sleeping apparel?"

She arched a brow. "Only about a hundred times. You are an extremely possessive man."

He shrugged. "All Beaumonts are." He walked around and sat down on the bed. "And I'd like to possess you again, but unfortunately, I have to go to work. We've got to get the catalog out ASAP."

"Go to work." She straightened his tie. "I think you've done enough possessing." After getting home late from

Napa on Saturday night, they had spent all day Sunday in bed—and not sleeping.

"I'll never get enough." He kissed her before he got to his feet. "So what are you going to do on your first morning free from captivity?"

"I haven't really thought about it. I guess I need to find a new job. And I probably should move back to my apartment—"

Grayson cut her off. "No."

It was funny how one word could make her so giddy. "No? And why not?"

She was hoping for some kind of declaration. She should've known better. Grayson wasn't the type to express his emotions through words. Which explained the outrageous lie.

"Bugs?" He shook his head. "A horrible infestation. Which means that you'll have to live with me until Nash can get those creepy, hairy spiders under control."

She bit back a grin. "Well, I guess I don't have any other choice. I hate spiders. But I'm not going to live here without contributing something. I'll go to the grocery store and make dinner."

"Perfect." Grayson gave her another quick kiss before he headed for the door. "I'll see you tonight."

When he was gone, Chloe didn't waste any time showering and getting dressed. She had been cooped up in the house for too long. She couldn't wait to get outside in the hustle and bustle of San Francisco. It felt like a new city. Or maybe she just felt like a new person. A person who was no longer hiding from the past. It was funny, but as she made her way to the grocery store, people treated her like a new person.

The young man working at the newspaper stand did a

double take and gave her a free morning paper. The businesswoman she passed on the street spoke as if she knew her. "You're as beautiful as the picture." And the cashier at the grocery store who rang up her groceries couldn't stop looking at her. "I know you from somewhere," she said. "I just can't think of where. What's your name?"

"Chloe," she said with pride. "Chloe Cameron."

The woman only shook her head. "Nope, the name's not familiar. Maybe it's because you look like Audrey Hepburn."

"Thank you." Chloe gave her a bright smile as she collected her bags and headed out the door.

The bags were heavy. Obviously she'd bought more than she should have. Especially when she was on foot, and when she had only a couple hundred dollars to last her until she got a job. Her father had wanted to give her money before she left Napa, but she had refused. She wanted to make her own success, not live off her father. Which had her thinking about Eden's idea. Why couldn't Chloe start a flower nursery? It would take getting investors, but she already had one in Eden. And there were those acres of her father's land that were too rocky for grapevines. They would be perfect for greenhouses.

After another block she decided to part with some more of her money and take the bus. She sat down on a bench next to a teenage girl. At first the girl didn't acknowledge her. She was more interested in texting on her cell phone. But after a few moments, she glanced up, and her mouth dropped open.

"OMG! I didn't realize supermodels take the bus. I thought you took limos and private jets."

Chloe glanced behind her. When she didn't see anyone, she turned back around. "Sorry, but you must have mistaken me for someone else."

The girl looked confused for only a second before she

leaned closer. "Yeah, I get it. You don't want the paparazzi showing up and going all ballistic on you."

Obviously the girl had some mental issues. No doubt she was living on the streets like Chloe had. Which made Chloe instantly sympathetic. "Look," she said, "I know it's hard to take handouts." She pulled out her wallet. "But here's a few dollars—"

The bus pulled up to the curb, cutting off her words. Not because of the squeal of brakes as much as the huge picture on the side. A picture of Chloe in a black bra and panties with paint streaked across her cleavage and a pouting smile on her lips. While she stared at the side of the bus in complete horror, the girl held up her phone and took a picture.

"Sorry," she said as she got up. "But my friends aren't going to believe that I met a French Kiss model." She hurried onto the bus.

Chloe sat there stunned for a few seconds before unmitigated anger set in. Noticing a street person sitting next to a building, she set all three grocery bags next to him and headed for French Kiss. When she arrived in the lobby, she was still pissed off, and if the blonde behind the receptionist's desk had been as rude as she'd been the other day, Chloe would've clocked her. But the blonde wasn't rude. At least not overly rude.

"No need to check in," she said. "I think everyone knows who you are."

Chloe only rolled her eyes as she headed to the elevator. The old security guy hopped off his stool and pushed the button. "I knew you were somebody special the moment I saw you," he said with a wink.

Once she got to the executive floor, she headed straight for Grayson's office. When he wasn't there, she moved down the hallway, peeking into every office along the way.

"Looking for someone?"

She glanced behind her to see a woman walking toward her with a tray of coffee cups. The same woman who had shown up when she and Grayson were being arrested. She took a closer look at Chloe and smiled.

"So I finally get to meet our new top model. I'm Kelly Melvin, Deacon Beaumont's executive assistant. Although I seem to be the assistant to all the Beaumonts." She shook her head, and her Hello Kitty earrings swayed. "I really need to ask for a raise. So who are you looking for?"

"Grayson?"

"He's in the photo studio, which is on the seventh floor."

"Thank you." Chloe turned and headed back to the elevators.

"You're welcome," Kelly called after her. "And when you're through yelling at Grayson for whatever he did to make you so angry, come back and I'll show you around. You're going to like working at French Kiss. The Beaumonts can be exasperating, but they're honest and fair employers."

Honest. Ha! That's what Chloe had thought, but she'd been completely wrong. Grayson had lied through his teeth.

The seventh floor had a lot of rooms, but it didn't take her long to find the one with Grayson in it. His voice greeted her ears as soon as she opened the door.

"Now stop it, Nat. I'm not going to kiss you."

Chloe hadn't thought she could get any madder. She'd been wrong. She felt livid when she stepped in the room to discover Grayson being mauled by a supermodel in skimpy pink lingerie.

"But Gar-a-son. Why won't you kiss me again? You can't tell me that you didn't like it."

Chloe walked in. "Oh, I'm sure he liked it. But his praise for your kisses will have to wait. Right now, Gar-a-

son is going to get his butt chewed out." She grabbed
Natalia's arm and hauled her to the door. Then, before the
skinny model could do more than sputter in Russian, Chloe
slammed the door in her face. When she turned, Grayson
was grinning.

"Before you chew my butt out, I want you to know that
nothing happened. Natalia and I were in the middle of a
photo shoot."

"And we all know how innocent your photo shoots are,
Grayson." She moved toward him. "To think that I believed
that virgin story."

"Calm down, Chloe. Nothing happened. I promise you."

"Just like you promised me that you'd delete all the pictures you took of me?"

Grayson looked confused. "What are you talking about?"

"The photos you took of me in your bedroom. The ones
you were supposed to delete but didn't."

A light dawned in his eyes. "Is that what has you so upset? You're mad because I didn't delete the pictures?"

"Not as mad as I am at you for putting them on every bus
in the city!"

Grayson's eyes widened. "What? I didn't put them anywhere but on my laptop."

"Don't you dare lie to me." She slugged him in the arm.
"Who else would do something like that?"

"I would."

She whirled around to see Grayson's brother standing
in the doorway. She had seen Deacon only in photos. And
no photo could capture the magnetic presence of the man.
He wasn't any bigger than Grayson, but he seemed to fill
the room. If Chloe hadn't been so angry, she might've been
intimidated.

"Deacon Beaumont," he said as he held out a hand. When

she refused to take it, he let it drop. "And you must be the elusive Chloe. I'm glad to finally meet you."

"Wait a minute." Grayson sent his brother a hard look. "What did you do, Deacon?"

"I did what I thought you and Samuel wanted me to do. I used Chloe's pictures for our new advertising campaign."

"You what?" Grayson yelled. Since she had never heard him raise his voice before, it made her jump. It also made her realize that Grayson hadn't betrayed her. He was still the honest, honorable man she'd thought he was. Just that quickly her anger left. Although she was still annoyed with his brother.

"You didn't even ask my permission," she said. "You could get sued for that, you know."

"But I believe Grayson did? And you gave it by signing your name on the dotted line."

"I never signed anything but the release for the picture you used on the cover of the summer catalog."

"You should learn to read the fine print," Deacon said. "That contract covered any photographs that were taken by a French Kiss photographer within the year. While Miles is our main photographer, Grayson sometimes fills in. And it's only been a little over six months since you signed. So that means that we still have control over all photographs that have been, or will be, taken in the next few months. Of course, we will pay you the designated fee for each photo we use." He held out his hand again. "Welcome to the French Kiss family, Miss McAlister."

Chloe stared at his hand, and then at Grayson. Grayson didn't seem to be as surprised and angry as he'd been before. In fact he looked a little too pleased.

"Oh no," she said. "I am not going to end up being sucked into modeling like Madison. I don't want to be a model. I want to go to college and take horticulture so I can start my own flower nursery."

Grayson took her hands and turned her to face him. "I think that's a great idea. But that doesn't mean you can't do a little modeling on the side. You don't have to have a schedule like Madison's. In fact, you don't have to do any more photo shoots if you don't want to. All you have to do is let us use the ones I already took."

"I don't concur, Gray," Deacon said. "From the buzz on social media, Chloe's pictures have caused quite a stir. I'd like more photographs, a few appearances, and the fashion show."

Chloe shook her head. "I'm not doing the fashion show. Being in front of big crowds is not my thing. But I'll let you use my pictures, especially since there's not much I can do about it." She looked at Deacon. "And I'll expect my money today since my butt is already plastered all over city buses."

"I think everyone should get paid for their butt being on a bus." A smile broke over Deacon's face, and it completely changed the intimidating businessman to a charismatic Beaumont. "Now I'll leave you two to get back to whatever I interrupted. Although I think you need to deal with Natalia, Grayson. She seems to be sobbing in the hallway." He walked out and closed the door behind him.

"Wow," Chloe said. "No wonder Madison reveres the guy. He knows how to take charge." Grayson spun her around and kissed her until she was breathless. When he finally pulled back, she asked, "What was that for?"

"I just don't want you thinking that my brother is the only one who knows how to take charge." He brushed back her bangs. "So are you still mad at me?"

"I should be. You told me you were going to delete the pictures."

"But how could I delete something so beautiful?"

Okay, so the guy knew exactly what to say to defuse her anger. And the hot, wet, deep kiss he gave her didn't hurt either.

"Oh, Gar-a-son!"

They pulled apart to find Natalia standing in the doorway. She stared at them with weepy eyes for only a second before she turned on a heel and left.

"I should probably go after her. We need more pictures for the catalog, and if you're not going to do another photo shoot—"

"Fine," she said. "I'll do it." She pointed a finger at him. "But there is no way in hell that I'm prancing down a fashion show runway."

CHAPTER TWENTY-ONE

"Your posture is horrendous. You look like my great-grandmother who has bad osteoporosis. How many times do I have to tell you to keep your shoulders back and your spine straight? And stop swinging your arms like a monkey."

Chloe glared at the short man in the bright-green suit and pink shirt. She wanted to demonstrate a swinging arm and punch him right in the face. She had been working on a proper runway walk for the past two hours, and nothing she did seemed to satisfy the man who'd been hired to get her ready for the French Kiss fall fashion show. Rudolph was an annoying little slave driver.

"How can a person stand straight in these torture chambers you've strapped on my feet?" She pointed to the bright blue platform shoes with their seven-inch heels. "I feel like a clown on stilts."

"You better figure out a way to walk in them," Rudolph snipped as he stood by the outline of the catwalk he'd taped off on the floor. "On the runway you'll be wearing stilettos."

Her eyes widened. "Like hell I will. I'm not falling off a three-foot-high runway and breaking my neck. I don't care how much money I'm getting paid." She clomped over to a chair and sat down to unbuckle her shoes.

"No, no." Rudolph rushed over. "What are you doing? You can't take those off. We're not finished."

"Oh, we're finished." She took off both shoes and handed them to him. "You can tell Samuel to shove those right up his—" A cough had her glancing at the door of the studio. Samuel stood there with the same unsmiling face he always wore. Although his eyes sparkled with humor.

"I see that your practice is going well," he said as he walked into the room.

She scowled. "I'm not runway material."

Samuel nodded dismissively. "That will be all for today, Rudolph." He took the shoes from Rudolph, then waited for him to leave before he sat down next to Chloe. "You said you weren't a catalog model either, but your pictures in the holiday catalog have caused quite a stir."

That was an understatement. Since the catalog had come out, she'd become a celebrity. It wasn't easy going from being a recluse no one knew to being a French Kiss model everyone seemed to know. The guy at the Starbucks that morning had almost fallen out of the drive-up window when he recognized her. And she didn't know who had been more embarrassed—she or the barista.

"There's nothing to letting someone take your picture," she said. "Grayson could make anyone look good."

"Grayson is a talented photographer, but it also takes a talented model to be able to communicate their feelings with just one look. You, my dear, are a natural. Although some things need practice." He handed her the shoes.

She rolled her eyes. "Fine, but you're never going to make me prance like a pony."

Samuel laughed. "Okay. No pony prancing. Let's just start with a simple walk."

With only a few grumbles, Chloe put the shoes back on and wobbled to the other side of the room and back again while Samuel watched her with one finger pressed to his bottom lip.

"Again," he said. "But this time I don't want you to worry about your shoulders or your arms. I only want you to think about placing one foot directly in front of the other. Don't look at your feet. In fact, close your eyes and just feel the walk."

She closed her eyes and tried to do as he asked, placing her right foot directly in front of her left, then her left in front of her right. She had just started to feel like she'd gotten the hang of it when she misjudged a step and stumbled over her clunky heels. She would've landed hard on the tile floor if Samuel hadn't caught her. At least she thought it was Samuel until she opened her eyes and looked into twin pools of violet. Not Grayson's twin pools, but a pair that were almost identical.

"I think the key to walking is to do it with your eyes open." Nash Beaumont gave her a charming smile.

Chloe quickly regained her balance and pulled away. Even after numerous Beaumont family dinners, she still felt awkward around Nash. Or maybe just embarrassed. He had been her one and only client as an escort. Something she would like to forget.

"Tell that to Samuel," she said. "He's the one who had me closing my eyes."

Nash glanced over his shoulder. "Are we now making our models walk the runway with closed eyes, Sam? Isn't that like walking the plank blindfolded?"

Samuel lifted an eyebrow. "I'm assuming you know a lot about pirates, Nash?"

Nash laughed. "About as much as I know about lingerie. I leave all of that to you. I just deal with the customer service and publicity side of things. Which is why I'm here."

Chloe was relieved that she had an excuse to stop her runway lessons…and to get away from Nash. "I'll just let you two talk," she said as she headed for the door. But Nash stopped her.

"Actually, I came to see you, Chloe."

She turned. "Me?"

"I would like to talk with you about getting on social media."

"I'm sorry, but I'm not very good at dealing with the public."

"I'm sure Madison won't mind helping you out. She's become quite the expert on tweeting, Facebooking, and blogging. And your presence on social media will help promote the fashion show—not to mention the art charity event on Thursday night." He glanced at Samuel. "I assume you're going to be there."

Samuel nodded as he got to his feet. "I don't have much choice. It's all Deirdre has talked about for the last two weeks. She thinks it's going to be quite the success." He glanced at Chloe. "Mostly because of your painting."

Chloe had mixed feelings about her naked painting being put on display. She was happy about helping cancer research, but it was still embarrassing to think that people were going to be bidding on her naked body. Even if Deirdre had promised that her name wasn't going to be released.

Her name.

After visiting Casa Selena, she had finally taken the steps to legally change her name. She had kept Selena as a tribute to her grandmother, and because her family would never call her anything else, but she'd added Chloe. Chloe Selena Cameron sounded right. It also sounded like a name a woman should be proud of.

"Okay," she said, "I'll do some social networking and promote the fashion show. Although I don't know why anyone would want to see me clomp down the catwalk."

"You won't be clomping," Samuel said. "We have plenty of time to get you looking like a pro." He winked at her. "Or a show pony." He moved toward the door. "Now if you two will excuse me, I have a luncheon date with a very domineering woman."

Chloe started to follow him, but Nash blocked her way. He was no longer all smiles. In fact his expression was as somber as Samuel's.

"I think we need to talk."

There was little doubt what he wanted to talk about. "So you really didn't want to talk to me about tweets and Instagram. Let me guess. This is where you try to get rid of the big, bad escort by offering me money to leave town."

Nash studied her, his eyes intense. "Would you blame me? He's my little brother, Chloe. And I've been responsible for him since our mother passed away. I taught him to bait a hook, make a peanut butter and jelly sandwich, and zip his coat."

"Where was his father?"

"Donny John didn't have much time for his kids after his wife died. So Deacon and I took on the job of raising Grayson—which wasn't that difficult. Grayson has always been unassuming and easygoing."

Chloe had to disagree. On the outside Grayson seemed unassuming and easygoing. But beneath his reserved persona was a complex, passionate man. All you had to do was look at one of his paintings to see his deep emotions...or spend a night in his arms. While Grayson had trouble communicating verbally, he had no trouble communicating physically.

"I'm not sure you know Grayson as well as you think you do," she said.

Nash tipped his head. "And you think you know him better?"

"Maybe not as a kid. But Grayson isn't a child anymore. He doesn't need you to bait his hook, make his sandwiches, or zip his coat."

Nash paused for a second. "And what about saving him from broken hearts?"

"Is that what you think? You think I want to break Grayson's heart?"

"That's why I'm here. I don't know what you want." He walked over to the small window and looked out. "All I know is your history. And we both know that it's not exactly stellar."

"And from what I've heard, neither is yours," she snapped.

Nash released his breath and ran a hand through his hair before turning. "Okay, I deserved that. I've made more than my share of mistakes in the past. And whether you believe me or not, I'm not trying to judge you for yours. I'm just trying to protect Grayson from getting hurt. So I'm asking you...how do you feel about my brother?"

A few weeks ago, Chloe would've told him that it was none of his damned business. But since reuniting with her family, she realized how much her leaving had hurt them. How much they'd worried about her. How much money they'd spent to find her. And wasn't Nash doing the same thing? He wanted to protect his brother from pain and hurt just like her family had wanted to find and protect her. Chloe couldn't go back and ease their fears, but she could ease Nash's. It surprised her how easily the words came out.

"I love Grayson," she said. "And the last thing I want to do is hurt him."

Nash studied her long and hard before a smile stretched his lips. "Well, why in the hell didn't you say that in the first place?" He strode over and lifted her into his arms, giving her a bear hug.

"Okay, okay," she said as she pushed back, "you don't have to crack a rib."

He was still grinning when he set her on her feet. "So why hasn't that brother of mine mentioned you guys were in love?"

Chloe felt her face heat and looked down at her painful high heels. "Because maybe he doesn't feel the same way. And I wouldn't blame him. As you said, my past isn't exactly stellar. Grayson deserves better."

"Bullshit!" Nash said. "Grayson deserves to be with the woman he loves. By the sappy smile that's been on his face the last couple weeks, I'd say that he loves you. He's just having a hard time saying it. Have you told him?"

"No."

He tossed up his hands. "Well, there you have it. Guys have extremely fragile egos, Chloe. He's probably just waiting for you to say it first." He took her arm. "Come on, let's go find him."

"Now? I'm not telling him now."

"Why not?" He pulled her toward the door. "There's no time like the present."

She tried to dig in her heels, but it was hard with platforms. So she had to slug him hard in the arm to get him to stop.

He released her and rubbed the spot. "Damn, you've got quite a punch for a skinny girl." He grinned. "No wonder my brother loves you. You remind him of me."

She rolled her eyes. "There's more where that came from if you don't keep your mouth shut. I'll tell Grayson in my own time."

He held up his hands. "Fine, but I think the sooner the better. Now come on, I'll take you to lunch and teach you how to use Twitter."

Twitter with all its hashtags and following was almost as difficult to figure out as runway walking. But Nash wasn't as much of a taskmaster as Rudolph. Once he'd helped her set up an account and explained the basics, they moved on to another subject.

"Have you talked to Grayson about my dad getting married?" Nash asked.

"He mentioned it."

"So I guess you got that he's not real happy about it. Being the youngest, Grayson was extremely close to my mom. He didn't talk for a week after she passed away." He studied her. "I understand that your mother died of cancer as well. So you understand what Grayson went through . . . what he still seems to be going through."

Chloe nodded. "But I was older than Grayson so I have more memories to hold on to. Grayson doesn't even have those. Which is probably why he's having such a hard time with your father remarrying."

"I agree. But if I've learned anything from life, it's that you need to let go of the past and move on. From the phone conversations I've had with Dad's fiancée, I like her. I think Grayson would too if he gave her a chance." He motioned to the waitress. "Could you bring us a slice of that chocolate cake in the front display window?" Once the waitress was gone, he glanced at Chloe and smiled. "I saw you eyeballing it when we walked in."

Chloe understood why the man had gotten the nickname of the Dark Seducer. He seemed to be able to read women's minds and give them exactly what they wanted.

"Anyway," he continued. "I was hoping you could talk him into going to Louisiana for the wedding on Saturday."

"So the chocolate cake is really bribery."

"Of course." He flashed her a megawatt smile. "We Beaumonts are willing to do whatever it takes to get our way."

It was pretty good bribery. The cake came with a big scoop of vanilla ice cream and a drizzle of chocolate syrup. Since Nash didn't like chocolate, she ate every last crumb herself. After she finished they headed back to the office.

Chloe should've continued her runway lessons. Instead she went in search of Grayson. She found him in his office studio painting. He had removed his tie, and smudges of paint stained his dress shirt and suit pants. He worked with such total concentration that he didn't even look up when Chloe walked in. Which had her quickly glancing at the divan. If there was a naked female model stretched out on it, she wasn't quite sure what she would do. Grayson was an artist. She couldn't expect him never to paint another nude woman. And yet she heaved a sigh of relief when she saw who was curled up naked on the divan.

Michael Paris Beaumont was sound asleep with his chubby cheek pressed against the fuzzy material of his blanket and his sweet butt cheeks sticking up in the air like two small loaves of undercooked bread. Chloe didn't know why tears came to her eyes. She just couldn't keep them in. Nor could she keep in the tiny sob that escaped. A sob that had Grayson's hand stopping in mid-stroke and his gaze traveling to her.

"Chloe?"

With emotions clogging her throat, all she could do was nod. Setting down his brush, he got off his stool and had her in his arms only seconds later.

"Okay," he said against the top of her head, "whose ass do I need to kick?"

She laughed through her tears. "How many times do I have to tell you that I can fight my own battles?"

He pulled back, his eyes serious. "Who or what upset you?"

She released a wobbly breath. "No one upset me. Girls can cry at the drop of a hat. Didn't you know that?"

"I knew that about other girls. I didn't know that about you."

She sniffed. "Well, now you do." She smiled, just because she felt like smiling. "I like your new subject."

He returned her smile, and she felt even happier. "Deacon wants to give it to Olivia for her birthday."

"She'll love it. I bet she'll love it as much as your dad would love you coming to his wedding."

His eyes narrowed. "Deacon or Nash?"

"Nash, but I really do think you should go, Grayson. Family is important. You helped me figure that out. It's only fair that I reciprocate."

He released a sigh. "I'll think about it. That's all I can—"

Before he could finish, there was a noise that had both of them turning to the divan. The sight that greeted them was not pretty. It was, however, funny. At least to Chloe. While she burst out laughing, Grayson stared in horror at the mess his nephew had made of the couch.

"I am not cleaning that up."

CHAPTER TWENTY-TWO

Deirdre Beaumont knew how to throw a party. Everything about the charity benefit, from the gallery she'd chosen as the venue to the champagne being passed around by the waiters, was top-notch. Grayson had to admire the woman for pulling it all together so quickly and making it such a big success. Everyone who was anyone was in attendance, including the mayor, a senator, and a famous actress whose name escaped Grayson at the moment.

"She's more beautiful in person than she is in the movies, isn't she?"

He pulled his gaze away from the actress and turned to Chloe. Talk about beautiful, she looked like a movie star herself. The red evening gown she wore clung to her slim body like a second skin and offset her dark features. Her hair had been cut short again and was moussed back in a chic style that made her brown eyes appear twice as large...and twice as captivating. A man could lose himself in those eyes. Although as he stared into the chocolate depths, Grayson didn't feel lost. For the first time in his life, he felt found. Like he knew who he was and where he was going.

"Did I tell you how stunning you look tonight?" he asked as he brushed a finger over her cheek.

She rolled her eyes, but a smile teased her lips. Lips that had been painted the ruby red of her dress. "Only about a hundred times. And those compliments would work much better if you weren't staring at other women."

"I was just trying to remember the actress's name. But I love it when you're jealous."

Her brow knotted. "I am not jealous."

"Really? Then why did you inform all the models at French Kiss to keep their hands off me or you'd punch their lights out?"

Her lips pouted. "I should've known they were all tattletales."

He couldn't help the satisfied grin that split his face. "So you did say it."

"You should talk," she grumbled. "At least I'm willing to let them pose for you. You won't let anyone else photograph me but you."

Grayson could've justified himself by saying that he had a certain vision for her photo shoots that only he could pull off. That's what he had told his brothers—although if the smirk on Nash's face was any indication, he hadn't fallen for it. But maybe the time for justifying himself was over.

He slipped his hands around her waist and pulled her close. "I don't want you posing for anyone else because I'm jealous as hell. Because I don't want you giving them the same smiles...the same sexy looks...the same intense feelings you give me when you pose."

It was hard to read the emotion that flickered in her eyes. Especially when she lowered them so quickly. But her words gave him the confirmation that he needed. The confirmation that she was falling as hard for him as he was for her.

"Okay then," she said in a soft voice. "I won't pose for anyone but you." She carefully adjusted his tuxedo bow tie. "And I would appreciate it if you didn't touch the women who pose for you."

"No one has posed for me since you—except Michael. And that is the last time I paint that poopy kid. I still can't get the smell out of my studio."

She laughed. "It will be well worth it when Olivia sees the painting. It's amazing, Grayson. And it proves that you don't need to paint me to paint well."

Unable to resist, he brushed a kiss over her lips. "I might not need to paint you, but I love to paint you. You are my muse, Chloe Cameron. Without you by my side, my painting means nothing." He leaned in for another kiss, but before he could deepen it, Deirdre Beaumont walked up, displaying more diamonds than a Cartier store window. The only things not sparkling were her eyes.

"That will be enough of that," she said. "As the artist, you need to be mingling and pushing people to bid on your paintings, Grayson." She looked at Chloe. "And as the model of the main attraction, you need to be doing the same thing." She glanced over her shoulder at the crowd that had formed around Chloe's painting. "Although I don't think they're going to need much pushing. We already have numerous bidders on the painting of the famous French Kiss model Chloe Cameron."

Chloe eyes widened. "You told people that I'm the model? But I asked you not to use my name."

Deirdre waved a hand. "I do not honor ridiculous requests. And that was a ridiculous request. Your body is beautiful, and the painting is breathtaking. People knowing that it's a famous model's body will make it sell twice as fast."

"Well, I'd like to know how you'd feel if everyone in this room knew what you looked like naked," Chloe said.

"Posh." Deirdre took a flute of champagne from a passing waiter. "You're not exactly naked. The sheet covers more of your body than your catalog photos. Which seems rather odd since Grayson's other paintings of women show a lot more skin." Her eyes narrowed on Grayson. "It almost makes me wonder if there's not another painting."

There were several paintings he'd refused to show her, and all displayed a lot more skin than the one he'd given Deirdre for the auction. But those paintings were for his viewing pleasure. He didn't like sharing Chloe. Even now he had to stifle the strong urge to walk over and take the painting off the wall and carry it right out the door. There were only two things that kept him from doing it: The money it was making for charity. And the plan he'd devised to be the winner of the silent auction.

"I promised you a painting, Deirdre," he said, "and you got one."

She studied him. "Yes, I did, didn't I? Well, enough of this chitchat." She downed the champagne and handed the glass to a waiter before she took Chloe's arm. "Come on, dear. It's time to get over your shyness and make some money for cancer research."

"If one guy says anything sexual to me, I'm punching him," Chloe said.

"If anyone is that vulgar," Deirdre said, "I'll hold him while you do so."

Once they were gone, Grayson headed over to the painting to see how the bidding was going. Deirdre was right. There were numerous bids on the auction sheet right next to the bidders' numbers. He looked for the number he'd been assigned and was happy to see it numerous times, including in the very last entry for a hundred thousand dollars. His eyes widened. It looked like he was going to have to part with more money than he'd planned.

"Checking to see how much your talent is worth, little brother?"

He looked up to see Nash walking toward him with Deacon. Both of his brothers wore the same style of black tuxedo he had on, and standing all together, they must've looked like identical penguins. Nash elbowed Grayson out of the way and glanced at the bid sheet before releasing a low whistle through his teeth.

"Looks like your paintings are worth much more than the pictures of Batman you used to sell to the kids at Cypress Elementary. What did you sell those for? Ten cents?"

Grayson grinned at the memory. "Twenty-five cents. I made a good fifteen dollars and sixty-five cents on that venture."

Always the businessman, Deacon questioned the number. "How did you end up with fifteen sixty-five if each picture sold for twenty-five cents?"

"Cheryl Tate only had fifteen cents, so I made an exception."

Deacon laughed. "You've come a long way since then, haven't you?"

Nash slapped both his brothers on the back. "We all have."

They exchanged smiles and enjoyed their success for a moment before Deacon brought them back to the present. "You've certainly outdone yourself tonight, Gray. I thought Nash was the marketing genius, but this charity event was a brilliant idea. And with the buzz this painting has caused, people are going to be chomping at the bit to watch Chloe walk the runway."

"I'm interested to see how that goes myself," Nash said with a mischievous sparkle in his eye.

"What are you up to, Nash?" Grayson asked. "You've had that same devious look in your eye for the last few days. It's like you know something that no one else does."

"Now what would I know that you don't, little brother?" Nash said before he quickly changed the subject. "Dad called today and wants to make sure that we're all there for the wedding on Saturday. So are you done throwing a tantrum, Gray?"

Grayson should be done throwing his tantrum. He knew he was being childish and ridiculous, but he just couldn't come to terms with Donny John's remarrying. Which was why he grasped for any reason not to attend the wedding. "I just think that someone needs to stay here and hold down the fort. Especially with the fashion show being so close."

Deacon studied him for no more than a second before issuing an order. "We'll all be at the wedding, and that's final."

"Deke is right," Nash said. "Donny John wasn't exactly the best father after Mom died, but lately he's been making the effort to change. So I think it's only fair that we make the effort too. And speaking of fathers." He glanced at Deacon. "You're looking a little more alert these days, Deke. Is Michael finally sleeping?"

"Not the entire night, but at least for a few hours at a pop."

"So I guess all those books you read finally paid off."

Deacon started to nod, but then stopped and released his breath. "To be honest, they didn't help worth a damn. Newborn babies seem to have a mind of their own. They eat when they want. They poop when they want. And they sleep when they want. The only thing parents can do is try to survive."

Grayson and Nash exchanged looks before they laughed.

"I don't know what you two think is so funny," Deacon said. "It won't be long before both of you will be sleepless in San Francisco."

"We're not laughing about your predicament, Deke," Nash said. "We're laughing because you were so convinced that you had everything handled. That you could train Mikey like a hunting dog."

"A hunting dog?" Olivia strolled up, looking radiant for a new mother who had had little sleep. She kissed Grayson on the cheek before doing the same to Nash. "I certainly hope you don't think that you can train our son like a hunting dog, Deacon Beaumont."

"Of course not, Livy," Deacon said as he tucked his wife against his side. "Nash was just being a wiseass. And speaking of Michael, you need to call the sitter and tell her that she read him the wrong book. *The Very Hungry Caterpillar* gives him indigestion if you read it to him before he goes to sleep."

"And just how do you know what book the sitter read him?"

Deacon pulled out his phone. "Because I had Nash set up cameras in his room. You didn't think I'd leave my only son with some random sitter you hired without being able to keep an eye on things, did you?" He tapped his phone and turned it so they could see. The screen was divided into two pictures of Michael's room. One showed Michael swaddled in a blanket and sleeping in his crib, and the other showed a grandmotherly woman knitting in the rocking chair next to the crib.

Olivia looked at the pictures for a long moment before

she stood on her tiptoes and kissed Deacon's cheek. "Has anyone ever told you that you're a very loving man? Controlling, but loving." She rested her head on his shoulder as they both studied the phone as if their sleeping son were the number one YouTube sensation.

Grayson had never given much thought to kids until he'd had Michael for an hour so he could paint him. Despite the pooping incident, he was a cute little guy. And looking at Deacon and Olivia's awed faces, he couldn't stop the longing that welled up inside him. A longing to one day stand next to his child's crib and watch him, or her, sleep while Chloe rested her head on his shoulder.

"I guess he only stays awake with his parents," Deacon said.

Olivia smiled. "Probably because we're such interesting people." She lifted her head. "And speaking of interesting people, Mother certainly invited some tonight. I just met an extremely interesting older gentleman when I stopped to bid on Chloe's painting."

"You bid on Chloe's painting?" Deacon asked as he slipped his phone back in his tuxedo pocket. "As proud as I am of Grayson's talent, we already have three of his nudes that we're going to have to figure out where to hide when Michael gets older. And he just painted a picture of— anyway, I don't understand why we need another one."

"I didn't bid for us." She looked at Grayson, and he had little doubt that she was about to spill the beans. "Eden, Madison, and I have been doing exactly what you asked. We've been staking out the silent auction sheet and outbidding the highest bid, but there seems to be another person who wants the painting as much as you do. And we weren't sure how high you wanted us to go."

"Who's the bidder?" he asked, now more concerned

about being outbid than about what his brothers thought of his bidding on his own painting.

"I'm not sure. But I think it could be the man I was telling you about. Bob seemed very interested in the painting—even if his grandson Gavin wasn't."

Grayson wasn't surprised that some of Chloe's relatives were in attendance. Especially Gavin. He'd been expecting a visit from the older cousin since he and Chloe had gone to the vineyard. Although he would've preferred their first meeting to have taken place without the nude picture of Chloe. But since there was no help for it now, he excused himself and went in search of the Camerons.

He found Chloe's grandfather first. Bob had dressed for the occasion and looked like a typical Texas millionaire in his expensive Western suit and big tan cowboy hat. He stood at the bar with Madison, telling her a story that had her laughing so hard that tears rolled down her cheeks.

"... I kid you not," he said. "That bull chased me all the way to Drucker's farm—me dodging his horns and yelling at the top of my lungs." Bob finally noticed Grayson. "Well, there is the man of the hour." He clapped an arm over Grayson's shoulders. "Good to see you, son." He winked at Madison. "Why didn't you tell me that San Francisco had such pretty ladies? I would've been to visit much sooner."

Madison sent him a flirty smile. "I'm sure you say that to all the ladies, Bobby."

"Only the ones that laugh at my stories." He glanced at Grayson. "Can I get you a drink, son?"

"No, thank you," he said. "I heard you brought Gavin with you, and I wanted to introduce myself."

"You might want to wait on that, son. Gavin isn't quite as forgiving as Cain is. I figure he's giving her a piece of his mind as we speak."

Grayson bristled. He didn't agree with Chloe's having kept her whereabouts a secret from her family for all these years, but regardless, Grayson couldn't sit back and let her be bullied.

He glanced around. "Where are they?"

"Last I saw, they were headed out that back door." He pointed to the door in the far corner. "But it might be best if you let them have it out, Grayson. Gavin is as mad as a bull with a toothache, but he would never hurt Chloe."

Grayson didn't heed the advice. After excusing himself he headed straight to the door in the corner. The back alleyway was well lit, so it took only a quick glance to locate Chloe and Gavin. From the looks of things, Chloe wasn't getting bullied as much as doing the bullying. She was leaning toward Gavin, giving him hell.

"What did you expect, Gavin?" she yelled. "I was a fifteen-year-old girl who just lost my mother and, I thought, my father in one fell swoop. I was hurt and confused and grieving. Yes, I should've spoken to you before I left, but you were busy in Texas and Cain was busy with college. I just thought my leaving would be best for everyone."

"Well, it wasn't!" Gavin bellowed. "I would never blame you for mistakes your mother made, Selena—or whatever the hell you go by now. We grew up together. You were like a little sister to me." He leaned closer so they were nose to nose. "And I've missed the hell out of you."

"Well, I've missed you too!"

"You have a funny way of showing it. It's been six years. Six years of worrying about where you were and if you were okay. Not to mention all the money we spent trying to track you down."

Chloe's voice lost its angry edge. "I'm sorry. But the private investigator you hired did find me. I just left before he could come back."

"I thought that old guy who lives in your building was telling the truth when he said he'd never set eyes on you. If he had been truthful, I would've found you a lot sooner and gotten it through that thick skull of yours to come home. In case you didn't know this, I love you."

"I love you too, Gav." Chloe hugged him.

Now that he knew Chloe was okay, Grayson would've left them if Chloe hadn't glanced over and seen him.

"Grayson." The way she said his name never failed to make his heart beat faster. She took Gavin's hand and pulled him along with her. "Gavin, this is Grayson Beaumont."

Grayson held out his hand. "It's nice to meet you—" Before he could even finish, a fist slammed into his face and sent him reeling back against the door.

"Gavin!" Chloe screamed. "What are you doing?"

"I'm kicking the guy's ass who exploited my little cousin." Gavin swung again, but this time Grayson was ready. He ducked the punch and circled around. He really didn't want to fight with Chloe's relative, but Gavin didn't give him much choice. Her cousin wasn't as good at boxing as Grayson's brothers, but he was quick. He swung repeatedly until his fist clipped Grayson's jaw. Between the pain in his jaw and the one in his throbbing eye, Grayson was just pissed enough to punch back. He did a combination of a left uppercut followed by a hard right jab that had Gavin folding at the waist before his head snapped back from the punch to his face.

"Grayson!" Chloe yelled. "Have you two lost your minds?" She stepped between them.

Gavin straightened. "What did you expect me to do to the guy who painted you naked? Shake his hand?" His eyes narrowed on Grayson. "Wait a minute, you're the one I saw outside of Selena's apartment. The one I showed her picture to."

Grayson cringed as Chloe turned to him. "You never mentioned meeting Gavin."

"How else do you think he found the winery?" Gavin said. "Although I don't know why he didn't bring you with him the first time he came."

Chloe's eyes widened. "You went to the winery?" When he didn't say anything, she drew her own conclusions. "So you knew who I was and never mentioned a word." Her eyes snapped with anger, and she slugged him hard in the arm. "You jerk! You lied and manipulated me."

Before Grayson could explain, Deirdre stepped out the door.

"Would someone like to tell me what's going on? I was informed by one of the waitstaff that a brawl was going on in the alley." She looked between Gavin and Grayson. "Now, I don't have the time to find out what has caused this little show of testosterone. Nor do I care. But I do care about the success of my benefit. So I suggest you put this dispute on ice, gentlemen, before I give you each a butt-kicking."

She looked at Chloe. "The man who bought your painting would like to speak with you, dear." She held the door, and after one nasty glance at Grayson, Chloe didn't hesitate to walk inside.

Once the door closed behind Deirdre, Gavin spoke. "So Uncle Davis and Granddad were right. We do have you to thank for getting Chloe to the winery."

Grayson nodded as he tentatively touched the spot beneath his eye. "But obviously my manipulation didn't work out so well."

A look of smug satisfaction crossed Gavin's face. "Yeah, she looked pretty pissed." He tested his jaw. "Where did you learn to fight?"

"My father. Where did you?"

"Texas honky-tonks. And speaking of which, I could sure use a drink...and a bag of ice."

Since his eye was swelling shut, Grayson nodded. "But first I need to talk to Chloe."

The smirk that Gavin sent him was as annoying as hell. "Good luck with that."

Once inside, Grayson followed Gavin to the bar, thinking Chloe would be bawling out her grandfather for not telling her about Grayson's visit. But Bob was still talking to Madison, and Chloe was nowhere in sight. When he saw Grayson and Gavin, he laughed. "Looks like you boys could use a drink."

Grayson was about to ask where Chloe was when Eden came hustling over. "I'm sorry, Grayson. I tried to get in the last bid, but someone beat me to it."

It didn't take a genius to figure out who had wanted the painting that badly. Grayson glanced at Gavin. "So how much did you pay for it?"

Gavin looked nonplussed. "Are you kidding? That's creepy. Why do you think that Uncle Davis and Cain refused to come with us? They didn't even want to glance at the painting."

Grayson looked at Bob, who shook his head. "Not me."

Confused, Grayson looked around the room. But who else would want it so badly?

CHAPTER TWENTY-THREE

Chloe was so upset that Grayson had lied that she paid very little attention to where Deirdre was taking her until they started up the stairs.

"Where are we going?" she asked. "I thought I was going to talk to the guy who bought the painting."

"You are." Deirdre held her gown in one hand as she continued up the stairs. "He's on the phone. A lot of art buyers bid by phone."

"So why does he want to talk with me?"

"Buyers enjoy meeting the subjects and painters. It's all part of the experience. I'm sure he'll want to talk to Grayson next." She stepped into the office, where a pretty young woman sat behind the desk. "Chloe, this is Beverly Hart. She runs the gallery and took Mr. Rogers's bid."

The young woman got up and held out a hand. "It's a pleasure to meet you," she said before lifting a cell phone to her ear. "I have Ms. Cameron right here, Mr. Rogers." She handed the phone to Chloe with a smile.

Feeling extremely awkward, Chloe placed the phone to her ear. "This is Chloe Cameron." There was a long stretch of silence, and she wondered if the guy had hung up. "Hello?"

"My, my, but haven't we moved up in the world."

The voice had Chloe's heartbeat accelerating and her knees turning to liquid. She wanted to hang up, but with Deirdre and Beverly looking on, there was nothing she could do but grip the phone in her hand and try to keep her knees from buckling.

"Are you there, sweet?" Zac said in a voice that was filled with smugness.

"Yes, I'm here," she said as she glanced at Deirdre and Beverly. Deirdre had moved over to the desk, but they were still within hearing range. So Chloe kept up the charade. "I want to thank you for your generous donation, but I'm afraid I need to get back to the party...Mr. Rogers."

Zac laughed the same humorless laugh he'd used right before he started hitting her, and Chloe couldn't keep chill bumps from rising on her arms. "Yes, by all means, get back to your little party, Chloe. We can talk tomorrow—let's say around noon at our favorite Chinese restaurant."

She'd hoped Zac was still in jail and only yanking her chain. But it appeared she was wrong. If he could meet her, he was out of jail. Which meant he could get to her whenever he wanted to. The terrifying thought had the phone slipping from her hand. But before it hit the floor, she caught it. She glanced at Deirdre and Beverly to see if they had noticed, but thankfully they were engrossed in something on Beverly's laptop.

Chloe turned her back to them and lowered her voice. "I'm not meeting you."

There was a long pause before Zac spoke. "Then I guess I'll just have to show up at French Kiss."

Just the thought of such evil being around the people she'd come to care for made her sick to her stomach. "Fine. I'll be there at noon." She could almost hear Zac's gloating smirk.

"Until tomorrow, my sweet." The phone clicked.

It took a moment for Chloe to collect herself. When she turned, Deirdre and Beverly were still looking at the computer. They glanced up when she set the phone on the desk.

"So did everything go okay?" Deirdre asked. "He didn't want to talk with Grayson?"

Chloe plastered on a smile. "I guess not. Now if you'll excuse me, I better get back to the party."

Except she didn't go back to the party. Instead she walked down the stairs and straight out the door. It was cold outside, too cold for a skimpy evening gown. And yet it seemed appropriate that the outside temperature was as cold as her inside temperature.

Zac was back, and there was little doubt in her mind that he still believed that she had turned him in to the cops and that he wanted revenge. She just didn't know in what form his revenge would come. And that was the scary part.

The front door to the gallery opened, and Grayson stepped out. His face showed relief when he saw her. It quickly changed to concern when he noticed her shivering. Without a word he took off his tuxedo jacket and slipped it around her shoulders. It still held his body heat, and she clung to it like a grapevine to a trellis as he pulled his phone from his pants pocket and called for the limo. It pulled up in front only minutes later, the chauffeur jumping out to open the door. The inside was blissfully warm, and yet Chloe continued to shiver long after they pulled away from the curb.

She could feel Grayson's eyes on her, but she refused to

look at him. Instead she stared out the window at the passing buildings. A few moments later, something nudged her arm. She looked down at the glass filled with amber liquid.

"It will help warm you up," he said.

Since she still felt cold, she accepted it and took a healthy drink, enjoying the burn as it slid down her throat. She had finished the glass when Grayson finally spoke.

"I know you're upset, Chloe. And you have every right to be." She turned to find him sitting in the corner of the limo watching her intently. For a second she thought he knew about Zac's phone call, but she realized her mistake when he continued. "I should've talked to you after I ran into Gavin at your apartment," he said. "I'm sorry. But I was worried that, if I told you, you would run."

Chloe had forgotten all about Grayson's betrayal. At the moment it seemed like a petty thing to be worried about, especially in comparison to Zac's getting out of jail. She wanted to tell Grayson about Zac's phone call. But she couldn't. Grayson would be pissed and want to do something about it. And while he'd proven he could whip Zac's butt in the past, this time Zac would be ready for him. In fact she wasn't so sure that wasn't Zac's plan. He was extremely possessive and jealous, and with all the publicity, there was little doubt that he knew she was dating Grayson. Maybe he wanted Grayson to show up at the restaurant instead of her. Just the thought of Grayson's being hurt, or worse, made Chloe feel sick. Her face must've reflected her tortured thoughts because Grayson pulled her into his arms.

"I'm so sorry, baby," he whispered against her hair. "You're right, I should've told you that I went to Casa Selena and spoke to your grandfather." He leaned back and brushed a finger over her cheek. "But I worried that it would make you run. And I can't stand the thought of you leaving me."

His beautiful eyes held an emotion that made her heart tighten. "I love you, Chloe."

Just that quickly the fear that had been eating away at her mind dissolved. There was no room for thoughts of Zac when her mind was filled with Grayson. He loved her. No matter how belligerent and mean she'd been to him. No matter how sordid her past. Grayson loved her. And at that moment nothing else mattered. She opened her mouth to repeat his words of love, but he placed a finger on her lips.

"You don't need to say it just because I did," he said. "When you say it, I want you to mean it with all your heart." Before she could tell him that she did mean it, he kissed her. It was similar to all the other kisses they had shared, and yet completely different. Because in this kiss he communicated all his love... and she communicated all of hers.

His hands cradled her face as their lips melded and their tongues mated. The kiss took her breath away, and she didn't care. She didn't need to breathe. She only needed Grayson. Moving her hands between them, she untied his bow tie, then worked on the buttons of his shirt until it fell open. Her hands were cold compared to the heat of his skin, but they warmed up quickly as she strummed over each sculpted muscle. She took her time, enjoying the sensation of touching his hard body while he continued to take possession of her mouth. But when she flicked a nail over one of his nipples, he groaned and pulled away from the kiss, his breath coming out in harsh puffs that made her feel even more excited.

Lowering her head, she took his nipple in her mouth and gently sucked. He tipped his head back and ran his fingers through her hair.

"Damn, Chloe."

She smiled, then continued to suckle as she reached for

the button on his fly. With a flick and zip, she released him into her hand. He groaned, and she kissed her way down his chest, her lips sipping over his hard stomach, around his navel, to the base of his penis. She moved her hand and licked the entire rigid length before she swirled her tongue over the tip and took him deep in her mouth. The sound he made was part tortured groan and part satisfied sigh. But he allowed her mouth only a few full strokes before his hands tugged on her hair and pulled her away.

"Not without you," he whispered as he dipped his head and gave her a kiss. As the kiss deepened, he moved her to his lap and slid up her dress. He froze with his lips pressed to hers when he realized she wasn't wearing any panties.

He lifted his head and gave her a sexy smile. "Why, Miss Cameron, what a naughty little girl you are." His one hand remained on her bare butt cheek while the other unzipped the back of her dress. "Don't tell me you're completely naked beneath these sequins."

Chloe returned his smile. "Not completely." She shrugged her shoulders and the dress slipped to her waist, revealing the lavender satin corset with the pretty pink lace that was part of Grayson's Romeo Collection. It just took a minor adjustment to release her breasts from the cups. With his gaze lowered, she couldn't see the expression in his eyes. But she could feel the lengthening of his penis beneath her naked butt.

"Good God," he mumbled before he lowered his head. He trailed heated kisses across each breast before taking her nipple between his lips. He wasn't as gentle as she had been. He pulled it into his mouth with a hard suck, then used his tongue to roll it against the roof of his mouth. The heat spiraling from that point to the spot between her legs made her gasp. He answered the gasp with another suck and roll.

When she thought she couldn't take a second more, he adjusted her legs around his hips and thrust. The tight stretch was soon followed by a deep pull as he lifted her up and then reseated her with another hard thrust. He repeated the process again and again until her head lolled back and her body tightened, searching for release. It took only the brush of his thumb over her clitoris to find it.

As she hit orgasm, she started to yell his name, but he kissed her, the word mingling with his own groan of satisfaction. After the last of the tingles melted from her body, he lifted her off his lap, adjusting her corset and zipping her dress. She wanted to confess her love. Then she wanted to tell him about Zac. But when he pulled her back in his arms and snuggled her close, all she had the strength to do was allow his heartbeat to lull her to sleep.

Chloe awoke the next morning with only a vague memory of Grayson carrying her from the limo, undressing her, and tucking her into bed. What she did remember was his "I love you." She rolled over, intending to shower him with those words, but Grayson wasn't there. Instead, propped up on the pillow was a drawing of her standing at a Juliet balcony completely naked. At the bottom of the drawing, Grayson had taken liberties with Shakespeare:

What light from yonder window breaks? It is my sun.
It is my Chloe.

The words made Chloe's heart swell. Especially when she read the rest of it:

Sorry I had to leave. Deacon called and needed me
at work, but I'll be back as soon as I can. I love you,
Romeo

Chloe wanted to stay right there until Grayson got home. Unfortunately, there was something she needed to take care of. And her Romeo's love had given her the strength she needed to do it.

The Chinese restaurant was squeezed between the tattoo parlor where Chloe had gotten her only tattoo and a tourist shop that sold cheap San Francisco T-shirts and souvenirs. It was the Chinese restaurant where Chloe had been working when she first met Zac. She was still living on the streets at the time, sleeping in an abandoned office building that had no heat, lights, or running water, hoping to find a place to live on the tips she made busing tables.

Compared to the transients and thugs she had to deal with on the streets, Zac had seemed like a perfect gentleman. He dressed nicely, tipped well, and always had a compliment for her. After only a few months of coming into the restaurant, he offered her a room in his upscale apartment with no strings attached. Or so she'd thought. But there had been strings. Strings that Chloe didn't even realize were there until she was tangled in their web.

"There's my princess."

The voice sent shivers up Chloe's spine. But when she lifted her gaze from the cup of ginseng tea she'd ordered, all she saw was an average guy in an ill-fitting suit. And suddenly she realized that the monster she'd created in her mind didn't exist. Just as her father's hatred hadn't. They were both just figments of a scared young girl's imagination. But Chloe wasn't that scared young girl anymore. She was a woman who realized that she didn't have to fear her past. Nor did she have to hide from it.

"Hello, Zac," she said.

Zac must've read her nonchalance, because he grabbed her chin and ground his lips against hers in a painful kiss.

She wanted to slap his face but she knew that if she did, it would only make things worse. So she endured the kiss until he pulled back with a grin. "You always tasted like sin."

She ignored the comment and grabbed some packets of sugar for her tea. "So I guess your lawyers got the charges dropped."

"The undercover cops who set up the sting operation fucked up, and I got off on a technicality. Although I'm stuck with probation after I punched out that cop." He pulled out the chair across from her and sat down. "Which only leaves one question: Who tipped the cops off in the first place?" His knee brushed hers under the table, and she pulled away.

"I didn't turn you in, Zac," she said. She had wanted to, but fear of her true identity getting out had stopped her.

"Then who did?"

"I don't have a clue."

"Probably that bitch Madison."

"If Madison was too scared to testify, she'd be too scared to turn you in."

His knees captured her legs. "And are you scared of me, Chloe?"

It was a trick question if ever she'd heard one, so she decided not to answer. She stirred the sugar into her tea. "What do you want, Zac?"

He picked up her cup and took a sip, then shivered with disgust. "You always used too much sugar. Which always made me wonder if there was some sweetness under your prickly personality." He set down her cup and motioned for a waitress. Once he placed his order, he waited for the waitress to leave before he looked back at Chloe. "What did I always want?"

"Money and power."

He grinned. "Exactly. And it looks like you have both. Which just doesn't seem fair," he said in a deceptively soft voice. "Just not fair, at all."

The waitress arrived with Zac's water. When she was gone, Chloe opened her purse and pulled out the envelope that was filled with the cash she'd gotten out of her bank account. It was every penny she'd received for the holiday catalog pictures. She had earmarked it for college tuition, but at the moment, getting rid of Zac seemed like a better way to spend it.

"Here." She shoved it at him. "Consider it rent for the years I lived with you."

He took the envelope and opened it, and his eyebrows lifted. "Why, that's real sweet of you." He closed the envelope and took a sip of his water. "But I hope you don't think this makes us even."

Chloe's temper finally snapped, and she didn't care if he was a dangerous man. "This is all you're going to get from me. So if I were you, I'd take the money and run." She pushed back her chair and got up. "And if you contact me again, I will call the cops and tell them everything I know."

Once outside, she wasted no time heading up the street. She had just started to feel proud of herself, as if she'd faced the dragon from her past and survived, when a hand closed around her arm and she was jerked into an alleyway. Zac shoved her against the wall of a building with teeth-jarring force and pressed a gun to her temple.

"Did you actually think you could hand me a few measly thousand and walk away scot-free?" he hissed as his hand tightened painfully on her arm and the barrel of the gun dug into her head. "Not fuckin' likely, bitch. Not after you ruined my business and my life. You might not have called the cops, but I don't doubt for a second that one of your Beaumont boyfriends did. Or that bitch of a reporter. Which means you owe me, Chloe, and you're going to pay. Not with money, but with your flesh."

It was hard to get words out of her suddenly dry throat. "What are you talking about?"

His hand tightened until she could almost feel the bruises forming beneath each of his fingers. "You're going to do exactly what I spent all those years grooming you to do. You're going to be my number one whore."

"Like hell I am." She tried to jerk free, but he moved closer, pinning her against the building with his body. He leaned in, his breath hot and rancid-smelling.

"Now, now, Chloe, is that any way to talk to the man who took you off the streets and gave you a place to live and food to eat?" His eyes narrowed. "Or are the rumors true? Have you found a new billionaire sugar daddy? One who keeps his whore in satin panties for blow jobs?"

"I don't whore for Grayson. He loves me."

"He loves you?" he said. "Sort of like I loved you, Chloe?" He laughed, his bad breath ruffling her bangs. "Regardless of the tough exterior, you are nothing but a little weak princess. A little weak princess who is waiting for her prince to come sweep her off her feet and rescue her from all the badness in the world." He pressed the gun into her temple. "But there's no such thing as princes. Just like there's no such thing as princesses. And no man is going to fall in love with a whore. Especially one who whored for his brother."

Chloe flinched. "It wasn't like that. I left before anything happened."

"Do you think that will make a difference to your billionaire sugar daddy when he finds out?"

The seed of doubt he put in her mind hurt worse than his fingers squeezing her arm or the gun digging into her temple. "Let me go, Zac." She hated that her voice quivered on each word. "I'm not going to be with you—not ever again."

His gaze narrowed. While Grayson's eyes reminded her of a garden of lavender, Zac's were like bottomless pits with no color at all. "Oh, you're going to be with me. Because if you don't come with me, I'm going to spill your entire sordid past to the newspapers. And not just your past, but Madison's. And how do you think people will feel about their two favorite lingerie models being hookers? How will your new boyfriend feel?"

She'd thought she was so tough because she'd faced Zac alone. Now she realized her mistake: You can never meet with the Devil and keep your soul. All hope of getting away from Zac drained right out of Chloe.

He must've read the defeat on her face because his hand relaxed on her arm, and he lowered the gun. "Now don't look so sad, sweetheart. Haven't I always shown you a good time? Unfortunately, we won't be able to have it here in San Francisco."

"But I thought you were on probation."

"I don't like people keeping tabs on me and telling me where I can go and where I can't." He grinned slyly. "So I'm starting over in a new country. I think wealthy foreign men would pay dearly for the chance to be with a top model, don't you?"

CHAPTER TWENTY-FOUR

"Did Babies 'R' Us change locations?" Grayson asked as soon as he stepped into Deacon's office. There were baby things everywhere: A crib in one corner. A changing table in another. An infant seat on the couch. Baby bottles lined the bar. And all kinds of rattles and stuffed animals cluttered Deacon's desk.

Deacon sat behind the desk, holding Michael in the crook of his arm. "Olivia wanted to be here this afternoon for the fashion show fittings, and since the sitter was sound asleep last night when we got home, I refuse to trust Michael with her again. So I'm glad you could make the board meeting this morning."

"I didn't think I had a choice."

If Grayson had had a choice, he would still be tucked in bed with Chloe. Now that he'd confessed his love, he wanted to spend every single second with her. In fact he was thinking about taking her on a trip to Fiji. Since they had started their relationship there, it only made sense. And this time he didn't intend to sneak around lusting after her with a camera. This time he planned on being very open about his lusting.

"You didn't have a choice," Deacon said. "Nash wouldn't answer his phone, and Michael was having a bad morning."

Grayson moved around the desk to look at his nephew. "Well, he doesn't look like he's having a bad afternoon."

Deacon stared lovingly at his son. "He seems to like the office better than being at home."

Grayson laughed. "Somehow that doesn't surprise me." He leaned closer. "Hey, little dude. Are you going to be a businessman like your daddy?" He made to tap Mikey's nose, but Deacon stopped him.

"Wash your hands."

"I just washed them when I went to the bathroom."

"I don't care. Since then you've touched door handles and who knows what, and I don't want him getting germs."

With a shake of his head, Grayson took a seat across from Deacon's desk. "Michael will have to deal with germs eventually, you know."

"I know. But not on my watch. Which reminds me." He leaned forward and pushed a button on the phone panel. "Kelly, you need to have the private jet disinfected before we take it to Louisiana this weekend. Kelly?"

"She's not there, Deke. She always has lunch with her parents in Chinatown on Fridays."

"Damn. I forgot." Adjusting Michael in his arms, he scribbled a note on a piece of paper. "And I'll expect you to be on that plane, Gray. You need to accept the fact that Dad is getting married."

It was funny, but since telling Chloe that he loved her, he didn't feel as hurt about his father's getting remarried. While he was still sad that he had no memories of his mother, he now had other memories to fill the gap.

Happy memories that were all centered around Chloe:
The sleepy, sexy way she smiled at him when she woke
up every morning. The way she tried to beat him back
to the house on their morning runs and thought it was so
funny to snap his butt with a towel when they were getting ready for work. The way she ate as if she enjoyed
every single bite—whether it was lobster at an expensive
restaurant or pizza on the couch. The way she called out
his name when she reached orgasm—as if he'd given her
the most precious of gifts.

She still hadn't told him that she loved him, but he didn't
need the words. Every one of her actions said that she did.

"I'll be at Dad's wedding," he said. "And I'm thinking
about bringing someone."

Deacon lifted his eyebrows. "Who? And don't tell me it's
that stupid seagull."

Grayson grinned at the thought of Josephine sitting in
a plush leather seat in French Kiss's private jet. "No, I'm
bringing Chloe."

"So this thing between you two is serious?" When
Grayson nodded, Deacon visibly relaxed in his chair.
"Thank God. You had me worried there for a while."

"Worried about what?"

"About the fact that all you seemed to want to do with
women was paint them."

Grayson stared at his brother. "You thought I was gay?"

"More like asexual. And I couldn't really blame you after
all the women that Donny John brought home and my poor
parenting skills. Still, it's nice to know that I didn't screw
you up too badly."

It didn't surprise him that Deacon still felt responsible for
his littlest brother. Deacon was just that kind of a man. "You
didn't screw up at all, Deke. I know I probably didn't tell

you this enough, but I appreciate everything you and Nash did for me. You're my family, and I love you."

Deacon gave one quick nod before he cleared his throat. "Well, I love you too. Now tell me about Chloe. I had no idea that her family owned a winery."

Since it was a subject he loved, Grayson had no problem talking about Chloe. He told Deacon about Casa Selena and Chloe's reasons for running away from home. And he told him the story of how he'd met Chloe and about Zac's abuse. The only thing he left out was the part about the escort service.

"Well, I'm glad that you kicked the guy's ass," Deacon said. "It sounds like he deserved it. And I'm glad that you helped Chloe reconcile with her father. Family is important. Something I've realized even more since Michael's birth. Although I probably could've done without Dad's little care package for Michael."

"Let me guess. A new fishing boat?"

Deacon laughed. "He didn't go that far. He sent him boxing equipment."

"That sounds like Dad, all right."

"What sounds like Dad?" Olivia walked into the office, and immediately Michael started to fuss.

"He knows when his food source has arrived." Deacon got up and handed the baby to Olivia. "I was just telling Grayson about Dad's gift for Michael."

Olivia cuddled Michael close and kissed his head. "I will admit that it was a little unconventional, but it was also very sweet. And I can't really say anything when my father sent his new grandson an entire box of lemon juicers."

It was true. Olivia's father was even more unconventional than Donny John. Due to his issues with walls and roofs, he lived on the streets and supported himself by selling lemon juicers. According to Deacon he did pretty well for himself.

"How is your father?" Grayson asked.

"He's doing well. I'm trying to get him to come home for the holidays. But Mexico nights are a lot warmer than San Francisco's at this time of year." She walked over and brushed a kiss over Grayson's cheek. "That's from Mother. I guess the art benefit was a huge success."

"It would've been an even bigger success if I had gotten Chloe's painting."

Olivia pulled back. "Didn't you hear? The winning bid was nothing but a hoax. The guy who called it in didn't even exist. Although Mother isn't too upset, since his bids jacked up the price."

Grayson shook his head. "So I guess I'll be paying twice as much for my own work?"

"Exactly." Olivia laughed. "Now let me just change and feed Michael, and we can head over to the design studio. I can't wait to see the designs Samuel has come up with for the show. Especially the designs he themed after characters from famous old movies. He e-mailed me his sketches, and it's an amazing idea. Madison is going to be Marilyn Monroe in *Some Like It Hot*. Natalia will be Jane Russell in *The Outlaw*—"

Deacon cut her off. "Natalia's back? I thought she refused to come back because Grayson had broken her heart."

Olivia placed Michael on the changing table. "It would appear that her heart heals quickly. I hear she's dating the lead singer of some European band. Anyway, she'll be Jane Russell, and Chloe will be Audrey Hepburn from *Breakfast at Tiffany's*. Although we won't get to see the diamond-studded bra modeled. Not only because Tiffany's won't let it out of their sight before the fashion show but also because Chloe's not here to model it."

Grayson sat up. "Chloe's not coming for the fitting?"

Olivia picked up Mikey and turned. "Samuel said she

called and said that she had to take care of some personal business." She grinned. "Until I saw you, I thought I knew what *personal business* meant."

Grayson didn't acknowledge the teasing remark. He was too disappointed that he wasn't going to see Chloe this afternoon. And that she hadn't called him to tell him she wasn't coming in.

"I'm sure she wanted to spend time with Gavin and her grandfather while they were here," he said.

"Well, that explains it," Olivia said. "Still, I was looking forward to seeing how she looked in some of our new designs." Mikey started fussing, and she walked over to the couch and sat down, then started unbuttoning her blouse.

It took Deacon's gruff order for Grayson to figure out what was going on. "It's time for you to leave, Gray."

Wanting no part of a nursing mother, Grayson got to his feet. "I'll just meet you two in the design studio."

But when he stepped into the hallway, he didn't head for the elevators. Instead he pulled out his cell phone and dialed Chloe's number. He was being clingy, but he couldn't seem to help himself. He just needed to hear her voice. Instead her voice mail picked up. He was about to text her when Kelly appeared around the corner. And since she looked a little upset, he put his phone away.

"So how did lunch go with your parents?" he asked.

"Fine." She set a takeout container on her desk, then removed her coat and hooked it over the back of her chair. Beneath she wore a purple dress with no Hello Kitty accessories that he could see. If that wasn't enough to worry Grayson, Kelly's face lost all color when Mikey's wails came through Deacon's office door.

"Here"—he moved around her desk and held out the chair—"sit down. You don't look like you feel well."

Kelly slumped in the chair and covered her face with her hands. "I think I've made a big mistake, and there's no way to go back now."

Grayson leaned on the edge of her desk. "What mistake?"

She lowered her hands and picked at her fingernail. "Wanting to get pregnant. I thought it would be so much fun to start a family. Olivia looked so happy when she was pregnant, and her baby shower was so much fun. You should've seen all the cute little baby clothes." Her gaze moved over to Deacon's door. "But it doesn't look like they're having so much fun now." She looked at Grayson with a terrified look in her eyes. "And I just don't think I'm ready to change those awful, stinky diapers and clean up puke and go without sleep. I'm just not ready!"

Grayson placed a hand on her shoulder. "And what does Jason think?"

"He feels the same way. Until Mikey, we both didn't realize how much work having a baby is."

"Then the answer seems pretty simple to me," Grayson said. "If you're not ready, then wait."

Kelly sighed. "Unfortunately, it's not that easy. My parents are all excited about being grandparents. They told me today at lunch that they already bought me a crib."

"Well"—Grayson shrugged—"wouldn't it be easier to take back a crib, than take back a kid?"

Kelly studied him for a moment before she laughed. "That's a good point. And that's exactly what I'm going to tell my mother." She reached for her phone, but then stopped. "How involved are you with Chloe Cameron?"

The swift subject change made Grayson a little confused, and a little wary. "Why do you ask?"

"I know I'm not supposed to get involved in my boss's personal business. But when something in your personal life could affect your happiness here at work, I think it's my business to tell you."

A tingle of apprehension climbed up his spine. "Tell me what?"

"While I was eating lunch with my parents, Chloe walked into the restaurant. I knew she was supposed to be at the fittings today. So I figured she was playing hooky—not that I ever do that." She cleared her throat. "Anyway, she took a seat by the window, and not more than ten minutes later, this young guy with really scary eyes showed up. I'm sorry to tell you this, but it looks like your new girlfriend is cheating on you."

Grayson's shoulders relaxed, and he laughed. "I appreciate your loyalty, Kelly, but Chloe isn't cheating on me. The guy was her cousin Gavin."

Kelly sent him a pointed look. "I've heard of kissing cousins, but the kiss he gave her wasn't cousinly. And if his name is Gavin, then why did she call him Zac?"

CHAPTER TWENTY-FIVE

Chloe was going to Thailand. She didn't have a choice. If she didn't go, Zac would make good on his threat. And the news that French Kiss's top model had once been a prostitute would not only ruin Madison but could also ruin the Beaumont brothers. And consequently Eden and Olivia. Chloe wasn't about to let that happen. She loved Eden and Madison and had grown to love Grayson's brothers. But most of all she loved Grayson, and she couldn't stand to see him hurt when he found out the truth about her being an escort.

Zac must've known that he held all the cards because he didn't have any problem letting her go back to Grayson's to pack. She had three hours before she had to meet him at the airport. It wasn't nearly enough time. Especially when she spent most of it trying to compose a letter to Grayson.

Since she couldn't find any paper, she used his sketchpad and threw away so many drafts that she ran out of paper. She finally scrawled four words at the bottom of a sketch he had drawn of her feeding sardines to Josephine.

The picture reminded Chloe that she needed to feed the bird before she left. Leaving her duffel bag on the bed, she hurried up the stairs to the kitchen. She grabbed a can of sardines from the cupboard and took it out to the balcony. But Josephine wasn't sitting on her eggs. Which made Chloe worried. Especially when one egg looked as if it had a crack in it. Before she could bend over to check, Mr. Huckabee's voice drifted over from next door.

"So is that your granddaughter, Bob? Because her name is Candace, not Chloe."

Chloe looked over to find not only Mr. Huckabee sitting on his balcony naked but also her grandfather. "Granddad?"

He lifted a hand in greeting before he stood. Luckily, he had on a pair of boxer shorts with bronco-riding cowboys printed on them. "I stopped by to say goodbye to you, but you weren't home. Hammond here was nice enough to invite me over for some magic brownies." He waggled his gray eyebrows. "And I must say that they make you feel pretty magical—are those sardines you have in your hand? You got any crackers to go with them? This veggie plate that Doris fixed us just isn't filling up my gut."

Chloe rolled her eyes. She really didn't have time for this. "Please put your clothes on, Granddad, and I'll call Gavin. Is he still at the hotel?"

"Nope. He had a business meeting this morning, which is why I came to see you. So where were you?"

"I went to lunch. Now hurry and get dressed." Just in case Josephine came back, she opened the sardines and put them on the coffee table, then went inside to call Gavin. Her cell phone was in her room, and as she waited for him to answer, she started tossing clothes in her duffel bag. Gavin's voice mail clicked on, and she had just started to leave a message when a voice behind her made her freeze.

"Let me guess. You're leaving."

Chloe slowly turned to find Grayson standing in the doorway. He wore a gray suit without the jacket. His tie was loose and hung at an odd angle and his hair was mussed. But it was his eyes that held her captive. They were filled with hurt.

She hung up the phone. "You came home early."

He jerked off his tie and tossed it on the dresser. "Which I guess screwed up your plans to leave without a word."

"I was going to call you."

"Just like you called your family after you ran away from home?"

She wanted to explain, but she knew that if she did, Grayson would go after Zac. While Grayson could take Zac in a fistfight, he wouldn't stand a chance in a gunfight. So instead of answering the question, she turned and continued to pack. Although it wasn't easy when her hands shook and the backs of her eyes burned with unshed tears.

"So it's true," Grayson said. "You're going back to Zac."

She turned. "How did you know?"

He stared at her, as the hurt look morphed into hate. "What an idiot I am for believing that we had something special. But there was nothing special about it, was there? You were just biding your time until the guy you really do care about got out of jail."

The tears she was trying so hard to hold back filled her eyes. "It's not like that, Grayson."

"Really?" He took a step closer. "Then what is it like?" When she didn't answer, he shook his head and stared up at the ceiling. "I actually believed that you didn't have any choice in the way your life has turned out. Poor, pitiful Chloe just got dealt a bad hand. But on the drive over here, I realized that life didn't deal you anything. You chose your own hand. You chose to run away from home. You chose to move in with an abusive asshole. You chose to go to Nash's hotel room. And you're choosing to go back to that abusive asshole who sent you there."

"You know about me going to Nash's hotel room?"

"I've known all along, but before now, I thought that Zac had forced you. I thought you didn't have a choice."

Her shoulders wilted. "I didn't…I don't."

He stared at her for only a second before he spoke in a voice barely above a whisper. "Yes, you do, Chloe. You had a choice then, and you have a choice now. You can stay. But the truth is that you don't want to." He turned and walked out. A moment later there was the loud slam of a door, followed by the roar of a car engine and the squeal of tires.

Heartbroken, Chloe sat down on the bed and released her tears. She might've continued to cry if a loud crunching hadn't drawn her attention to the doorway. Granddad stood there eating a bag of Cheetos.

"Well, it looks like you've gotten yourself in quite a pickle this time, Selena Cameron." He pulled out another Cheeto and munched on it. "And I might take your side if I didn't agree with Grayson. Everybody has a choice. But sometimes we just do a bad job of choosing." He glanced at her duffel bag on the bed. "And it looks like you're making another one."

She released her breath on a quivery sigh. "You don't understand, Granddad."

He walked over and sat down next to her. "Then enlighten me."

With only a couple of hours before she had to be at the airport, Chloe really didn't have the time. But there was something about her grandfather's understanding eyes that made her start talking. She told him all about moving in with

Zac, and his abuse. She told him about Zac's pretending to buy the painting and wanting to meet for lunch. She ended with Zac's ultimatum.

When she was finished, she expected her grandfather to be disappointed in her for getting involved with such a thug. Instead he only nodded. "Sometimes it's hard to tell a bad apple until you bite into it."

"And by then it's too late," she said.

Granddad took her hand and gave it a squeeze, leaving Cheeto-dust fingerprints on her skin. "It's never too late to toss a bad apple in the trash. But after his abuse, I understand why you're hesitant."

"I'm not really scared of him. I'm more afraid of him telling people about Madison being a prostitute and ruining French Kiss."

Her grandfather looked thoughtful. "But isn't that putting the cart before the horse?"

"What do you mean?"

"I mean that you don't know for sure that people finding out about Madison will ruin her or French Kiss. It seems to me that people would want to buy lingerie from an expert on seduction."

Put that way, it did make sense. "But what if people don't?" She shook her head. "I'm afraid I can't take that chance."

Her grandfather sent her a pointed look as he polished off another Cheeto. "Just like you left home because you were afraid that your family would hate you once we found out you weren't our blood relative? For a woman who acts so tough, it seems to me that you've spent an awful lot of time being afraid of things that might not happen. Which makes you a bit of a chickenshit."

Chloe's eyes widened. "Granddad!"

He shrugged. "I don't know what else you'd call it. Only a chickenshit would run instead of staying and fighting for what they want."

"And exactly how am I supposed to fight a hoodlum with a gun?"

For a moment it looked as if her grandfather had zoned out and wasn't going to answer. A Cheeto hung from his mouth, and his eyes were dazed.

"Granddad?"

He blinked, and the Cheeto dropped to his lap as he continued the conversation as if he'd never taken a break. "That's your problem, Selena. As an only child, you think everything is about you. But the truth is that no man, or woman, is an island. A truly strong person welcomes the help of their friends."

Her grandfather's wisdom struck such a chord of truth in Chloe that she was too stunned to reply. He was right. She had always thought that asking for help was a sign of weakness. Which probably explained why she had never had many friends. She had refused to go to Cain and Gavin when she was upset over her mother dying and her dad not being her dad. Fought against Eden and Madison's friendship and refused to accept any help that they'd offered. She'd even resented Grayson for helping her get away from Zac. And if he hadn't kidnapped her, she would now be living in some strange country without any friends or family. Which was exactly what was going to happen to her if she went with Zac. All because she couldn't get it through her thick skull that asking for help when you couldn't handle something on your own made you stronger rather than weaker.

She sat there for a moment absorbing the epiphany before a loud snore startled her out of her reverie. She turned to see her grandfather flopped back on the bed sound asleep.

The empty Cheetos bag rested on his chest, and cheese dust ringed his mouth. She smiled, but the smile faded as soon as she realized that she now had a choice to make. She could run like a chickenshit or she could rally her friends and fight.

* * *

Chloe was late getting to the airport. So late that she didn't even wait for her cab driver to give her change. She hurried to the airline counter where she was supposed to meet Zac. At first it looked like he wasn't there, then a hand curled around her arm, digging deep into her flesh.

"You're late," he growled.

"Sorry." She held up her bulging duffel bag. "I guess I had more to pack than I thought."

He stared at her for a moment before he smiled. "I hope it's filled with sexy lingerie."

"Of course, what else would it be filled with?"

It didn't take them long to check in and get their boarding passes. Zac had purchased the tickets using the same name he'd used to purchase the painting. And the counter clerk didn't even look twice at the fake passport he handed her. He handed her another one for Chloe that had the same last name as his. And when they left the counter, he glanced at her and winked. "Until death do us part, Mrs. Rogers."

Chloe tried to smile as they made their way to security, but she was nervous about getting through the X-ray machines with what she carried in her duffel. Fortunately, she was sent to the TSA-approved line, while Zac had to go through regular security and get thoroughly searched. The TSA woman who scanned her bag stopped the conveyor belt only briefly before she nodded at Chloe and allowed her to move on.

Once through security Zac seemed to relax. He bought them a couple of bottles of soda from a kiosk and found two seats by the window. Chloe sat down next to him and made sure to position her bag on her lap so the closed zipper tab was closest to Zac.

"So what exactly do you intend to do when we get to Thailand?" she asked. "Do you know someone there?"

Zac grinned. "I met a guy while I was in jail who has connections. He's the one who made us the fake IDs. He left on the previous flight to Thailand and will meet us at the airport."

"So are you going to do the same thing there that you did here? Are you going to run a prostitution ring?"

He unscrewed the cap and downed half of his cola. "Better. Here I had to worry about every prostitute I hired giving me problems. There the women do what they're told or they get the crap knocked out of them."

Chloe knew exactly who would be doing the knocking. She cleared her throat and spoke as loudly and clearly as she could without drawing attention from the people around them. "So you're going to prostitute women for money. Just like you did here."

He studied her, and for a moment she worried that she had given herself away. But then he took her hand. "I would never prostitute you, sweet one. You're mine." His fingers tightened, and he gave her a smile. "But if there's a lonely businessman who just wants a little company, I'm sure you wouldn't mind spending some time with him."

For a moment Chloe really wanted to punch him right in the face. Instead she returned his smile. "Of course I wouldn't mind."

It seemed to take forever for the first boarding call to come over the speakers. They got in line behind an older woman with a carry-on roller bag.

"So why are you going to Thailand?" the woman asked. "I'm going to visit my daughter. She got a job there teaching English." She glanced at Chloe's duffel bag. "It looks like you brought plenty to keep you occupied on the long trip too. Mine is mostly filled with books." She shook her head as the line started to move. "I just can't get used to those new e-readers. I like to do the page turning myself." She handed her boarding pass to the airline attendant. "Do you have an e-reader?"

Chloe was a little too preoccupied to reply. Something wasn't right. She wasn't supposed to get on the plane. She was just supposed to come to the airport. But unless she wanted to alert Zac, she had to hand the attendant her boarding pass. Once they were in the Jetway, she became even more nervous. But the book woman didn't seem to notice and kept right on talking as they waited to board the plane.

"Have you read this one?" She leaned down and unzipped her bag, pulling out a hardcover book. "It's about this guy who becomes a stalker after his wife leaves him. When she gets a restraining order and moves, he ends up getting facial reconstruction surgery and following her. He moves in right next door to her, and she falls in love with him all over again. But when they finally get around to having sex, he unzips his pants and she instantly recognizes his penis and calls the cops."

Zac, who had been listening, burst out laughing. "Now that's a book you need to read, honey."

The woman shoved the book at Chloe. "Here, you can read it on the plane. I have plenty of others."

Since Chloe had no plans of flying to Thailand, she shook her head. "No, thank you. I'm not much of a reader."

"I wouldn't mind reading it." Zac took the book. "It sounds kind of interesting." Before Chloe realized what he was doing, he'd reached for the zipper on her bag and unzipped it. "Could you hold it for me, sweet—" He abruptly cut off when the microphone popped out through the opening.

Holy shit. Okay, now Chloe was scared. Especially when Zac's eyes darkened.

"What the hell is that?" he growled in a low voice. But not low enough for the book woman not to hear.

"Well, it looks like some listening device to me," she said. "I read this spy novel about a device like that. This CIA agent posed as a hotel maid and got all kinds of info—"

"Shut the fuck up," Zac said.

The woman blinked. "Excuse me?"

Zac grabbed Chloe's arm and jerked her close. "Where are the cops?"

Chloe wished she knew. When she had called her FBI agent friend from The Lemon Drop and asked for his help, Jeff had notified SFPD, and they had quickly set up the sting. Jeff had said that he and the other officers would be watching her the entire time and assured her that Zac would be arrested as soon as she got him to confess to running the escort service. Now it looked as if she would have to deal with Zac by herself.

"Stop being paranoid," she said with a laugh. "That's the microphone for my new video camera. I've never been to Thailand, and I wanted to film—"

Zac hooked an arm around her throat, cutting off her words and breathing. "You fuckin' bitch. I should snap your neck right here and now."

"Hey," the book lady said, "you let go of that young woman right now." She grabbed his arm, but Zac shoved her away, causing her to trip over her roller bag and sit down hard on the floor of the Jetway. People raced to help her, oblivious to the fact that Chloe was the one in danger.

Although she didn't feel scared. She just felt pissed. Pissed at Zac for shoving a nice lady. And pissed at herself for ever having gotten involved with such a jerk.

Lowering her chin, she bit Zac's arm, and at the same time rammed her elbow into his ribs. He released her, but instead of running, she did what she'd wanted to for a long time. She beat the shit out of him. She kicked and punched and kneed him in the nuts. And she would've continued to pummel him if Jeff hadn't stopped her.

"That's good, Chloe." He hooked an arm around her waist and pulled her off Zac. "We'll take things from here." He waited for the two uniformed cops to handcuff Zac before he released her. "Are you okay?"

She looked at Zac, who was still bent over in pain, and smiled. "Yeah, I think I am. I think I'm finally okay."

CHAPTER TWENTY-SIX

With the way his father loved flashy cars and gold jew-elry, Grayson thought Donny John's wedding would rival George Clooney's. Instead his father wore a simple gray suit and got married in the gazebo of his new backyard with only family in attendance. Although he did wear plenty of diamonds and gold that flashed in the late-afternoon sun. Standing next to his bride, who was wearing a modest floral dress with no jewelry, he looked like an old rapper. He also looked happy. Happier than Grayson had ever seen him. Which left Grayson feeling even more depressed and angry. And when the cake had been cut and Deacon had made the toast, Grayson headed to his rental car. But he didn't even make it to the back door before his father stopped him.

"Grayson Romeo!" When he turned, Donny John at-tempted to give him a stern-father look. But since he had never been a stern father, it fell short. "You're not thinking about leaving, are you? Suzanne would be very disappointed if you did."

"I'm sure she'll live. She has her own family to visit with." He continued to the back door.

Donny John followed. "Well, if your mind's made up, I guess it's made up. But before you leave, I want to show you my man cave."

While the wedding had surprised him, Donny John's man cave was exactly what Grayson had expected. It was over the top. There were a pool table, a poker table, slot and pinball machines, a carnival popcorn machine, and a long saloon-style bar that ran the length of one entire wall. On the other side of the massive room was a theater, complete with a large-screen television and a row of cushioned recliners.

Donny John held out his arms. "Well, what do you think?"

"I think Deacon's giving you too much of an allowance."

Donny John chuckled. "Mikey's birth has made him a lot more generous. Is that the cutest kid you've ever seen?" He walked behind the bar and poured two glasses of Johnnie Walker whisky. Since it didn't look like he was going to get away without a drink, Grayson took a seat on one of the leather barstools and accepted the glass.

"To family." Donny John clicked their glasses. "And finding love." Since Grayson couldn't drink to that, he set his glass on the bar without taking a sip. Donny John downed his drink and released a sigh before studying Grayson. "So Deacon told me that you were going to bring a girl with you to the wedding. What happened? Did you two break up? Is that why you look like you just lost your best friend?"

Grayson had never had a best friend—he'd had his brothers and his art—and if losing one felt like this, he didn't want one. When he had seen Chloe packing, he'd felt like someone had reached into his chest and ripped his heart out, leaving him with a gaping hole that nothing seemed to fill. After Kelly had told him about Chloe meeting Zac, he still hadn't believed it. He'd thought that all he had to do was go home and Chloe would be waiting to explain everything. But she hadn't been waiting...she'd been leaving. And her inability to explain had made him realize that he'd put his trust in the wrong woman.

After leaving his house, he'd driven all the way down the coast and into Mexico, not stopping until he was so tired he couldn't keep his eyes open. He got a room in a fleabag hotel and was awakened early in the morning by the couple in the next room having wall-banging sex. Which made Grayson think of Chloe and the gaping hole in his chest. Unable to get back to sleep, he'd checked out and would've continued to drive south if Deacon hadn't called and bawled him out for not being at the private airfield where French Kiss kept their jet. And when he found out that Grayson wasn't planning on attending their father's wedding after all, the shit really hit the fan. So Grayson had turned around and driven to San Diego, where he'd hopped a plane to Louisiana. Now he wished he'd stayed in Mexico.

"Look"—he got up from his barstool—"I really need to get going."

"Now, not so fast. There's something that I wanted to give you." His father reached beneath the bar and pulled out a thin wrapped package. "This was all Suzanne's idea, and I'm still not so sure it's a good one. It's hard to rehash old memories—especially painful ones."

Suddenly wary, Grayson only stared at the package. "What is it?"

"Old movies that I took when you boys were little. We found them in a box when Suzanne was helping me move, and she thought she'd surprise me and have them put on a DVD."

Grayson swallowed hard as he continued to look at the present. "Is Mom in them?"

Donny John nodded solemnly. "That's why they were hidden in a box. After she died I couldn't bring myself to watch them." He blinked as if fighting tears. Grayson knew how he felt. His own eyes suddenly felt hot and heavy.

"So you haven't looked at it?"

"I watched it, but I sure put up a fight." Donny John shook his head. "It's the darned stubborn Beaumont streak that we all have. Poor Suzanne doesn't know what she's in for. Although she certainly got a taste of it the night she gave me that DVD. I threw quite the tantrum. I yelled at her for taking the movies without my permission and told her to get the hell out of my house and never come back. Once she left I grabbed all the movies and DVD and threw them in the trash." A smile tipped his lips. "But God had other plans. On my trip to San Francisco for Nash's wedding, I couldn't stop thinking about the hurt way Suzanne had looked before she walked out. And then when Mikey was born, I was reminded of you boys' births and the joy I'd felt the first time I held you in my arms. So when I got back to Louisiana, I watched the damned DVD."

Tears flooded Donny John's eyes. "And as painful as it was seeing your mother so happy and full of life, it also made me realize how much she loved us. And how much she would want us to be happy." He smiled. "I proposed to Suzanne that very next morning. As soon as she accepted, this overwhelming feeling of peace surrounded me. Like your mama had given us her blessing. Which makes sense after the promise she made me give her."

"What promise?" Grayson asked.

Donny John released his breath in a long sigh. "Before she died, your mother made me promise to find a good woman who would love me and her boys like she did. I think she knew that I would need some help raising you." A tear splashed down his cheek. "And I guess she was right."

Grayson had never seen Donny John cry. His father had always been bright smiles and clever jokes. And he didn't know how to react to his father's tears. But what he did know was that he couldn't deal with watching a movie of his mom.

"I don't want it," he said.

Donny John studied him for a moment before he nodded. "Suit yourself." He grabbed a handkerchief out of his back pocket and wiped his eyes. Grayson recognized the white cotton with the little embroidered purple flowers immediately. It was identical to the ones Nash and Deacon carried. Grayson had one too, but he didn't carry it. Just the sight of the delicate flowers made him angry that he couldn't remember his mother stitching them on. But the fact that his father still carried the hankie, even on his wedding day, made Grayson realize that Donny John would never forget his first wife. She would always hold a place in his heart, and he would always cherish his memories of her. It seemed the only one refusing to keep Althea in his heart was Grayson.

"Well, I better get back to the party." Donny John moved around the bar. "Just leave the DVD there."

While Donny John went back upstairs to enjoy his wedding reception, Grayson sat and stared at the DVD as he sipped his drink. When the glass was empty, he poured himself another. After he finished that drink, he unwrapped the DVD and stared at it some more.

Finally he carried it over to the shelf of electronics beneath the flat-screen television and placed it in the DVD player. It took him a while to figure out how to turn on the television, and a little while longer to figure out the remotes. Once he had everything working, he sat in a recliner and pushed the play button.

The first images were of Deacon as a baby. It was surprising how much he looked like Mikey. But Grayson forgot all about the similarities when an image of his mother flashed up on the screen. She was leaning over Deacon's crib. His father was right. She looked young and happy, and the expression of happiness and love grew as she helped Deacon learn how to build block towers, then walk, then ride a trike. Nash arrived next. And once again his mother was in almost every frame, smiling and laughing. Finally Grayson showed up.

After all the time he'd spent trying to remember his mother, here she was, cradling him close to her breast, singing him to sleep, laughing as he made a mess of his first birthday cake, and beaming when she stood over him as he colored a picture. Grayson wanted to reach out and touch the screen to see if her skin felt as soft as it looked—if her hair was as silky. Instead he just sat there enthralled.

Until the final scene flashed on the screen. A scene where a little boy hesitantly brought a picture into a room and held it out to the woman in the bed. A woman who didn't look like the smiling young mother in the previous clips. This woman looked pale and thin. Like a swift wind could easily carry her away.

And it had.

Just that quickly the memories came flooding back like water from a dam that had just been released. Grayson remembered. He remembered the warmth of her arms, and the fresh scent of her skin, and the way her smile could make him feel like everything was going to be okay. And he also remembered the last few days of her life. When she'd turned into someone he hadn't recognized. Someone who scared him. Suddenly he realized why he'd suppressed the memory of his mom. He hadn't wanted to remember those last few months and the frail, pale woman his mother had become. He'd wanted to remember the youthful, pretty mother he'd loved.

Now he understood perfectly why Chloe had run away. Grayson had done the same thing. He had run from the memories of a sickly mother who couldn't love him. But he'd been just as wrong as Chloe. Because now that Grayson was older, he could see beyond the pale, sickly skin and frail body and see the love shining in his mother's eyes. Love that filled the gap in his heart and made him realize that his biggest fear had been nothing but a lie. He had a mother. A mother who had loved him, and cherished him, and cradled him. He hadn't gotten to keep her for as long as some people did, but he'd been blessed to have her, even for so short a time.

Long after the DVD was over, he continued to stare at the blank screen. Finally he wiped the tears from his eyes and got up. He took the DVD out of the player and put it back in the case, then carefully placed it on the bar. He would retrieve it before he left, but for now there was something he needed to do.

When he stepped out the back door, night had fallen, and the party was in full swing. The chairs had been removed from the gazebo, and it had been turned into a dance floor with strings of white lights draped overhead. It seemed everyone was dancing. Suzanne's relatives had paired off. Nash swung a laughing Eden around. Deacon held Mikey with one arm and Olivia with the other as they swayed back and forth to the music. And in the midst Grayson finally spotted Donny John doing a graceful waltz with his bride.

Grayson crossed the lawn to the gazebo and wove through the dancers until he reached his father. When Donny John saw him, he stopped dancing.

"I thought you left, Grayson."

"I changed my mind." He nodded at Suzanne. "Could I cut in?"

Donny John looked surprised for only a second before a bright smile spread across his face. "Of course." He pointed a finger. "But don't even think about stealing my girl." With a wink at Suzanne, he headed over to Deacon and took his sleeping grandson.

Grayson held a hand out to Suzanne, who looked a little skeptical. He couldn't blame her. He hadn't said more than two words to her since they'd been introduced. "Would you do me the honor?"

It took Suzanne a moment to nod. Grayson had never been as good a dancer as his father and Nash. In fact he had two left feet. So he didn't try for anything fancy. He just shuffled in an awkward circle and tried to figure out where to start. Suzanne helped him out.

"So your father told me that he gave you one of the DVDs I had made," she said. "And I want you to know, Grayson, that I didn't do it to hurt anyone. I just thought that you'd want a keepsake of your mother."

For the first time, Grayson really looked at Suzanne. After his mother died, his father had always dated big-busted blondes, but Suzanne was neither. She had gray hair that was short and stylish and a petite body similar to Grayson's mom's. She didn't dress sexily or flamboyantly. Her floral dress was nice but conservative, the neckline high and the hem low. The wrinkles around her eyes spoke of years of laughter as the kindness in their blue depths spoke of a good heart. The kindness gave him the courage to say what needed to be said.

"It was the best gift anyone has ever given me. And I would like to apologize for my behavior. I have no excuse but Beaumont stubbornness. Something I'm sure you're aware of, since you married my dad."

She laughed. It wasn't as musical-sounding as his

mother's, but it was close. "I figured out he was stubborn the first time his dog treed my cat. When I knocked on his door to tell him, he just smiled that wicked smile of his and said, 'You can't change a leopard's spots or a dog's instincts.'" She grinned. "At the time I was madder than a wet hen, but looking back, I have to agree. Your father is as stubborn as the day is long, but I wouldn't change him for the world. I like his spots just as they are."

Grayson laughed. "Then you have more patience than me and my brothers."

"Oh, I don't know if that's true," she said with a twinkle in her eyes. "The man can make me lose my temper faster than anyone I've ever met. But I think the best relationships have a little spice with their sugar." She straightened his tie. "Now what happened to this young lady that you were supposed to bring?"

The last person Grayson wanted to talk about was Chloe, yet he wasn't about to be rude to Suzanne again. "She left me."

"Oh no. I'm so sorry. No wonder you look so hurt. And here I thought it was due to your father marrying me."

He blushed guiltily and apologized again. "I had no business letting my problems put a rain cloud over your wedding."

She swatted his shoulder. "Now you stop that. We're family now, Grayson. And family share in each other's problems. That's just how it works." She glanced down at her feet. "And right now, my main problem is my swollen feet in these new shoes. Do you mind if we sit this one out?"

Thankful for the reprieve from dancing, he guided her down the steps of the gazebo and over to a wrought iron bench, where she slipped her shoes off with a sigh. "So tell me about this young woman of yours. Eden speaks of her in glowing terms and was very disappointed that she didn't come with you. From what I gather, both she and her friend Madison tried to talk Chloe into surprising you and just showing up."

The news didn't make sense. Not that Madison and Eden would try to talk Chloe into coming, but that they would do so after she had gotten back with Zac.

"So you are trying to steal my girl, Grayson." Donny John walked up. He quickly handed a sleeping Mikey to Grayson and pulled Suzanne into his arms. "I think they're playing our song."

"I'm afraid I'll have to pass," Suzanne said. "My feet are killing me."

Donny John grinned evilly as he pulled her away. "That's even better. There's a chaise lounge right over here in the dark that would be perfect for a little slap and tickle."

Suzanne swatted him and giggled. "You are too bad, Don Juan. Just too bad."

Once they were gone, Grayson looked down at Mikey. If the baby had been any other baby, Grayson might've sat down and let him sleep. But he'd heard Mikey's screams, and he wasn't about to be stuck without help close by. Unfortunately, Deacon and Olivia had left the dance floor, and it took some hunting to finally locate them. They were cuddled in one of Donny John's recliners sound asleep, not even waking to the sound of steel balls pinging as Nash and Eden played pinball on the other side of the room. Or Eden was playing pinball. Nash was standing behind her, nuzzling her neck.

The flashing lights and bouncing pinball might not bother Deacon and Olivia, but Grayson was worried that they might wake up Mikey. So he'd started to head back upstairs when the pinging stopped and Eden spoke.

"I can't believe you would leave Chloe."

Grayson turned to see Eden giving him a hard, mean look. Now that he thought about it, she had been glaring at him since he'd arrived. He'd just been too upset to notice. He walked over and handed Mikey to Nash, who wasn't very receptive to the idea.

"What do I do with the kid?" Nash whispered.

"Since you probably will be having one of your own, you better figure it out." Grayson adjusted Nash's hand on Mikey's back. "Just don't drop the pacifier, and if Deacon wakes up, tell him you washed your hands before you took him."

Nash studied the baby for a second. "He is kinda cute." He glanced at his wife, who read his expression immediately.

"No. Not until I become a best-selling author and travel the world."

Nash winked at her. "As long as you take me along for the ride, babies can wait." He moved over to one of the recliners and sat down.

"So?" Eden said. "Do you want to explain why you left Chloe and broke her heart?"

"I think Chloe hasn't been honest with you. I didn't leave her. She left me to go back to Zac."

Eden's mean expression didn't soften one bit. "Of course she did. She didn't think she had much of a choice. Zac had convinced her that he was going to anonymously tip off the newspapers about Madison and her working for an escort service. Which would not only ruin Madison's modeling career but also French Kiss."

So that was what Chloe had meant when she'd said she didn't have a choice. Grayson didn't know whom he was madder at: Zac for threatening Chloe or Chloe for not telling him. Probably Chloe. All roads led back to her.

"But she had a choice, Eden," he said. "She could've told me what was going on. She could've trusted me. Instead she was going to leave without a word. Which tells me that she cares for Zac more than she cares for me."

"Well, if she cares about him, then she has a funny way of showing it," she said. "Zac is now back in jail for trying to break his probation, and with his confession about running a prostitution ring on tape, he won't be getting out anytime soon."

"What does that have to do with Chloe?"

"She was the one who set him up. The one who was wired and got him to confess on tape."

Hope flared to life inside Grayson, but he refused to let it catch. "Then why didn't she call me and tell me?"

Eden sent him an exasperated look. "For being the Woman Whisperer, you certainly can't read Chloe. It's hard for her to show her love with words and hugs. She's much better at showing her love through actions. When you get home, you'll find her waiting."

"I don't believe it." Grayson pulled out his cell phone. Since it would be too painful to call and not get an answer, he texted.

Where are you?

The answer came only seconds later. Not in words, but in a picture. A picture of three little speckled seagull chicks.

CHAPTER TWENTY-SEVEN

Chloe was going to be sick. Literally sick. And it would be bad enough if she hurled backstage. There was no way she was going to hurl in front of millions of people.

She pushed the makeup brush away from her face. "I'm not doing this."

The makeup artist who held the brush stared at her in confusion. "I'm so sorry, luv," he said. "Did I accidentally poke you in the eye?"

"No..." She tried to remember his name, but her brain was too consumed with fear. "It's not you. I just can't do this." She got up from the stool, forcing the hairstylist who had been fluffing her bangs to step out of the way.

She pushed through the makeup artists, hairstylists, and designers who surrounded her, only to have to push through the ones who clustered around Madison. Though this was her first runway show, Madison didn't look nervous at all. In fact she looked as if she was thoroughly enjoying all the face painting, hair teasing, body bronzing, and skimpy-lingerie adjusting.

That didn't surprise Chloe. Madison owned her lifestyle—whatever that lifestyle might be. Whether she was an escort or a supermodel, she believed in enjoying every second and making no excuses for past mistakes. After Zac had been arrested, Chloe had contacted her friend and told her that Zac was probably going to tell the world that she had worked for him as an escort. Instead of being upset, Madison had only laughed.

"Too late," she'd said. "I blogged about being an escort months ago. And the majority of the response was positive. Most people viewed it as a *Pretty Woman* story and are waiting for me to find my Richard Gere."

Chloe wished Madison had mentioned that before Zac had threatened her. But sometimes things work out a certain way for a reason. Chloe had needed to overcome her fear of Zac and realize that running was never the answer. She froze at the doors that led out of the hotel ballroom and rolled her eyes. She was running again. Obviously, habits were hard to break. She took a few deep, even breaths to calm her stomach before she turned around.

When she got to the small area that had been designated as her dressing room, the stylists and makeup artists were gone. There was only one person standing next to her rack of lingerie with his back to her. One person who made the queasy feeling return and her heart thwack hard against her rib cage.

"Grayson." The name came out on a puff of air filled with embarrassing longing.

He turned, and the longing grew. He wore a deep gray suit that fit his body to perfection and a crisp lavender shirt with a light-gray-striped tie. His hair was longer, as was the stubble on his face, but the contrast of tousled artist with starched businessman made him all the more breath-stealing. When his beautiful forget-me-not eyes locked with hers, everything inside her stilled and her chest rose and fell as she struggled to catch her breath.

His gaze wandered down to the purple corset she'd been laced into—the same one she'd worn when they made love in the limo. "Did they lace you in too tight? Is that why you can't breathe?"

She could've lied, but she was through keeping secrets from Grayson. "It has nothing to do with the corset."

His gaze snapped up to hers, and *hot* didn't begin to describe his eyes. *Scorching. Sizzling. Flaming twin torches of molten heat* were more accurate. They seemed to burn straight through her and brand her heart with the initials GRB. Or maybe he'd branded her with those initials from the moment he had first rescued her from Zac. He moved closer, and her world narrowed to the uneven curves of his top lip as he spoke. "So Josephine's a mother."

It was hard to talk around all the emotions that clamored inside her. "I thought you would come home after I sent you the picture."

He cleared his throat as if he was having a hard time talking too. "I needed some time to think. And I was still angry that you hadn't trusted me."

"I should have, but I've always been a slow learner. It took me this long to realize that running never solves anything—that in life you have to face your biggest fears."

"And what is your biggest fear, Chloe?" He studied her with eyes that were so intense she had to look away before she could speak.

"Losing you."

He moved closer. But he didn't touch her. His hands remained at his sides. "Funny, but that's my biggest fear as well. And I think my fear is more justified than yours. You weren't exactly nice when we first met. Which is why I raced off to Paris and couldn't paint. Being rejected by the love of your life hurts like hell."

She looked at him. "You loved me before Paris?"

"I've loved you from the moment I first set eyes on you. At first I thought I was looking for the perfect model to pose for me. But now I realize that I wasn't looking for the perfect model. I was looking for the perfect woman. Not to paint. But to love."

Chloe couldn't help the tears that sprang to her eyes. "I love you, Grayson."

"I'm sure glad to hear it." He dipped his head to kiss her, but before his lips could touch hers, Samuel came charging up, more freaked out and emotional than she had ever seen him.

"Oh no, you don't, Grayson Beaumont! I will not have you ruin Chloe's lipstick with kisses." He looked at Chloe, and his eyes narrowed. "Or her mascara with tears. Whatever you two have going on will have to wait until the last rhinestone and feather have paraded down that runway." He clapped his hands. "Now get out of here while I try to repair the damage."

Grayson looked as happy as Chloe felt about the interruption, but he finally nodded. "Okay. I won't kiss her until after the show, but I'm not going anywhere." He looked at Chloe. "You're not getting out of my sight again."

He wasn't kidding. He stood in her tiny dressing area and watched her with a possessive look while the makeup artist repaired her mascara and the hairstylist plumped up her hair. Chloe couldn't take her eyes off him either. She felt buoyant. Like she'd eaten one of Mrs. Huckabee's magic brownies.

Until Samuel called for her and she realized she was going to be the first model on the catwalk.

Once she caught a glimpse of the long runway, which was lit up like an airplane landing strip at night, she wanted to hurl all over again. Grayson must've read her fear because he moved up next to her. Taking her hand, he turned her until all she could see was his face. The warmth of his hand coupled with the love in his eyes calmed her stomach and her nerves.

Obviously she wasn't as immune to the Woman Whisperer as she'd thought.

Taking a deep breath, she nodded. "Okay, but if I do a nosedive out there, it's all your fault."

Chloe didn't do a nosedive. She wasn't as graceful as some of the models in their high heels, but at least she didn't fall. And when she got to the end of the runway, she was so relieved that she broke out in a bright smile that had the entire audience applauding. Or maybe they were just applauding because the awkward girl had made it. Either way it gave her confidence, and she actually started to have fun. Chloe modeled the next few outfits without a hitch. But when she put on the diamond-studded Audrey Hepburn bra and thong, Grayson's eyes widened, and he became as bossy as Deacon.

"I don't think so. You are not wearing that on the runway. Your entire butt is hanging out." He took off his jacket and draped it over her shoulders as the other models looked on with little smirks. Madison was the only one to out-and-out laugh.

"I don't know what you're worried about, Grayson," she said. "Chloe had on less than this in the painting you auctioned."

"That's art," Grayson said. "Not to mention that the painting is back where it belongs—with me." Chloe had wondered if Zac had ever gotten his hands on the painting. She was relieved that he hadn't. "This show is being broadcast to millions of people. And I'm not going to have some pervert getting his jollies from my girl's butt."

The *my girl* made Chloe feel all giddy, but she still stopped him when he started to button his jacket. "Grayson, we both know that I can't wear this on the runway."

He stubbornly crossed his arms. "Then you're not going out."

"Of course I'm going—"

Samuel hurried up with his clipboard and headset. "Why isn't Chloe lined up? And why is she wearing that suit jacket?"

"It seems that Grayson thinks your design is a little too skimpy in the butt area," Madison said.

Samuel shook his head as he pulled off the suit jacket and tossed it at Grayson. "Don't be ridiculous. Not only is this the grand finale of the Romeo Collection, it's the most expensive piece in the show. There are close to two-million dollars' worth of diamonds on the brassiere alone." He nodded at the two armed guards standing to the side. "Which explains Mutt and Jeff. And Tiffany's will be extremely upset if this piece isn't on television."

"Then I'll buy it," Grayson said.

Samuel studied his stubborn stance for only a moment before he released an exasperated sigh. "Very well. I'll find something to cover her backside, but she has to go out. And not in your jacket." He placed a finger on his bottom lip and studied Chloe for only a moment before his gaze returned to Grayson. "Although you might be wearing something that will work."

Chloe wasn't sure how the audience would react to a model walking out in a purple dress shirt. But they seemed to love it. At the end of the runway, she pushed back the shirt as Samuel had instructed and let the lights flash off the diamonds in brilliant rays. The applause became deafening. Although, when she made her turn, she realized it had more to do with the man who confidently walked down the runway toward her. And Chloe had to admit that Grayson was applause-worthy with his bare chest showing beneath the suit coat and tie. He might look confident, but when he met her in the middle of the runway, his face held a bright blush.

"You are so shy, Grayson Beaumont." Chloe couldn't help but giggle as she took his arm and walked with him to the end of the runway. "And this coming from a man who paints nude women."

"Haven't you heard?" He smiled for the television cameras. Although it was more a baring of teeth. "I'm giving up painting nude women."

She glanced at him. "Don't tell me that you're going back to apples."

"I'm thinking I'll try my hand at landscapes. Although there's one nude woman I might have to paint on occasion."

"And who would that be?" she asked as they turned and headed back down the runway.

He sent her a smile, and a dimple appeared. "My wife."

That was all it took for Chloe Cameron to stumble in her heels and almost take a nosedive. Fortunately, there was someone there to catch her.

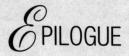

EPILOGUE

The house that sat only steps away from the Louisiana bayou looked nothing like an old fishing shack. The front steps that led up to the large porch didn't have one missing board or protruding rusty nail. In fact they were made with some newfangled composite material that looked like wood but wouldn't warp or peel in the humid temperatures...or in a flood like the one they'd had last fall. The multitude of windows on both levels had not one crack. The pristine white siding no peels. And the screen door no squeaks...even after all the use it received every summer, when the entire Beaumont family converged on the vacation home for three weeks.

Donny John didn't even jump anymore when the screen door slammed. He just sat there sipping his sweet tea as two little girls came charging out the door.

"Mine!" three-year-old Althea yelled as she tried to grab the doll from her cousin's hands. But Tulip was having none of it.

"But you said you would share," Tulip whined. "'Sides, you already have a baby in yours tummy."

A little surprised by the statement, Donny John leaned forward in his rocker. Sure enough, Althea's shirt showed the lumpy outline of a baby doll. He tried not to laugh as his granddaughters continued to bicker.

"But I wants two babies like Aunt Chloe." Althea jerked the doll away from Tulip and stuffed it under her shirt with the other doll, completely oblivious to the fact that the dolls' plastic legs were dangling beneath.

Tulip started to bawl, and the little girl could cry louder than an evangelist's wife giving testimony. Donny John was about to get up from his rocker and comfort her when the screen door opened and the Beaumont women stepped out. There was Olivia looking cool and collected in her pretty sundress. Eden looking like the writer she was with her glasses perched on her head. And Chloe looking extremely pregnant in her maternity muumuu, which appeared to be dusted with potting soil. The woman loved playing in the dirt. So much so that Grayson had built her a flower nursery on her father's vineyard when she'd graduated from college.

But of all the women who stepped out the door, it was Donny John's wife who reached Tulip first. Suzanne looked as beautiful as the day he had married her. She scooped their granddaughter up in her arms and gave her a kiss.

"What's the matter, angel? Did you fall?"

Tulip shook her head. "Noooo, Gamma...I just want a baby in my tummy too."

The women exchanged shocked looks before turning to Donny John, who was having a hard time keeping his laughter in check. "Don't look at me," he said. "I didn't put that idea in her head. I think it has more to do with wanting to be like her aunt Chloe."

Chloe looked down at her protruding stomach and frowned. "Believe me, Tulip, it's not as fun as you think," she said. "Especially in this awful heat."

"I'll get you some iced tea," Eden said before she glanced at her daughter. "And if you'll stop crying, I'll get you girls some of your grandmother's homemade peach ice cream." Tulip stopped crying, but only long enough for the screen door to slam behind her mother.

"But I don't want ice cream. I want a baby!" She pointed at Althea, who was trying to conceal the dolls under her shirt...but not very successfully. Her mother quickly zeroed in on her daughter.

"Althea Deirdre Beaumont," Olivia said. "You get those dolls out of your shirt right now and give one to your cousin."

Althea's lip protruded, but she listened to her mother and took the dolls out, holding one up to Tulip. The crying stopped instantly, and within minutes the two girls were sitting on the steps playing. Now that the crisis was over, the ladies went back inside to help Eden. And only moments later Donny John was enjoying peach ice cream with his sweet tea as he watched his granddaughters. Because of the heat, the women had opted to eat their ice cream inside. But Donny John enjoyed the humid heat. Of course he had also come to enjoy the cool ocean breezes of San Francisco—not to mention the big ol' boat his boys had bought him for his last birthday.

Having finished their ice cream, Tulip and Althea came and crawled onto his lap with their dolls, bringing with them the smell of fresh peaches and precious little girls.

"Tell us a story, Gampa," Tulip said.

"Yes," Althea agreed. "Tell us the story of the three little hillbilly boys who became princes."

Donny John gave each of his granddaughters a kiss on the head. "Are you sure you want to hear that one again?"

"Ple-e-ease!" they sang out in chorus.

Donny John smiled. "Once upon a time, there were three little hillbilly brothers named Valentino, Lothario, and Romeo. They lived in a run-down shack next to a bayou very much like this one. And one day the brothers decided to go fishing."

"Just like Daddy and Uncle Nash and Uncle Grayson did today," Althea said.

"Yes, just like that. But instead of catching fish in the bayou, each brother caught a—"

"Magical mermaid!" Tulip yelled as she looked up at him.

Donny John tapped her button nose. "Exactly. And each mermaid granted each brother only one wish. They could have money. They could have fame. Or they could have love."

Althea sat up and raised her hand. "I know what they chose! I know what they chose!"

Before Donny could call on her, three little hillbilly brothers walked out of the big cypress trees that surrounded the house, looking nothing like the lingerie billionaires they were in their camo pants, tattered T-shirts, and full beards. Like everything else, the beards had become a little bit of a competition among the brothers, to see who could grow the fullest beard by the end of the month. Surprisingly, it looked as if Grayson was winning this time.

Tagging behind the Beaumont brothers, with fishing poles on their shoulders and a string of fish in hand, were three little boys. Each with the dark hair and violet eyes of their fathers. His granddaughters finally noticed their fathers and brothers and released earsplitting squeals as they clamored off Donny John's lap and headed down the porch steps. Their feet had barely hit the bottom stair before Deacon and Nash were there to scoop their squealing daughters up. The noise alerted the womenfolk, and they came out the screen door and stood on the porch. At the sight of their moms, the boys stopped lollygagging and ran past their fathers and sisters, thumping up the porch steps like a herd of fishy-smelling elephants, each punching and pushing to get the honor of showing his catch first.

It was the youngest grandson who won the scuffle.

"Lookee what I caught, Mommy." Cameron Picasso held up his string of fish.

Chloe looked duly impressed by her son's accomplishments. "All of those? Why, I think you're a better fisherman than your uncle Nash. Now the question is who is going to clean them and cook them?"

"I'll be happy to clean." Grayson climbed the porch steps and took a handkerchief out of his back pocket, a white handkerchief with tiny purple flowers embroidered on it, and wiped the smudge of dirt off his wife's nose. "But Nash will have to do the cooking."

Nash carried Tulip up the stairs and placed an arm around Eden. "I don't mind frying up some fish." He looked at his son. "Do you want to help, Cash?"

Cash Tristan didn't exactly look thrilled by the prospect. "Do I have to, Dad? Mikey and I were going to set up a lemonade stand like Grandpa Harrington's. He gave me three juicers the last time I saw him, and we want to try them out."

Michael Paris nodded in agreement. "I figure if we set up next to that construction site in town we could sell ten glasses every fifteen minutes. And at a dollar a glass that would be forty dollars an hour."

"That's a fortune," Cameron said in awe.

"Can I help?" Althea wiggled out of Deacon's arms.

"Me too," said Tulip, before she looked at Donny John. "But first Gampa has to finish the story. What do the brothers choose?"

With his heart and eyes brimming with joy, Donny John got up from the rocker and made his way over to his family. A family that had survived and thrived...and would continue to survive and thrive.

Taking Suzanne's hand, he smiled. "Why, the brothers chose love, of course. Because only love can give you this kind of happily ever after."

Born to be the boss, billionaire Deacon Beaumont vows to save the failing lingerie company French Kiss. But bold and beautiful Olivia Harrington dares to question his authority in the boardroom—and the bedroom...

Please see the next page for an excerpt from *A Billionaire Between the Sheets*.

CHAPTER TWO

$\mathscr{D}$eacon Beaumont had pictured his second meeting with Olivia Harrington much differently. In his fantasies he was always dressed in an expensive designer suit and either helping a supermodel out of his brand-new Maserati or sitting behind a massive desk in his penthouse office. Olivia was always dressed in hand-me-downs and begging for money...and mercy. Of course in the fantasy he gave her neither. Money and mercy were for people who deserved them. And as far as he was concerned, Olivia didn't deserve anything but his strong dislike.

His hatred was reserved for her stepfather.

Nash took a towel off the rack and handed it to him. "I'm going to make a guess and say that you and our cousin decided to take a swim. And while I would love to hear the story, I think it can wait until after we show Olivia some Southern hospitality and let her get out of those wet clothes."

Olivia's clothes were soaked. Her white T-shirt was

completely transparent, showing every detail of the lacy bra beneath. And when Nash's gaze lowered, Deacon had to squelch the desire to wrap the towel around her. Fortunately, his brother had never been much of a gawker and quickly averted his gaze.

Grayson, on the other hand, was out-and-out gawking. He had always had an almost reverent fixation on women. He had trouble talking to them, but he loved to look at them. And paint them. It didn't matter if they were beautiful or plain. Skinny or fat. Young or old. Or covered in bug bites and lichen. If you were a woman, Grayson wanted you as one of his subjects. For some reason—his brother's pretty-boy good looks or his innocent blushes—women didn't mind posing for him, usually with their clothes off.

Well, it wasn't happening with Olivia. She wasn't staying long enough for Grayson to paint her, or for Nash to show off his Southern hospitality. And Deacon made that perfectly clear when he shoved both his brothers out of the bathroom and slammed the door behind him.

"She's not staying," he said as he strode into his bedroom.

Nash and Blue followed, Nash flopping down on the bed Deacon had painstakingly made that morning and Blue dropping to the floor in a puddle of loose bloodhound skin. "We can't just throw her out, Deke," Nash said. "Especially when she came all the way here to visit her Louisiana cousins."

Deacon glanced back to see Grayson standing in front of the closed bathroom door, his hand twitching as if he were sketching Olivia. "Jesus." He walked into the hallway and grabbed his brother by the collar of his shirt and pulled him into the bedroom before closing the door. "There is no way prissy Miss Olivia Harrington trekked from California just for a visit. Especially after the way she treated us the first time we met. And we're not her cousins. Her gold-digging mother just happened to marry our filthy-rich asshole of an uncle."

"I don't remember being treated that badly." Nash stretched out on the bed and tucked a pillow behind his head. "If Donny John had shown up at my California mansion begging for money with his three urchin sons in tow, I would've called the cops too."

Deacon pointed a finger at him. "Get your dirty boots off my bed." After Nash rolled his eyes and complied, Deacon pulled open the top dresser drawer and took a clean pair of boxers from the neatly folded stack. "No, instead good-hearted Uncle Michael took pity on his poor hillbilly relatives and invited us to stay the night before kicking us out the following morning."

"Only after you molested his stepdaughter." Grayson finally pulled his head out of the clouds and entered the conversation.

Deacon slammed the drawer. "I did not molest Olivia!"

Grayson raised his hands. "I believe you, Deke. But you have to admit that the evidence was pretty damning."

"Damning evidence seems to be the bane of the Beaumont brothers," Nash said dryly. And if anyone knew about damning evidence, it was Nash. He had spent months in jail after being falsely accused of a crime.

Olivia hadn't accused Deacon, but she hadn't spoken up for him either. She had just stood on the balcony like a spoiled Juliet and watched as the neighborhood security officers escorted him and his family off the property. Now she wanted to offer him and his brothers some kind of proposition. Well, as far as he was concerned, she'd had her chance to talk.

"One of you can take her back to town." He pulled on the boxers. "I need to head out to the work site."

"What work site?" Nash asked. "I thought you couldn't break ground until you reeled in a new investor. Did you find one?"

Deacon had. Unfortunately, the one investor he had on the line was the one he didn't want to reel in. Francesca Devereux had made it very clear what she wanted from the deal. And it wasn't a return on her investment. She wanted a cougar cub—a man she could parade around her social events like her froufrou pet poodle. Deacon had never been pet material. But he wasn't the type of guy to give up either. The project had taken him years to pull together, and he was convinced the lakeside condos would make money. If he had to prove it by becoming some rich woman's arm candy, then so be it.

He pulled open another drawer. "Speaking of catching, you need to catch a job, Nash—instead of living here for free."

"Free? I cook all the meals, and I believe Grandpa willed this house to all of us. Besides, I'm working on an idea that could make us filthy rich."

"Is that what you've been doing on your laptop? And here I thought you'd been playing games."

Nash grinned. "Maybe a few. But I'm telling you, big brother, that apps are the wave of the future. And I have this idea for a great app that will work in conjunction with all the new electronic sensors they have out. With just a tap of your phone, you can dim your lights, turn on music, and start up your gas logs."

"Dim your lights, turn on music, and start a fire? Are we talking business or seduction, Nash?"

Nash laughed. "Why can't we talk both? And I don't need an app to seduce women, Deke."

It was the truth. Nash didn't need anything to seduce women. There was something in his DNA that made women do things they would never do with another man.

"And when will this app be ready to make money?"

Nash got to his feet. "Unfortunately, I find myself in the same boat as you're in. In order to start making money, I'll need an investor."

Great. Maybe Francesca wouldn't mind three pet poodles.

Grayson, on the other hand, wasn't thinking about needing money or making it. As if he were sleepwalking, he opened the bedroom door and moved out into the hallway. "I need to paint her. Now. While the afternoon light is still good."

Nash laughed. "I don't blame you, baby brother. Despite the bug bites, she looked pretty hot in that wet T-shirt. Of course I'm interested in doing something other than painting her . . . now, while the light is good." He glanced at Deacon. "Or would that be considered incestuous?"

"She's not our damned cousin!" Deacon snapped just as the door to the bathroom opened and Olivia's head peeked out. She looked much cleaner. Almost squeaky-clean with her wet hair and steam-flushed skin. Her eyes were as green as he remembered them and still seemed to cover half her face.

"Do you think I could get something to wear until my clothes dry?" she asked. "A robe? Or a T-shirt, perhaps?" Her gaze drifted over to Deacon and then sizzled down his bare chest to his boxers. "Ahh, I was right. Cotton boxer briefs mid-cut." She tipped her head to the side and the door cracked open a little more, revealing a naked shoulder. "Nice fit in the butt, although they're a little too snug in the crotch area."

Before those innocent eyes could make his crotch area even snugger, Deacon grabbed a pair of jeans from the drawer and held them in front of himself. "Grayson, find Olivia something to wear."

While Grayson went to do his bidding, her gaze finally lifted to Deacon's eyes. "You're right. I'm not your flesh-and-blood cousin." She looked at Nash, who now stood next to Deacon. "But alas, I still can't have sex with you, Nash. I'm in a relationship." Grayson returned with a stack of clothes, and she gave him a soft smile as she took them. "And yes, you may paint me. But only if you bring me a comb." With that she pulled her head in and closed the door.

While Deacon's features hardened, Nash laughed.

"I think I like her better now that she's all grown up."

* * *

Deacon had always thought of California girls as having long, straight, bleach-blond hair and tanned, leathery skin. Olivia had neither. Her hair was shoulder-length, but a deep golden wheat color and wavy, and her skin was pale and smooth. She wasn't what he would call a stunner, especially in the baggy T-shirt and jeans Grayson had loaned her. Which didn't explain why he couldn't seem to look away.

"Thank you," she said as Nash handed her a glass of sweet tea before sitting down at the table across from her. Grayson sat on the couch, flicking a nubby piece of charcoal over his sketchpad. Deacon preferred to stand. He leaned against the old stove with his arms crossed, trying to look bored and uninterested. It was difficult when every cell in his body seemed to be on high alert.

The shower had helped Olivia's hair, but only agitated the leech hickey on her neck and the bug bites on her arms. Deacon didn't doubt for a second that they itched like hell. Or that she was sweating her butt off in the humid heat. But Olivia showed no signs of discomfort. She sat with a placid smile on her face as she took a sip of her tea.

"So the reason I'm here is because—"

"Don't move," Grayson said as his hand flew over the sketchpad. "Stay right where you are for just a second."

"I apologize for my baby brother," Nash said. "He's so busy thinking with the right side of his brain that he doesn't know how to socialize."

"Because we all know which brain you think with, Nash," Deacon cut in. "Now if you'll excuse me, I'm going to work." He took a step toward the door, but she stopped him.

"Please, Deacon. Just give me five minutes."

The *please* had him taking his cell phone from his back pocket and glancing at the time. With the crack running down the center, it wasn't easy to read. "You've got two."

Taking another sip of her tea, Olivia cleared her throat as if preparing for a long speech. "I'm sure you were surprised by Uncle Michael's death and the details of his—"

Nash cut her off before Deacon could get his mouth closed. "Uncle Michael is dead?"

Her eyes widened in surprise. "Michael's lawyers haven't contacted you?" She glanced around, and then answered the question herself. "I guess it makes sense, seeing how hard it was for me to find you." She looked back at Nash, and tears flooded her eyes. "I'm sorry. Michael died two weeks ago after a severe stroke had hospitalized him."

Deacon waited to feel something. Hurt. Pain. But all he felt was disappointment. Disappointment that he hadn't been able to achieve success before Michael died. Disappointment that he could never rub that success in his uncle's face.

"So if lawyers were supposed to tell us about Uncle Michael, why are you here?" he asked.

She turned her gaze on him. "Michael put you in his will."

And there it was. After all the years Deacon had waited to be recognized by Michael, the man had waited until he was dead to do it. There was a moment when Deacon wanted to hit something. Instead he shoved down the anger and spoke in a deceptively calm voice. "Now why would he do that?"

Olivia shrugged. "Believe me when I tell you that I don't have a clue. I can only guess that with you being his blood relatives, he thought it was the right thing to do."

"The right thing to do?" His anger flared. "Your stepfather wouldn't have known the right thing to do if it bit him in the ass. He disowned his family and never looked back—even when they needed him most. And I will never forgive him for that."

"Stop it, Deacon." Nash got up from his chair. "The man is dead. You don't need to point out his flaws now. And you certainly don't need to take it out on Olivia."

But that's exactly what Deacon wanted to do. Now that he could no longer confront his uncle, there was only one person to take his anger out on. He glared at her, but she only stared right back with those deceptively innocent eyes.

"I don't know what happened between my stepfather and your father," she said, "but Michael must've felt badly about it because he put you in his will."

"I have no use for guilt money," he said. "So you can take the will and go to hell." He strode to the door, but again she stopped him.

"Not even for fifty million dollars?"

Olivia's words had his hand freezing on the worn wood of the screen door. He slowly turned. "Fifty million dollars? Uncle Michael willed me fifty million?"

She shook her head. "Not just you, but your brothers as well. And he didn't will you money. He willed you shares of his lingerie company."

"How does that equate to fifty million?"

Instead of answering she reached for the backpack by her feet. The same one that had been strapped to her back when he'd pulled her from the swamp. It was soaked, so it took her a while to get it unzipped. Once she had it open, she pulled out a damp file folder. She unhooked the loop and opened it, taking out a stack of legal papers that were surprisingly dry.

"I'm willing to offer you and your brothers fifty million dollars each for your shares." She set the stack of papers on the table before pulling out a pen. "All you have to do is sign these contracts, and then once the will goes through probate and the shares transfer, I'll give you the money."

"Fifty million dollars?" Nash's chair creaked as he sat back. "This is a joke, right?" He glanced around. "There has to be a hidden camera somewhere around here."

"It's no joke." Olivia held out the pen. "With a simple signature, you could be a millionaire."

"So what's the catch?" Deacon asked.

"No catch." Her innocent eyes stared back at him. "I want your shares of the company."

It was rumored that the Beaumont men had an uncanny ability to read women's minds. Deacon didn't believe in such hocus-pocus. He believed in General Patton's theory of knowing your enemies. He'd done his research on Michael...and Olivia. In numerous interviews she had made no bones about the fact that she ate, slept, and breathed her job. She loved the company. Loved it enough that she wouldn't want three men who knew nothing about the lingerie business having any kind of control over it.

He should be elated. This was what he'd dreamed of, wasn't it? To make his first million before he turned thirty-five? And even with Francesca's backing, it was unlikely that he would achieve the goal in three years. Now fifty million had landed on his doorstep. It was just unfortunate that the windfall had come from the same family he wanted nothing from.

He glanced at the contracts. "I'll need to read through it and then talk to my brothers before we sign anything."

She nodded and got up, picking up her glass of tea. "I'll be on the front porch." She paused on her way out the door and looked at Deacon. "Do you think I could use your cell phone? Mine got wet and isn't working."

Deacon took his phone from his pocket, swiped the touch screen, and tapped in his passcode before handing it to her. Then, because he couldn't seem to help himself, he held open the screen door. She stopped on her way out. So close that he could smell the scent of his shampoo that she'd used and see the splash of gold that lined the pupils of her green eyes.

"I know you don't like me, Deacon," she said, "but please don't let that keep you from getting money you obviously need."

The word *need* annoyed the hell out of him. He didn't *need* anything from Olivia. But he kept his cool and waited for her to walk out onto the porch before he let the screen door slam and closed the heavy wood door with a decisive click. When he turned, he found his brothers staring at the legitimate-looking documents on the table as if they were a pot of gold at the end of a life that had been anything but rainbows.

Unfortunately, Deacon didn't believe in pots of gold, rainbows, or women with innocent green eyes. He believed that you worked for everything you got, and life was a bitch and then you died. Walking over, he picked up the contracts and handed one to each of his brothers.

"Let's not count our chickens before they hatch."

FALL IN LOVE WITH FOREVER ROMANCE

NACHO FIGUERAS PRESENTS: RIDE FREE

World-renowned polo player and global face of Ralph Lauren, Nacho Figueras dives into the world of scandal and seduction with this third book in The Polo Season. Antonia Black has always known her place in the Del Campo family—a bastard daughter. And it will take a lot more than her skill with horses to truly belong within the wealthy polo dynasty. She's been shuttled around so much in her life, she doesn't even know what "home" means. Until one man shows her exactly how it feels to be safe, to be free, to be loved.

FALL IN LOVE WITH FOREVER ROMANCE

ULTIMATE COURAGE
By Piper J. Drake

Retired Navy SEAL Alex Rojas is putting his life back together, one piece at a time. Being a single dad to his young daughter and working at Hope's Crossing Kennels to help rehab a former guard dog, he struggles every day to control his PTSD. But when Elisa Hall shows up, on the run and way too cautious, she unleashes his every protective instinct.

WAKING UP WITH A BILLIONAIRE
By Katie Lane

Famed artist Grayson is the most elusive of the billionaire Beaumont brothers. He has a reputation of being able to seduce any woman with only a look, word, or sensual stroke of his brush. But now Grayson has lost all his desire to paint...unless he can find a muse to unlock his creative—and erotic—imagination...Fans of Jennifer Probst will love the newest novel from *USA Today* bestselling author Katie Lane.

FALL IN LOVE WITH FOREVER ROMANCE

"A warm, tender story overflowing with emotion."
—RaeAnne Thayne, *New York Times*
bestselling author, on *Hope Springs on Main Street*

**LOVE BLOOMS
ON MAIN STREET
by Olivia Miles**

Brett Hastings has one plan for Briar Creek—to get out as quickly as possible. But when he's asked to oversee the hospital fundraiser with Ivy Birch, a beautiful woman from his past, will he find a reason to stay? Fans of Jill Shalvis, Susan Mallery, and RaeAnne Thayne will love the next in Olivia Miles's Briar Creek series!

**A DUKE TO REMEMBER
By Kelly Bowen**

Elise deVries is not what she seems. By night, the actress captivates London theatergoers with her chameleon-like ability to slip inside her characters. By day, she uses her mastery of disguise to work undercover for Chegarre & Associates, an elite agency known for its discreet handling of indelicate scandals. But when Elise is tasked to find the missing Duke of Ashbury, she finds herself center stage in a real-life romance as tumultuous as any drama.

GREAT SERIES! GREAT LOW PRICE!

"A charming, clever, and engaging storyteller not to be missed."
—SARAH MACLEAN, *New York Times* bestselling author